PRAISE FOR *WEELI'S SMILE*

"A witty and thought-provoking tale told with a unique and sharp voice."

*– Dave Saraiva, The Brushback*

"A modern-day journey of discovery, love, and spiritual revolution, *Weeli's Smile* pulls on the heart, challenges the intellect, and shamelessly pokes at the funny bone. A must read."

*– Raymond Media Group*

# WEELI'S SMILE

## *The Revolution*

**A Novel**

*W.g.Cordaro*

ISBN 13: 9780997433609
ISBN 10: 0997433604
First Edition 2017

Cover design by Laura Moyer of thebookcovermachine.com

Ormus Publishing
Taunton, MA
ormuspublishing.com
34 North Precinct St.
Lakeville, MA

10 9 8 7 6 5 4 3 2 1

# WEELI'S SMILE

*The Revolution*

*Dedicated to Dad, Mom, Ted, Larry, Duster, Jasmine, Terrapin, and the energy of all that inspire the cosmos.*

# CHAPTER 1

# CLEOPATRA'S LAMPSHADE

*Fear will do that. Hopelessness will do that.*
*When fear is so great that hopelessness becomes*
*desperation, apathy gives way to revolution.*

– LINDA DRESNICK
EXCERPT FROM MAYORAL CAMPAIGN SPEECH

Veiled by bastions of volcanic ash, deep in the womb of the lush American desert, the most advanced civilization conspires to the common cosmic good and the survival of the human race. The rewards of evolution, theirs to reap. How my mundane fortune landed me in that golden paradise, worlds away from the money-mongers and city worms, is the story of The Revolution.

Cosmologists piece together fragments of string theory, quarks, bosons, and Planck's constant to barely glimpse what that civilization has known for more than a thousand years. In human terms, infinite universes exist within universes, the 'God' particle isn't random and isn't a particle, but is in a constant state of creation, and all things animate and not, perceivable and not, are finitely connected.

While physicists try to break down 'love' by the predictability and randomness of hadrons, the Tibetans try to meditate away 'hate,' and the greedy look for any chance to turn a dime on both, it was 'love' that consumed me.

＝⇥ ⇤＝

As I grew into my own skin, everything became deadly serious. It was then that we crashed into each other's lives like comets colliding in the great wide open. The Revolution would have to wait.

It had been four years since I saw her last, yet it was as though no time had passed, as though neither of us had grown or shrunk at all, suffered or celebrated at all. Just as though no time had passed. As I stood outside the McCarthy Federal Building, bag in hand, Iraq on my mind, there she was sparkling with life, light green eyes guarding that splendid, slender face. She lowered a sign that read 'Will We Ever Learn? Burn Bones, Not Bodies.'

"I would've never imagined," she said with a gentle, curious expression.

"Life's a mystery," I replied. "I never figured I'd see you again." I can't relay what sort of expression I wore at that moment because it was all a haze. I had run the fantasy through my mind countless times. It was different every time. Sometimes with words that said it all. Sometimes without words, just an energy too perfect to refuse. In no version had I imagined I would be carrying a duffle bag, en route to war, while she was promoting weed and protesting...me.

A haze.

Time did not allow the luxury of exchanging philosophies and motives. Instead, she gave me her address and I headed to Fort Benning, address unknown.

When Castaneda wasn't manipulating women and preaching the virtues of a clean-shaven, hairless body as the 'way' to attain connection to the source, he was closing in on a hint of truth with what he called 'stopping the world.'

Every year, more than four hundred billion dollars exchange hands for 'legitimate drugs.' Cancer drugs account for more than one hundred billion dollars in revenue each year. There is more money in the treatment than the cure. The average wage of a pharmaceutical employee in the Philippines is one dollar an hour. Thirty dollars is the average price for one Ciagra tablet, with no rebate if the erection doesn't last four hours. The only thing more profitable than creating an incurable disease is creating an unwinnable war.

One company reported thirty billion in profits over the course of two years during the Iraq War. There are many more companies and many more wars. Economic disparity across the globe is greater than it has ever been in recorded human history. Terrorism has become a norm. Quantum physics, the Dalai Lama, and the internet tell us that it is all directly connected. Still, there is confusion as to why eighty percent of the first world population relies on prescription drugs to make it through a normal day.

⇥ ⇤

When I left for Fort Benning, visions of Sophia haunting me, I wasn't thinking about stopping the world, income disparity, or revolutions. I was thinking of fighting for my country and my love, Sophia.

We wrote religiously.

Though I believed I loved her once, as much as one can love, it was through those letters that I really fell in love with her ideas, her energy, all of her.

In response to my letters and emails full of Shakespearian romanticism, Sophia responded with Dickinson or Plath. On a particularly vulnerable day, in response to the sweetest of poems, Sophia sent me a taste of her Antarctic Tundra Love.

*He put the belt around my life, –*
*I heard the buckle snap,*
*And turned away, imperial,*
*My lifetime folding up*
*Deliberate, as a duke would do*
*A kingdom's title-deed, –*
*Henceforth a dedicated sort,*
*A member of the cloud.*

*Yet not too far to come at call,*
*And do the little toils*
*That make the circuit of the rest,*
*And deal occasional smiles*
*To lives that stoop to notice mine,*
*And kindly ask it in, –*
*Whose invitation, knew you not*
*For whom I must decline?*

– Emily Dickinson

Her coalition of blood and flesh was like Cleopatra and Madonna molded together into the body of a five-foot-seven-inch queen whose head rested perfectly beneath my own when we stood together. She was radiant. If the eyes truly say anything about the soul, then she was everything that is true and beautiful.

'Beauty and truth, truth and beauty.' Oh, how we rambled on with the philosophy and poetry. How we spoke of art and life, of truth and worth. We were excited to share thoughts, ideas, passions. We were excited. Eventually, for me, everything became dangerously serious. She was a nuclear magnet. After one of our long chats regarding how tragically we could destroy our friendship by taking things to the next level, I emailed her this.

*Let me not to the marriage, of true minds*
*Admit impediments. Love is not love*
*Which alters when it alteration finds,*
*Or bends with the remover to remove.*

*O no! it is an ever-fixed mark*
*That looks on tempests and is never shaken;*

*It is the star to every wandering bark,*
*Whose worth's unknown, although his*
*height be taken.*
*Love's not Time's fool, though rosy lips and cheeks*
*Within his bending sickle's compass come;*
*Love alters not with his brief hours and weeks,*
*But bears it out even to the edge of doom.*

*If this be error and upon me proved,*
*I never writ, nor no man ever loved.*

– William Shakespeare

Whispering come closer and laughing good fucking luck at once, Sophia's face was inviting and intimidating. Sometimes her response to my most intimate emails, full of quotes and thoughtfulness, would be one-liners or worse. She responded to Shakespeare.

*H–*

*"Your tongue a cancerous lump on my breast. My lungs collapse from your second-hand spit. Your memory stabs through my vision until permanently impaired."* Guess who? ...See you soon.

*–S*

A cancerous lump on my breast? How goddamn sweet. I give Shakespeare, I get Burinskas. I give love, I get collapsed lungs and second-hand spit. Flattered that Sophia respected my intellect, I was encouraged. No man ever wanted to be The *Friend* of Sophia, but I was willing because I was The Shit. Who could resist The Shit? When truth wrapped her unrelenting grip around that Nefertiti-like neck of Sophia's, I knew she'd realize life without my love would merely be survival.

A cancerous lump for God's sake. There were occasions when I was overwhelmed by something greater than myself, and sick-to-my-stomach lonely, wishing she was there. I stood on the canyon wall at Bryce, rain falling, a half rainbow over the horizon, and witnessed lightning rise out of the canyon into the heavens. I thought of my father, but he was gone. I wondered if my mother had ever witnessed such a spectacle, but she, too, was gone. It was that sort of sick-to-my-stomach, out-of-the-blue loneliness that Sophia inspired.

It was all brand-new again. Sophia was in town. Excited, I waited patiently on the couch, staring blankly at the television. My thoughts faded away from whatever was flashing in front of me until a dark circle engulfed my view.

# CHAPTER 2

# THE MERRY FRANKSTER

### *Hominid Zephyr*

*To my recess*
*vanity scampers hastily,*
*or runs*
*wild in human wind.*
*Proud,*
*she stands tall,*
*Foul*
*with human sin.*

– POOR JOHN, 1961

"Solar Cult lunar freaks wrapped in satin sheets, selling the souls of their own children, the spawn of their personal genetic mutations to this suicidal insanity. This shit's no joke. This is The Revolution."

Crazy Frank.

Raised from the ashes of Kesey's Merry Pranksters, he was a potpourri of genius and lunacy, part horn-blower, part wolf-whisperer and, according to him, part alien. A powerful mass of flesh and blood. Fatuously ensnared in the past, yet ahead of his time, he was all about The Revolution. For him it was personal.

"Evolution's catching up with us all. It's one way or the other. You better be prepared for The Revolution, man. You think this shit is new? Old as the Bible. Just follow the money, man. In sixty-one, Eisenhower gave the first televised farewell address by any president. He warns the planet that the military money-mongers are the greatest threat to democracy and human civilization. That we're all just pawns. No one cared. The ones that did are dead now or threw in with the cronies and got rich. It's coming. You better be prepared."

Life takes strange twists on occasion, landing us in the midst of relationships with people we'd have never imagined. Crazy Frank was one of these twists.

"War on drugs? What a money-grabbing farce that is. You know who waged a war on drugs? The Taliban. There wasn't a poppy seed to be found in all of the Helmand Province 'till the U.S. dropped back into town. Fifty billion dollars in war profits later and a wide-open free trade route from the poppy fields in Afghanistan direct to Commercial Street, U.S.A. Heroin epidemic, my ass. Naltrexone, buprenorphine, methadone...they were just waiting to open up the bake sale. Addict the society. Sell the treatment, but never the cure. Hell, before they even released methadone they had already spent twenty million on a marketing campaign to sell the anti-constipation medication that would be a smash hit once they addicted everyone to the opioids. You think this is all an accident?"

Worn like old rawhide, Frank's massive hands whipped through the air with a violent passion. His Popeye-thick arms bulged with the mature muscle only an older man could build over many years of hard labor.

"Some sort of cruel joke?" he continued. "Wake up. Joke's on you, man. Ha fucking ha. Accident? War on drugs, my ass. It's a war on humanity. The second fastest growing market in the U.S. is incarceration. Privatized prisons. In the god-forsaken name of free markets, prisons have been turned over to the service industry. That's a simple model. More accounts to service, more profit. There's no incentive pay for early release or rehabilitation rates. They get paid by the number of bodies they house, feed, and rape. No shit the U.S. has the highest incarceration rate per capita on the planet. On the bright side, we have the most profitable prisons in the whole wide world. Too bad Americans don't own those companies. Those poor bastards addicted to the mass-produced-for-profit opioids are incarcerated in unprecedented numbers, and the same company addicting them profits from imprisoning them. It's a war on humanity!"

Frank shouted. He shouted at us, the horses, his wolves, and the looming mountains of the Southern Vermont countryside. His intensity was tempered by the sincerity and compassion in his bright blue eyes.

"Even the Buddhists have lost their cosmic shit," he mumbled, squishing his lips together as if he was using his face to control his emotion. "Rohingya Genocide," he said, bowing his head, slowly shaking it back and forth as if to say, 'no, no accident at all.'

"The energy is amiss. When the military needs to be called in because the Buddhist monks have decided that wiping out an entire people is the only answer, well..." he paused. Looked skyward. "The shit has hit the cosmic fan. They'll tell you Russia and China are enemies. They're not enemies. They're minority shareholders of these United States of America. Saudi terrorists are our enemies? Do you know who the majority owners of this great nation are? Do you speak Arabic? German? French? Propaganda-purporting freaks leading us all to hell in a hacky sack." His intensity rose.

"You know what the fastest growing market in the U.S. is? Of course you do. Cannabis. As soon as Monsanto and Pfizer have the infrastructure in place, cannabis will be legal everywhere. They're divesting their interests in private prisons and preparing to mass-produce, price-gouge, and corner the market. But before they do that, there will be as much mass incarceration as possible to squeeze every last dime out of that scam before marijuana goes legal. Simple economics."

Frank stretched his arms, twisting his back as if the thought of it all was making his muscles hurt. He rubbed his head.

"You remember the old propaganda ads?" A pause. "Of course not, you're too young." Frank arched his back, took a deep breath, and in a nasal voice declared, "the only damaging effect of exposure to uranium is temporary balding.

It is perfectly fine that we test these weapons on you. Now get in there and secure the bomb site." His posture relaxed.

"Telling us that living within range of a nuclear test site was not harmful to our health, but being in the proximity of a 'reefer' addict could lead to mental illness, death, and demonic possession. Simple economics. Free medicine, straight from Mother Earth, isn't good for the market price."

Frank stopped. Squinted as if something were wrong or missing. He reached out his mitt of a hand and took the pipe from Weeli, exhaling a mushroom cloud.

"Temporary fucking balding. Like that's what we shoulda been worried 'bout when they used us at Bikini Beach. Dead or ball-less now, man. That's what all those poor, unsuspecting bastards are now. Dead or ball-less. How dare they?" Frank's mood shifted.

Dark.

Serious.

Angry.

It was personal. At the end of his stocky pipes, his leather hands shivered viciously.

"Serving their country and getting served up like sausage. It's still happening today, just new propaganda and different marketing tools. In California, gas fields are venting into towns introducing new cancers at rates that don't even pretend to hide the fact. Kids are playing on turf fields made of toxic shit while parents wonder why their child's experiencing random seizures and a deficit in their attention span. Entire towns and water supplies made toxic by fracking. But screw it, free markets; everybody's gotta work, right?" He looked at each one of us individually like a minister might.

Judgment.

A moment of silence.

The Vermont mountains whispered.

"Original sin. The blessed curse, consciousness," Frank pressed on. "A cosmic opportunity squandered. You really think the housing crisis was an accident? A twenty-two percent increase in personal debt across the lower ninety percent of the population, creating a more dependent, security-focused society and a monopolized rental market. Reform? There are more mortgage annuities and products now than before the so-called crisis. And now they've expanded to rental annuities. It's a riot. Almost funny." He shook his head and looked down at the earth. "Debtor society alive and well. America is just a pawn. A capitalist autocracy, under the guise of democracy, toting a flag of anti-government 'free markets,' and the autocrat isn't even American. Funny if it wasn't so tragic. Socrates said it, man, we need a new Sparta. A Sparta of the mind. Our Acropolis."

His voice softened.

"The Dalai Lama is saying humanity is on the verge of mass enlightenment. But energies can be hard to translate even for him. That little wannabe Buddha confuses energies of revolution with mass enlightenment. I'll tell you what those Buddhists have always been right about, though. It is all about The Now. Everything you do, do it all in. This three-dimensional human life is the greatest cosmic blessing, the biggest, sweetest piece of pussy you'll ever be lucky enough to fuck, and most people just don't get it. We can't let them genericize our taste buds, sanitize our cosmic senses. People are too afraid or just too stupid to fuck the shit out of life without a condom. We don't gotta teach our children safe sex, we gotta teach them to not be afraid to fuck the living shit outta life. To finger-fuck life 'till she's finger-licking good, you hear me?"

Frank fell silent. Almost smiled. He looked around for something. He focused thoughtfully until his expression was as if the truth, the answers to all, had washed over him.

"Are you good with that?" he asked. "I need a hit."

# CHAPTER 3

# THE FIRST DREAM, WAITING ON SOPHIA

### Dying Dreams

*Winter moon – cold and dry,*
*Goddess O' the night sky*
*You, my dream true do come*
*You, of all my fantasies' – sum*
*Who strikes earthly mouths dumb*
*Who feigns disdain – for the sun's*
*Warm embrace just passing by.*

– POOR JOHN, 1973

*W*rong…*wrong*…*wrong* zinged across my fragile senses, one nerve ending to the next until my synapses became dull, numbed by the notion that all I lived for, all I believed, was wrong…wrong…wrong.

I had never considered the possibility, but now it came from Her. I considered it. We meandered down the boardwalk, splashing our feet in the warm waters of the Pacific. Our brief call led me to assume the purpose of our rendezvous was for she and I to exchange gifts. I was wrong…wrong…wrong.

As we approached Santoria Park, a futuristic place where outdoor amusement mixed with twenty-first-century sit-in movie vans, my delusion came to an end. Sophia summoned a group of friends with a Queen Elizabeth sort of one-handed wave. All of the gifts from Sophia's pretty little bag landed in the unnaturally oversized hand of her steroid-head friend whom I'd never seen before. I had been reduced to 'a ride.'

"Oh, Herb, you don't think…" she flashed her most compassionate, humanitarian grin my way.

Patronizing.

Pitiful.

"You don't think I…when you picked me up I would–"

"I don't mind, just gotta go," I told her. I turned to open the car door.

"But, Herb, weren't we going to the pier later? I told everyone you'd take us to the pier. I'll call you later."

⇒· ·⇐

I rode the free lane up to the fifty-second floor. The old blanket hanging on the wall conjured images of the great American West. Bamboo drapes hung in front of the self-shading windows. My brother stood before me. He didn't look so well. He rarely did. The poor bastard. Nothing seemed to go right for him. More often than not, it was his own doing and less the universal conspiracy he believed formed against him. Either way, he was my brother.

"What are you doing here?"

"She always has to talk. Like, she gets mad at me just because I don't, like, tell her everything I did, or want to listen to every shit-ass experience she has every goddamn day. It doesn't mean I don't love her. I need to be alone for a little while, you know?" He rubbed his arm, nodded his head, and concluded pitifully, "we broke up." He dropped his cigarette into a half-empty beer can.

"Hey, at least now you got your freedom," I told him, playing along with the idea that this was his reason for showing up. "When she was with you all you did was complain about what a pain in the ass she was, man. You got your freedom. Right?"

"Freedom? I'm paying for a Hover GT-One I owned four years ago, man. I—"

"They repossessed it, huh?" I asked.

"I have to pay...I have to pay for what? A stupid Hover I don't have? Plus, supposedly I owe excise for that SkyCycle. Taxes are the ticks that suck the blood out of...out of...my ass, I guess."

"How did you end—"

"Don't even start with me, man," he cut me off. I didn't much care to fight him. I wanted to be alone to think, reconcile.

"Don't even start with that, you gotta, you could've bullshit, man. 'Cause you're wrong. You're dead wrong."

*Wrong…wrong…wrong.*
*Zing…zing…zing.*

"You know what I could've done? I could have sucked up to her at least 'till I had another Hover, you know? I mean, least 'till I could get around. Now I got no ride, no pussy, and I'm broke, man."

There it was. A hint of truth. Normally I'd leave it alone, but this whole being wrong thing was getting to me.

"Look at you, man. Who are you kidding? You don't care about losing her. You care about being broke and having no one to use for a ride. What do you need?"

"What do you mean, what do I need?" he snapped back at me. "Screw you. That look on your face, like you know everything. I'm not here 'cause I need anything, man. You're wrong."

*Wrong…wrong…wrong.*
*Zing…zing…zing.*

"You know, you're a condescending douche sometimes. Like you got it all figured out. What do you know? You couldn't be honest with yourself if you wanted to be."

"Really?" my tone shifted, "I'm condescending? Generous is what I am. Every time you get yourself into one of these shit jams, I bail you out and you have the nerve to call me condescending? And what the hell do you know about being honest?"

"What do I know?" he spat, his face lighting up like I just opened the pearly gates for him. "What do I know about being honest? You lie to yourself about Sophia. Never gonna happen and you know it, but you're too desperate to be honest with yourself. You pretend you're this great person, but you know you're the most selfish person on the face of the planet. You lie to yourself about me and Jenna so you can feel better about your own family. That's what I know."

Rage was rising within me. I wanted to thrust my fist right through his cheekbones.

"You take and take and take," my volume increased with each word, "and you have the gall to judge me? Why don't you be honest and say why you're really here. What do you need?"

His expression and tone softened. "Can't you be kind to your own brother for once? For once just pretend you don't know everything. I'm not here 'cause I need anything." His eyes looked sad, honest. "When did you start thinking so little of your own brother, man? When did you become so cynical?"

*Cynical?* The zinging gave way to self-scrutiny. Here I was, calling my own brother a liar and a good-for-nothing taker. It hadn't even occurred to me that he was being honest. *When was it exactly,* I wondered, *that I got to be so cynical, so skeptical? Was I wrong about this, too?*

*Wrong…wrong…wrong.*

My entire life, people have told me what an impressive person I am considering I come from poverty and lost my parents at a young age. Yet here is Anthony, my little brother, who lost his parents before he even really knew them. The closest thing he had to a parent was our sister Jenna and, despite doing the best she could, considering her own situation, I was even skeptical of her. *When did I become such a cynic?*

"It's not fair," Anthony went on, "you never believe a thing I say and…are you even listening to me? Herb? Herb!"

"Sorry, man. I hear you." He was right, though, I wasn't listening. I was scrutinizing myself and, at the same time, could not get Sophia out of my mind. "Really, man," I said, "that sucks. Is there anything you need?"

"Well," he said, his tone completely shifting, "I could really use your teleport to get to San Diego and a few bucks."

There it was. I was right, right, right. Somehow it didn't have the same impact.

"The teleport is expensive, you know? Every time you use it I get charged at least–"

"Forget it," he mumbled. A defeated expression. "I'm sorry, man. Forget it. You're right. I lied to you. I'm gonna see if Monica can help me out."

"Just use the thing. Here." I handed him three bills and the teleport.

"Thanks," he said. I felt sorry for him, that he could never look me in the eye while taking the money. He was gone.

⇒+ +⇐

The television rang. It was her.

"I was hoping I'd still see you tonight."

"Sure," I said, but I wasn't quite finished. I had to stipulate that we would be alone. This time it would be our time. I wanted to make sure it was clear. "Sure. But it's just going to be–"

"Hey, Herb." His big, fat muscle-head popped into view, taking up a quarter of the screen. He closed in behind her. "Pick us up at the park. We're going to the pier, man. The pier, you hear?" I wanted to vomit. She pushed his head out of the way.

"So, how long," she went on, entirely unfazed, "before you think you'll be here?"

There was a banging in the background. Maybe Bighead was hitting the telephone intake. "Stop that...huh...cut it out," she laughed, whispering to the oversized monkey behind her.

*Bang, bang, bang.*

His face grew larger and larger on the screen. He tickled her from behind. His face closed in on me. She giggled "cut it out," but she didn't mean it. He looked straight into me.

"Hey, Herb," Musclehead grinned, "You're wrong, Herb. Wrong, wrong, wrong."

*Bang, bang, bang.*

The image faded as the sound gave way to

*Bang, bang, bang.*

I woke. With the lingering hangover of a miserable heartbreak, I realized Sophia was at the door. Even in my dreams she broke my heart. I was in the worst of moods to see her.

"I'm so glad you're here."

# CHAPTER 4

# PROCESSING PARTNERS AND POLITICALLY CORRECT CANNIBALS

*I hope it will always be a subject of humiliating reflection to me, that I was, once, an active instrument, in a business at which my heart now shudders.*

– Reverend John Newton

Thousands of years of trial and error in ancient South American design led to crafting a perfect separation of light and space. That separation was now a part of my daily life. The sun, split beautifully by the Chilean blinds, rose in my bedroom. The white plaster had a few stains that stretched across the ceiling like the arms of an alien starfish floating and feeling her way through the Milky Way. The cherry-wood window frames grew along the center of the wall, climbing their way around doorways, windows and the covered fireplace. With the creeping light came morning, approaching slowly like a careful, steady predator. It was to be a doozy.

"Long," I sighed. With a single syllable, I explained my morning to a colleague standing at the threshold of my dull gray cubicle.

My journey began early. Bumper to bumper automobiles shifted like slow-moving waves rippling one car at a time. Snow fell like feathers from the heavens as a car rippled right into my rear end. There was no shouting and no real damage done to either of our cars, just a minor delay in both our travels. We didn't pass papers or information. I hoped to creep slowly back into the shifting sea of automobiles. In my rearview mirror, the mirror through which most things are seen, I saw a gray State Police cruiser slide right into the car that had just hit me. Before I had even inched one car length ahead, I heard the voice.

"You, in the gray Beamer, pull over to the side of the road." I couldn't believe this cop just caused an accident and had the nerve to pull me over. I quickly realized that the trooper had me pull over so that he could somehow blame our little bumper car episode for his accident. My gray sedan, the gray winter sky, and the gray of his State Trooper outfit was just too much shit gray for one morning. The officer was intimidating and rude until he discovered that Jim, the guy who just had a State Police cruiser jammed up his Mercedes' ass, was a lawyer. "Forget it," the cop said to Jim, "just give me your information." I gave him a pitiful look that was meant to say, 'and what about me?'

"Just go," he said. *Thank God*. Finally, I was on my gray old merry way.

When I arrived at work, my gray Entidot was missing, delaying me another fifteen minutes. All the reps had dots on a board, which we had to slide into 'In,' 'Out,' 'Bathroom,' 'Lunch,' or 'Meeting' columns. We were 'professionals.' Each group had its own color and ours, appropriately enough, was gray. Entidots at Entipop were very serious matters. I had to go down to Human Resources and pay five dollars for a new one. I also had to sign a 'Warning of Irresponsibility,' as they called it. My morning? Long.

Entipop.

The corporate crawl.

Globally, Entipop was the largest company of its kind. Its kind was the kind of manufacturing company that researches, makes, tests, markets, sells, lives, breathes, and dies lollipops. I started at the bottom of the barrel of monkey dung, the ladder, as it's called. I was worse than the monkeys. I was an intellectual orangutan. I ate the same bananas, swung from the same branches, but I spoke differently, with eloquent diatribes espousing the pitiful, mindless, zombie existence of corporate life. I was The Shit.

"Slaves to the dollar, man. These people sit idly as years of their precious lives just pass them by unnoticed, unattended. Pathetic. How can they buy this corporate whore bullshit?" With a commanding grasp of psychobabble vocabulary and an overly friendly, outgoing personality, I was a one hundred percent, fully-fledged master of orangutan business bullshit. Monkey sees, monkey does, orangutan or not, monkey fucking is. I pretended not to partake in the corporate atmosphere of Entipop. No golfing with the boys' club. No drinks up the street with the ladies whose bare legs helped catapult them up rungs. Thusly, I inspired a bit of a cult. Women who went out of their way to fuck me, The Shit, and men who thought I was beyond all the bullshit.

Entipop, the corporate crawl...

I started out as an E-1 Processing Partner.

A partner. Not bad at all. This was during that period of political correctness that led to ridiculous titles like 'Processing Partner.'

Titles even more asinine rose from the movement whose 'aim,' according to Crazy Frank, was to "effect the backsliding of evolution, man. Inspire bullshit instead of truth. But that's all right," he explained, "because ultimately, the lies will evidence the need for The Revolution."

A guide of politically correct terms to use when discussing terrorism and the war on terror cost six million dollars to develop, and fifteen million to communicate to government employees. In the two years it took to implement the guide, court filings and subpoenas were delayed. On the bright side, the shareholders of GoMessage, the company hired to develop and market the guide, saw an increase in dividends. The word 'terrorist' was replaced with the term 'anti-democracy radical.'

The neediest of American society, the handicapped, became the handi-capable. Barely capable of breathing and drooling, some couldn't move at all, and most could not support themselves by earning decent wages. Funding for the handi-capable was cut in half. Charitable donations were down by seventy percent.

A law first passed by the city council of San Francisco, California made its way through state legislatures and finally into law as Amendment Four Thousand Three Hundred and Seventy-One. Amendment FTSO, *Correction of Criminal Titles*, mandated that all government agencies, penal systems, and courts would "henceforth refer to those members of society, formerly referred to as 'criminals' as the 'law-abiding impaired.'" An appropriation bill for three point five billion dollars accompanied the amendment to pay for the correction or destruction of existing documents and software systems using not only the word 'criminal,' but also a slew of other terms including 'violator,' 'violators,' 'felon,' 'felons,' 'criminals,' 'villain,' 'villains,' 'transgressor,' 'transgressors,' 'bad or evil person,' and 'bad or evil people.' Of course, before the funds were allocated, the prisons would need to be transferred to private, for-profit companies. Frank said, "where there's a profit, there's a way."

James Mead raped and killed his own daughter. He sliced her up neatly and ate her. The day after the amendment passed, the California State Police caught Mead. He would 'be evaluated,' the commandant of police announced, so that 'proper treatment for his impairment could be assessed.' Truth itself was being openly raped. Energies were shifting. 'Devolution,' Frank called it.

School names, mascots, colors on buildings, flags, histories, uniforms, job titles, license plates, book titles, and

state slogans had to be changed. The United States Office
of Cost Estimation approximated the total cost at just above
three hundred billion dollars. Enough to pay off the debt of
all third world countries combined. These services were, of
course, outsourced to private, for-profit companies. Frank
called this, 'criminal.'

In Michigan, a judge ruled that the ULSA was to be
compensated by BFI Tires in the amount of twenty million dollars for selling black tires under the name 'White
Walls.' A court in Cheshire, England ruled that public officials could not use the term 'Radical Islam' to describe any
individual or group of individuals. Apparently, this term
was too inflammatory to terrorists. The lawsuit resulted in
a government payout of three million dollars, which was
later tracked to the purchase of Sarin gas used in Syria. So,
though I was an entry-level, bottom-of-the-barrel-of-shit,
piss-on-me phone rep, they called me 'Partner.' I was The
Shit.

The offer read:

*Dear Herb,*

*Entipop would like to inform you that we are extending an
offer to you for the position of E-1 Processing Partner.*

*E-1 Processing Partner annual salary starts at $20,500.*

*If you accept, please sign below.*

Right on! That sounded good. Some people spend eight
years in college, struggle through a bar exam, and still

don't get to be a partner. From the ghetto to partner. I *was* The Shit.

The letter should have read:

*Herb,*

*For less than $9 an hour, you can be a monkey at the bottom of the barrel of shit here at Entipop.*'

*Let us know.*

When I got the offer, bullshit or not, I was thrilled. I had been substitute teaching at the time. I entered corporate America as a partner for twenty-two hundred dollars a year more than a full-time first-year teacher would make in the Massachusetts public school system. Massachusetts' schools paid well compared to many other states. Frank called this, 'sinful.'

I've seen thousands of lollipops in my lifetime, but not one as a result of working for Entipop, the world's leading manufacturer of the candy. Like all good business experts, I never once came in contact with the lifeline of our business, our product, the lollipop.

The phone calls were riveting. People's lollipop likes and dislikes, wrappers gone bad, manufacturers ripping off distributors, Entipop shareholders, etc. The level of frustration a person could reach over the lack of quality in lollipops is entirely underestimated.

The complaints rolled in and I had the power to fix problems. The tools given to me: free lollipops (up to ten without supervisor approval) and coupons with no approval.

One free lollipop made many customers quite happy, even some of the rich shareholders.

"The stick on my lollipop gets soggy," a caller complained. "Why the fuck can't you all fix that? All this technology. I mean, we got emotional sensors on watches and you all can't figure out how to make the sticks stop getting fucking soggy?"

My climb up the corporate ladder began by chance and at the expense of an eager monkey.

"How do the orders get processed and tracked?" Mr. Garbway, CEO and majority owner of the company, called to test the phone reps. This morning he got me. It didn't take any time at all for my superior, who was monitoring my calls through his headset, to recognize the voice. The ardent little simian took over without warning.

"Mr. Garbway," Gomes interrupted, "let me tell–"

"Who is this?" Mr. Garbway shouted. My ears perked up. My gray Entipop day was about to get colorful. "Who is this? You're not the kid I was just talking to."

"No, Mr. Garbway, this is Mike Gomes. I'm the phone supervisor for this group and I just wanted to tell you that we here at Entipop are in the process of–"

"What the fuck?" Garbway cut him off. The rich folks were very sophisticated.

"…In the process of developing…" my monkey boss just kept right on talking. He didn't seem to mind interrupting. I was loving every second of it. Gomes was the type of person whose rare attempts at being nice were often unwittingly offensive and highlighted a certain ignorance. It was one thing to be an incompetent manager, but an entirely different, unacceptable thing to be an incompetent monkey and a prick. There were rules in corporate America that determined who could be the asshole. If one was intelligent, had a commanding grasp of the job, and good common sense, then asshole was acceptable. But if knowledge and intellect were lacking, it must be made up for with heaps of personality and charisma. Combining stupid and mean almost never worked. All rules have exceptions. Nepotism or extreme sex appeal could trump everything.

"Are you even listening to me? Where is the kid I was just talking to?" Garbway's tone shifted from angry to serious. "I guess it's moot now."

"But, Mr. Garbway, I was just–"

"Get me your goddamn supervisor. I'm sick of hearing you repeat my name like that's going to make me feel good or something. You don't think I've heard my own fucking name enough times in my life? I'm sixty-four years old, you little shit. I'm not impressed by the sound of my name, kid. Now get me your supervisor."

The area manager walked up behind my boss as he was telling Mr. Garbway, "my supervisor is in the, um, a management meeting this afternoon and I can answer any question you–"

She stripped the headset off me.

"Could you hold on for one second, sir, and I will take care of this?" she asked, interrupting Mr. Garbway in the middle of his sentence.

"Yes," I heard her say. "No, that was Mike Gomes. Absolutely. Really? I will do that. Not a problem. Thank you."

She glanced at me as she hung up the phone. "Thank you, Herb. Mike, I need to see you in my office, please."

That was the last time I ever saw Mike at Entipop. The next day, I was given Mike's job. So started my corporate climb. I was on my way up the lollipop ladder. Once I got promoted the first time, climbing just got easier. I was The Shit.

Within weeks, I proposed a new scheduling system that would handle more calls while allowing for more breaks, pleasing both management and the reps. Knowing nothing about computer systems, development, or testing, they made me Director of System Development.

In less than a year, I jumped seven levels. This is the equivalent of a Private in the U.S. Army being promoted to Master Sergeant in less than twelve months. To get to any grade in the Army, you have to have made the grade before it and held that grade for a specified amount of time. A Sergeant would have to first be a Private, then a Private First Class, then, in some cases, a Specialist, and then he or she would be eligible to make Sergeant. There were wartime exceptions and field promotions, but certainly no level of bullshit could get a Private promoted to Master Sergeant without first achieving all six previous grades. The quickest possible time that this can happen is six years. Usually, it took more like fifteen.

"I want to get out of here," I wrote my sister while sitting in a self-made foxhole at Fort Benning, Georgia. I was on a three-week AIT (Advanced Infantry Training) that consisted of spending sixteen days in the field, living in the dirt, trees, sand, and brush. "I need to get back to real life. This bullshit is really making me feel like I'm wasting my time. Our drill sergeants are the worst. They impose a hurry-up-and-wait technique on us daily. This is what most of the guys seem to complain about. Well, maybe that's second to getting laid. Hurry-up-and-wait is now getting to me. They run us for hours through the woods to get to a particular point for an ambush or something. Then we wait for hours and hope that someone shows up to be ambushed. If no one comes, we turn around and go back to our foxholes. We waste hours and days waiting to ambush an enemy that may never come."

The Army defined objectives clearly. If our objective was to cover an area in case the enemy crossed, then that is what we did. If, in fact, the enemy did cross, we would ambush that enemy. If not, we would practice the necessary patience by sitting and waiting for absolutely nothing. In the real world, however, when the appropriate time to hurry up and wait would come, bullshit would overrule common sense every time.

At Entipop, managers made bad decisions to keep up the appearance of progress. Hurry up and wait could have come in handy, but was never even a possibility in the corporate arena. Imagine if, instead of a seasoned Master Sergeant, an eager-to-please corporate monkey took command of an ambush.

"Hey, Private. Listen up. No one's out there to be ambushed. It will look like we just wasted all this time and money coming out here for nothing. Here's what I need you to do. Run out that way, east about two hundred yards, then start back this way, shooting like you're the enemy. Then we can ambush you."

"But, Drill Sergeant, if the enemy is out there it wouldn't be a good idea–"

"Shut up and start running or I'll shoot you myself."

"Yes, Drill Sergeant."

# CHAPTER 5

# WEELI AND THE BATHROOM PHILOSOPHER

*...In the days of your youth, before the evil days
come, and the years draw nigh, when you will
say, 'I have no pleasure in them;' before the sun
and the light and the moon and the stars are
darkened and the clouds return after no rain;
in the day when the keepers of the house tremble,
and the strong men are bent, and the grinders
cease because they are so few, and those that look
through the windows are dimmed, and the doors
on the street are shut; when the sound of the
grinding is low, and one rises up at the voice of
a bird, and all the daughters of song are brought
low; they are afraid also of what is high, and
terrors are in the way; the almond tree blossoms,
the grasshopper drags itself along and desire fails;
because man goes to his eternal home, and the
mourners go about the streets; before the silver*

*cord is snapped, or the golden bowl is broken, or the pitcher is broken at the fountain, or the wheel broken at the cistern, and the dust returns to the earth... Vanity of vanities...*

– [Ecclesiastes 12:1-8]

With the sun pushing through, the metallic silver drapes had a glow that gave the room a feeling of future and spirit. Electric. The one work of art hanging on the walls was a four-by-three-foot sheet of chrome, framed in gold. This was my first meeting with the executives; the CEO Mr. Garbway, and, most importantly, Weeli. I took immediate notice of Weeli, as he was the only attendee who appeared to be as young as I. He was slightly taller but I had a better nose, for sure. Appearance is key in corporate America.

"We're spending twenty-seven million dollars on this system and it's only now that someone finally develops procedures for ensuring Nacroya meets their end of the deal," Garbway said. Nacroya was contracted to build a new lollipop order system. The procedures he was referring to were those developed by yours truly, The Shit.

"Let this be a standard everyone lives up to around here."

Some standard. It was plagiarism mostly. I copied manuals from Nacroya and Microsoft, wiped out what I didn't like, and called them my own. Nonetheless, I was the highlight of the meeting.

In the atrium, I was smoking a cigarette, reveling in my greatness, when Weeli caught up with me.

"Less than a month into your new job and you already have the big boy's attention. Pretty impressive," he smiled.

"Thanks."

"You know what this means, don't you?"

"What's that?" I asked.

"Well, it means now I have to develop procedures." He shook his head, stepped in toward me, and lowered his volume. "I haven't even had to write a project plan. You just might make people get their shit together on this fucking project."

"Sorry."

"No, not at all." He reached his hand out to me. "Weeli."

"Herb," I replied.

"Herb?" he responded curiously. "Like Grape Crush or skunkweed?"

"Weeli? As in, you lie, I lie, we all lie?"

"Fair enough," he smiled.

Weeli opened up like a fifty-foot drain at the Metropolitan Commonwealth Sewerage Treatment Plant. He chose to work at Entipop because it had nothing to do with his family's name or influence. He didn't seem to believe me when I explained that I had no idea what he was talking about.

"I'm a Dresnick," he said. Then I understood.

"So, you?" he asked.

"What's that?"

"What's your master plan?" His tone, along with his own openness, made it seem natural to respond honestly.

"Don't know, really," I told him. "I thought I'd teach. I thought I might be president. I signed up for the war. I might join the Peace Corps. You know, save the world. But shit happens, I guess."

Wearing a terribly bright pair of lime-green slacks which, if the wind or his leg moved correctly, would barely touch the top of his loafers, and tucking in the back of his white short-sleeved polo with his stubby little fingers, Garbway approached.

Corporate folklore had it that Garbway was a loon. One story told how he called the president of Grandma Leary's Lollies a cunt right to her face at the previous year's annual Lovers of the Lollipop Conference. I'd heard that he spoke in bathroom analogies at board meetings, comparing staff members to urinals.

I was flattered that he remembered me and was sure he was coming over to tell me what a good job I had done. *What do I say to him?* I thought to myself. Then I heard myself say hello to the back of his head as he looked right past me and slapped Weeli on the shoulder.

"Hey, Weelee. What's going on there, Gum Cuddler? Did I put you to sleep in the meeting or what?"

"You know," Weeli answered, "this time you managed to keep me awake, actually giving someone credit for a change." He nodded my way.

Garbway looked curiously at Weeli for a second, then at me.

"Oh yeah," he said, reaching out his hand, "you're the new hotshot, aren't you? Good job, kid."

"Thank you, sir."

"Look at that, Weelee, someone still calls me sir. You see, not all you kids are lost causes."

"Oh sure," Weeli grinned, "next time you tell me one of your demented jokes I'll say, 'I don't know, sir, tell me, why is a piece of pussy like a Three Musketeers bar, sir?' You see, it doesn't sound quite right."

"That was a good one though, wasn't it?" Garbway's shoulders shuddered up and down in rhythm with his giggle.

"Oh yeah," Weeli replied, "my little sister just loved it."

A pause.

"Hey, asshole," Weeli said, "tell Herb the one about the cowboy that got the tassels caught up in his trousers." Weeli winked at me.

"I don't have time for that one. I've got big, important things to do today, you know?"

"Don't let him kid you, Herb. This is the same guy who once spent over an hour in the bathroom with me, detailing his philosophy on why people shouldn't wash their hands in a public restroom. I think I'm going to call you the Bathroom Philosopher from now on."

"You and your friend here can call me that when you buy this company. 'Till then, so long as I sign the checks, you'll stick to calling me Asshole, and that's that. You know though, that bathroom shit is serious business." He was serious.

*Your friend here,* I thought to myself. He had reduced me, the superstar from the meeting, The Shit, to 'your friend here.' Devastating.

"You listen to me," he shouted, pointing at me with his fat little finger, "this ain't bullshit. This is life and death stuff, kid. Never wash your hands in a public bathroom. You touch your dick when you piss, don't ya? If you're standing at a urinal and you're pissing, does your hand touch your dick?"

I couldn't believe he was asking me this in front of Weeli and whoever else was out having a cigarette, but he was. He got impatient as I did not respond immediately. I didn't imagine he really wanted a response. So much for my imagination.

"Do you touch your dick?"

"Of course," I mumbled nervously.

"Of course you touch your fucking dick when you piss. Would you want to touch my dick and the shit that dribbles from the tip while I piss?"

*Oh fuck,* I thought to myself, *where the fuck is this going?* Sometimes, I thought in even more vulgar language than I spoke.

"No, sir, I would not."

"Of course you would not. And when people sit in those little stalls taking a dump or jerking off or whatever it is they're doing, would you want to touch the leftover dribble shit spasm that they might get on their hands while wiping their little assholes? Would ya?"

"Of course not, sir."

"People don't think. I did my time in the Marine Corps. I ate and touched and slept in plenty of germ-infested shit, so don't go thinking I'm some kind of paranoid germ pussy, but I wouldn't wash my hands in a public bathroom. A man walks in and takes a piss or a shit, whatever it happens to be. He touches the faucet handle with all that dribble shit on his hands. Now the faucet handle is loaded with the shit. When he's done washing, what's he grab? The same nasty faucet handle. Now he spreads it to the door handle and anything else he touches on his way out, the nasty bastard. Then you walk in and take a little and give a little. Now you got his shit and piss on your hands and you leave some of your own behind for the rest of us. Now," Garbway snatched Weeli's cigarette, took a hit, then continued, "will you ever wash your hands in a public restroom again?"

"No," I told him.

"Don't know if I believe that, Herb, but one thing's for sure. If you do," he said as he reached for the door, his back fully to me, "if you do, you'll think of me."

# CHAPTER 6

# WHAT'S THE MATTER, JACOV?

*Capitalism, despite how well it may be
camouflaged, is not much different than socialism
or communism. Like the wolf dressed as the sheep,
our system hides the truth of capitalism behind
the shroud of democracy, equating freedom with
unhindered free markets. Because of our wealth
and influence, our son has had the best education
and healthcare money can buy. Fortunately, so far,
he has never needed the best legal representation
money can buy. Our son, Weeli, was offered a
full scholarship to Harvard while less fortunate
students will work three jobs with barely enough
time to sleep, never mind study, just to get a degree
from a community college.
St. Thomas Aquinas believed that knowledge arises as
a result of intellectual analysis of all things accessible
to one's perception. Access is key to knowledge,
education, and opportunity. Equal access is not even*

*possible within a capitalist society. We must, therefore, recognize, first and foremost, that our society is a democracy, founded on the belief of equality for all. Out of the necessity for a system of day-to-day trade, capitalism in its current form has evolved. Some mistake capitalism for democracy and equality for the right to make money.*

*Our constitution calls for everyone to have an equal opportunity for life, liberty, and the pursuit of happiness. On the local level, we fight for that equality now. Even here in our city, three very basic necessities to that pursuit remain dependent on monetary status, meaning they can never be equal. The poorest of poor receive the worst health care, if any at all. The poorest of poor must work ten times as hard as the well-to-do for even a nominal education. The poorest of poor have no, or pitiful, representation in legal matters. I should know, I've been a lawyer for what seems like my entire life. Try not to hold that against me. While the poorest of poor get the least and worst of all things, the well-to-do, like my family, get smarter, richer, and healthier, live longer, and can sometimes pay to get away with murder. I submit to each and every one of you that without equal healthcare, education, and legal representation, we do not enjoy the same opportunities for life, liberty, and the pursuit of happiness, exactly the sort of equal opportunities our constitution demands.*

*I submit to each and every one of you that these*

*needs must be met for all Americans, rich or
poor, completely outside of the monetary system.
Democracy, not capitalism, must be the foundation
of our society. I submit to all of you that capitalism
has allowed our democracy to be bought and sold.
These two things, democracy and capitalism, can
coexist so long as democracy drives a fair and just
constitutional version of capitalism. These two
things, democracy and capitalism, can coexist so
long as capitalism is not allowed to buy and sell
out our democracy.*
*This nation was born from the womb of a passion
so great, brothers killed brothers, fathers killed
sons, and mothers sent their children off to die,
all in defense of these ideas. We were not born
from the womb of Apathy. We lecture the world on
human rights, dictating our stipulations while,
right here in Brockton, Massachusetts, the sons
and daughters of America are deprived of their
constitutional rights to life, liberty, and the pursuit
of happiness.*

– Linda Dresnick
Excerpt from speech to the
City Council of Brockton, Massachusetts

The Word of God Church was a majestic structure
whose centuries-old bell had rung out faithfully since
the time of reconstruction. She sang her songs through

both world wars, the Great Depression, the Civil Rights Movement, and all the triumphs and tragedies of the modern day. Her proud, white steeple stood high above a small town as it transformed into a capital of commerce and manufacturing. Within the historic structure stood the second-largest pipe organ ever constructed in all of the Americas.

"They turned it into a Wal-Mart," Weeli explained.

The months following the day Weeli and I first met were intense. We spent very little time without the other nearby. Many nights after work we found ourselves up the road at the local dive, drinking and talking, thinking aloud, sometimes encouraging and sometimes smashing each other's ideas. We had grown up in the same city, but worlds apart. We would slowly turn each other on to The Revolution.

"Completely hypocritical," he told me during one of our after-work drinking-fests. "My mother, 'Ms. Equal Education, De-privatization,' preaching to the masses in Brockton, sends me to private school. They hated religion, too. Both of them. Yet they send me to The Word of God Christian Academy?"

I don't know which Weeli felt more cheated over, having to attend the school, or its destruction in favor of a Wal-Mart. The church was on the Historic Society's list of protected properties, but the combined political power of the church and the Dresnicks could not stop the destruction.

"Private school," I laughed as Weeli complained to me, "I couldn't even fathom it. I rode my sister's banana seat Huffy 'till sixth grade. I didn't have socks or shoes. We used to mix Ramen Pride noodles with ketchup and pretend it was spaghetti and sauce. But we're both from Brockton."

Sometimes, Weeli laughed at my ghetto stories. Sometimes, he was legitimately shocked and genuinely attempted to grasp what my experience had been like. "I rode a Suzuki DR-350 through two winters 'cause it was my only transportation. The starter didn't work. No shitting you. I used to have to run it downhill to start it. Try that in a blizzard. You know how many times I dropped that thing in the snow or in the middle of an intersection when it stalled? Good times. That's the funny thing. I didn't so much mind." Weeli's first car was an Eighty-Six Porsche, which he received as a birthday gift on his seventeenth birthday. It came with life lessons.

"Son," Weeli's father said to him as he handed the keys over, "let's take a ride." There was small talk, 'oohs' and 'ahhs,' before his father got down to it. "Think of this car as a metaphor for life, Son. What you put into it, how you take care of her, how much you respect the car and yourself as the driver, will dictate what this car can do for you. Put cheap gas into her instead of the good stuff and, well, she's not going to move too well. Don't change the oil, the water, the coolant, and she'll die. Don't pay attention while you're driving her, Son, and, well…you'll crash and burn. Do you understand?"

"Sure, Dad."

"I'm talking about life here, Son," Ronald Dresnick went on.

"Sure, Dad. What you put into it, you get out of it. I know."

"I'm talking about you, too, you know? Your life, your body, your brain…you've got to respect yourself as the driver, Son. You are the driver."

"Got it, Dad."

"I'm talking about women, Weeli...women...and you. You understand?"

"You mean Mom?"

"Weeli."

"Sure, Dad."

"Son, wear a condom. Now take me home."

That was it. That was the one and only birds and bees conversation Papa Ron would have with Weeli. Weeli's father was Brockton's Ward Six City Councilor, President of the New England Chapter of Lawyers for Civil Liberties, and Counsel to Brockton's second female mayor, Zahava Coleman. Ronald Dresnick was among New England's intellectual elite.

"My parents?" Weeli explained to me one drunken night, "two of the most intelligent people you could ever meet. But my father was a complete donkey with any father-son shit. Fortunately, my mom was great for father-son talks. I have a built-in respect for women that really helps me get laid."

Weeli's mother, Linda Dresnick, was the first female mayor of Brockton. Ronald and Linda met while trying a case in the Plymouth County District Court. Linda was prosecuting Joseph Graziano, largest known dealer of marijuana on the South Shore of the Commonwealth of Massachusetts. Weeli's father was the prominent defense attorney representing Graziano. It was a lunatic judge, I.C. Potcrack, who really brought the two of them together.

By the end of the trial, Potcrack had broken rules of court and villainized Ronald Dresnick as a criminal in his own right. There was no chance of a fair trial. Though

Graziano was convicted, Linda did not feel victorious. As a prosecutor, she was infuriated at the vigilante justice the judge exacted. She began putting together a case against the judge who she believed had broken several laws and ignored the code of ethics altogether. Ronald became her unpaid partner, assisting on the case.

Ron researched Potcrack's history, personally interviewing over three hundred witnesses. He listened to astonishing tales of police officers, district attorneys, the accused, and even the victims in various cases, who were verbally abused, held in contempt, fined, or worse. In one case, Potcrack purportedly fined his own bailiff for 'stupidity and incompetence,' banning him from the courtroom for three weeks.

Having to substantiate charges of alleged abuse, Ronald and Linda began pulling every piece of documentation, from newspaper articles to court transcripts, to help support their case. As luck and good fortune would have it, they stumbled upon an author by the name of Wildorf B. Crossbar. Crossbar wrote a series of fictional short stories. All of his stories, published monthly in *The Plymouth Rock Noise*, were allegedly based on real court cases, all of which were presided over by the honorable Judge Potcrack. They'd struck gold. This was the first of many of those stories.

*Issue IX, Volume III, September 1998*

*Jacov,*
*In the Matter Of*

*By Wildorf B. Crossbar*

The killer in the court
Of the wolf with the wart
Charms the shepherd's little sheep
Their soul, he takes for keep
All the while, children smile in a
playground of steel.

*– Ormus Shalinski*

*Nine months of confinement in the Walpole, Massachusetts maximum-security prison passed slowly for Jacov, but affected him little. Nine months of suffering and fighting for justice passed slowly for the Harsbros, and took a much greater toll. Finally, the Jacov matter came to an end.*

*The verdict:*

*'In the matter of* The State of Massachusetts vs. Jacov O. Dorsmell, *whereby the Prosteria County District Attorney charges that at or about four twenty, on the evening of February the fourteenth, in the year nineteen hundred and ninety-two, Mr. Jacov O. Dorsmell committed first-degree murder, second-degree murder, premeditated murder, and voluntary manslaughter, and that he, the accused, Mr. Jacov O. Dorsmell, was fully responsible for the homicidal death of the late Mr. J. L. Harsbro. We, the jury charged this day, November the twenty-second, in the year nineteen hundred and ninety-six, in the courtroom of the honorable Judge I.C. Potcrack, with our civic duty to subscribe swift and fair justice to this matter, do hereby find the defendant, Mr. Jacov O. Dorsmell, GUILTY of first-degree murder."*

The killer, Jacov O. Dorsmell, was about to address the court. The family, from left to right included: Maria Harsbro, the victim's wife of thirty years; Dana Harsbro, son of twenty-six years; Jennifer Pier Colletta Harsbro, daughter of twenty-five years.

"I," Jacov began to spew. His large, brash hands scrubbing the top of his bald head as if he were being eaten alive from the inside. The hands slowed. They lowered from the top of his head, sliding downward until they came into Jacov's mouth. He began to gnaw at his fingernails. The gnawing was temporary. His hands moved up his face, rubbing his eyes, then the back of his neck. As his posture relaxed he looked exhausted. His shoulders sank, resting naturally in their sockets. He began to squirm about his lower torso as if he had to relieve himself. He flattened his fingers on the wood podium, fixing his eyes on the honorable Potcrack, infiltrating him from a distance.

"I can say whatever I would like to say? That is, in addressing the court, Your Honor? I mean, so long as I am not to offend the court? But," Jacov's eyes remained fixed on the judge, "I do get to address the court freely?"

"That is accurate," Potcrack replied, "so long as you are reasonable."

"And," Jacov replied to His Honor, "I imagine you will alert me and stop me should I do anything to the contrary?"

"Correct."

"Well then, thank you, Your Honorable Crackpot… Potcrack."

"Potcrack, Jacov, Potcrack. Stick to Your Honor," His Honor said.

"I'm sorry, Your Honor." Jacov turned his focus on the family. His face became flush. His eyes bulged. His fingers crept slowly upward, knees came together, then apart, then together, and then apart again as he squirmed. Although restless and squirmy, Jacov looked sure, confident about something. Potcrack scratched at a hair hanging just below the left nostril of his wide nose. Jacov tilted his head slightly to the left, stretched out his neck, rolled the corner of his lip up toward his right eye, swallowed air, and fixed his stare on Mrs. Harsbro.

"I dreamt the other night," Jacov began, rubbing his forehead, "the worst dream of my entire life. I'm sick to my stomach just thinking about it. We are on the coast, but it isn't the coast. Me, my brother, and our little sister. Maybe it was the Pacific. It felt like that. We are walking. The three of us are happy. Waves are crashing. It's peaceful. Beautiful. It's daytime. You can see clear across the ocean." He shifted. A look of anguish. "I see it." His voice is on the verge of cracking, breaking into tears. He composes himself. "I see it. I'm excited at first. I'm excited to be the first to see it. It's massive and breathtaking. The volcano blows, but it is so far away. I call to the two of them. Then I realize it's not far enough away. It isn't a volcano. I can feel it. It's the earth. She's opening up all around. Under the ocean. Around our feet. Everywhere. The only chance we have to survive is the water. I tell them to jump into the water. I tell them it's our only chance, but..." his voice cracked. Tears. He tried to compose himself. "My brother doesn't listen. He just runs and there's nothing I can do. But my little sister looks at me. She's afraid, but she believes me. She trusts me. She doesn't run. She jumps in behind me. We're not dead, but the hot lava has reached the water. I pull myself out of the water. The lava's still coming. I feel a sting, but I am alive. I remember she is behind me. I turn to find her. She rises out of the water and...and as she comes out, I reach to grab her, hug her, to tell her we're alive. But her smile is all wrong. She has a hole through her cheek." Jacov put his right hand to his face as if to feel the hole. "All the way through. She looks at me. I can see it in her eyes. 'Why? Why?' That's what she wants to say, but she says nothing. She's burning, dying, right in front of me. She's not angry. She is so sad. So helpless. I am her only hope, but it's hopeless. I push her in front of me, up a hill. 'Run,' I tell her. I throw her over a rock. I am too selfish to let her die first. I can't watch her die. I know we're doomed. The lava catches up with me and I wake up." Jacov rubbed his head with both hands. "I was everything she trusted. In that moment she was all that mattered. I didn't care that I was dying.

"I tell you this dream to bring you comfort. Your husband died happy. He wasn't wearing the expression my sister had in my dream. He was truly happy. That fatal day, at Cran Deer Crossing, was as peaceful and pretty as a freshly-shaken snow globe. It was a magic day. He looked me as straight in the eye as I'm looking you right now and asked, 'Are you going to kill me?' Just like that, he said it. I shook my head. He said, 'You know, I don't think I could be any happier.' He looked around and said, 'What a stage to die on.' What a smile he wore." Jacov stared at Mrs. Harsbro.

"*Well, if that is all, Mr. Jaco—*"

"*No!*" *Jacov shouted, turning his eyes to Judge Potcrack.* "*No, I'm not done, Crockpot. There are two things I would like—*"

"*Your Honor, Jacov, just Your Honor. And for—*"

"*Yes, I'm sorry, Your Honor, but I was not finished,*" *Jacov cut His Honor off, turning his attention back to Mrs. Harsbro. "Your husband died happy. I could see it in his eyes, everything he loved was right there in that moment. He was happy. That's how any of us would want to go. It's how we'd want anyone we love to go. He didn't mind leaving you, leaving your children, leaving the—*"

"*Shut up!*" *Mrs. Harsbro cried.*

"*Maria,*" *Jacov tried to continue.*

"*Order, Mrs. Harsbro!*" *the judge bellowed.*

"*Maria, I am only telling you,*" *Jacov continued over the sound of Maria's voice, the judge's gavel, and the children calling out, "Mom, don't let him," and "Mom, it's all right."*

"*Order, order! I said order!*" *His Honor shouted.*

"*Don't you call me Maria, you sick bastard!*" *Maria Harsbro was now standing and shouting at Jacov.*

"*Order!*" *Potcrack roared in a deep, King Kong voice, dropping the gavel with force. The courtroom fell silent.*

*Potcrack tilted his head to the left, stretched his neck in every direction, brought his lips together, and rolled them up toward his nose, shifted slightly in his seat, finally bringing his right hand down over his face as if to wipe everything away. It worked. His face was straight now.*

"*This is my courtroom. This is a house of law and order. A sanctuary of justice.*" Potcrack leaned back in his leather chair. "*This is a house of justice. None of you will disgrace it. Mrs. Harsbro, if you have another outburst, I will hold you in contempt of court. Jacov, you will continue respectfully and the rest of you will control yourselves.*"

Jacov closed his eyes, stretched his head back, took a deep breath, and began again.

"*Even now I cry just thinking about it. About her. I could see on her face, in her eyes that she knew her life was over and for her, nothing could be worse. See,*" Jacov paused, focusing again on Mrs. Harsbro, "*that's the thing. It wasn't like that for him. His eyes were bright. He lit up. He looked happier than most of us ever look. I don't want pity. I want you to know that you don't have to feel any guilt or sadness because your husband, your father, didn't.*"

Mrs. Harsbro peered at the judge, then Jacov, her eyes blinking rapidly, nose twitching, her body struggling to restrain itself.

"*It's what I didn't see. That's what you need to know. His eyes were not sad that they would never look upon you again. Not sad that you would never see him again. Not sad that you would have to survive without him. All of you. You don't have to feel guilty. You can be okay with—*"

"*Shut up!*" Mrs. Harsbro was standing again.

"*Order, Mrs. Harsbro.*" The gavel crashed down.

"*How can you let him...*"

Potcrack rose to his feet and looked down upon her. "*Order, Mrs. Harsbro. This will be your last warning. All of you.*"

*She fell into her seat.*

"Jacov," Potcrack had lowered his voice, shifted his tone to something gentler, "have you anything further before sentencing?"

"Your Honor, I have been trying to put the family here at ease and I haven't had a chance to address the court regarding myself, my sentencing, Your Honor."

"This is your time, Jacov. Proceed."

"Thank you, Your Honor. Have you ever smoked cigarettes? You know, I mean, totally addicted?"

"Jacov, this is not a question and answer session. This time is for you to address the court with anything you believe should be considered when determining your sentence. What do you have to say?"

"Your Honor, I quit smoking cigarettes the day I killed Mr. Harsbro. That's what I'm trying to say. For the first time in my entire life, I really did it. I quit. I didn't hide cigarettes in the barrel of my shotgun. I didn't keep a tin of chewing tobacco in my pocket. I just flat out, cold turkey quit. Do you know what that's like?"

Potcrack reached for his glass, sipped slowly and responded with a nod. Jacov brought both of his hands up to his head.

"The pain was brutal. In my stomach, in my gut... in my head. I mean, it gets you angry. Angry as hell. The withdrawals are unbearable."

"Jacov," Potcrack interjected, "are you blaming what you've done on cigarettes?" His Honor's question was sincere.

"Your Honor, I'm not blaming cigarettes. But I believe that in sentencing me, any extenuating circumstances are supposed to be taken into consideration, Your Honor, and all I'm telling you is that nicotine is a powerful addiction. Cigarette companies are responsible for killing people, for the deaths of the addicted. If they can be blamed for people killing themselves then, at the very least, isn't it plausible that they are in some way responsible for my horrific behavior? The withdrawals are mind-altering and mood-altering. I know I would've made better decisions that day...I might have been somewhere entirely different even if I hadn't quit smoking, Your Honor. We might not even be here today if it weren't for goddamn cigarettes. I think the tobacco companies owe the Harsbro family an apology." Jacov raised his head proudly. He looked at the judge to make sure he had connected. Potcrack returned an affirming nod.

"Do you have anything further, Jacov?"

"Just one thing, Your Honor. You have been more than fair and understanding to all parties in this case. I will accept whatever sentence you impose, as I know it will be fair and just. Thank you, sir."

After a brief recess, Potcrack returned with his sentence.

"Let me begin by saying I am so very sorry to the Harsbro family. No one should ever endure such a tragedy. I think we can all take some comfort in knowing that not only has Mr. Dorsmell expressed genuine remorse for his actions, but it is very likely Mr. Harsbro, if nothing else, died a happy man. That is something the rest of us can only hope for. With regard to you, Mr. Dorsmell, I have found you to be refreshingly honest and open with this court through these proceedings. You have made extraordinary efforts to comfort the victim's family while lifting the ribbon of darkness from the facts of the matter. I have considered the extenuating circumstances and have found that, though you are ultimately responsible for your own actions, you are not the only one at fault. I will recommend that the district attorney pursue the tobacco angle as I would agree that, at the very least, it was a contributing factor and, at most, possibly an accomplice or worse. Nonetheless, sir, you have committed murder. I have considered that you have already served nine hard months in the Walpole Penitentiary.

"Mr. Dorsmell, you are hereby sentenced to nine months' time served, a five-year suspended sentence and lifetime probation. Should you violate the conditions of your parole at any time in your life, your five-year suspended sentence will be served at Bridgewater State House of Corrections. Good luck, Son."

# CHAPTER 7

# FAMILY MATTERS

*I need a cranberry bog of words submerged and twined up in muddy senses and swampy times to describe the utter perplexed-ness of family. And what of God? Oh, like those questions really matter in times like these. God isn't willing to stand at the threshold, to stave off the crackheads and piranhas that violate in dark caves, soul-suckers and molesters who creep along the fringe crevices of hell on earth. Welcome, everyone.*

– SAMUEL F. WILLIAMS
EXCERPT FROM *THE AFTERMATH, RELIGION*

Freelance writer Crossbar gave Weeli's parents high-lighted transcripts of every case Judge Potcrack presided over, but to simplify matters, he sorted out the 'Top Ten,' or what he called, 'the exceptionally absurd.'

"Take a guess," Weeli said to me, "whose case made it to the top ten? Someone we both know and love." I was befuddled.

"On behalf of the people of the Commonwealth and the entire civilized world," Weeli went on, "in the matter of our fearless CEO, *Garbway vs. The State of Massachusetts*, we demand self-cleaning, auto-flushing toilets, and automatic sinks in all public bathrooms."

"He did not?"

"He listed witnesses who would testify to when a public toilet flushed at the wrong time. He had medical reports of rashes caused by splashing toilet water. The thing is, my mother said if it weren't for Garbway, bathrooms wouldn't be nearly as sanitary as they are. So anyway, Crossbar helped them disbar Potcrack and, ever since, he's devoted his writing to the stories of my folks. I mean, that's really how all those cults started, and probably why my mother was able to win the election for mayor."

Weeli's mother was assassinated outside of the Brockton Police Station less than one year into her time in office. She had been reduced to a DOTS (dead on the scene). The cults intensified, and her popularity took off like the conspiracy theories zipping across the internet at light speed.

"Imagine what it's like," Weeli told me later, "reading this shit while you're preparing for the funeral. The police chief killed her because he wanted to be mayor. My father killed her because he wanted to fuck the police chief. A corporate conspiracy against de-privatization. The government assassinated her. The worst is when you start believing some of it. Some of them are still out there claiming she's alive and well. That's how all this Laura shit got started."

Weeli's sister Laura, who some referred to as Linda Jr., inherited a good many of Linda's cult fans. Because of her own accomplishments and political views, some looked to her to pick up where her mother left off. Like Weeli fought his wealth, Laura made conscious efforts to avoid the comparisons, but also capitalized on the notoriety.

With help from the various LMD (Linda Michelle Dresnick) cults, political friends, and a federal government program known as Secular Student Assistance for the Betterment of the Homeland, Laura Dresnick developed a program that provided temporary shelter, jobs, and training for the homeless. The program, including the shelters, was mobile and catered to those who would make a measurable effort. The system was designed to allow four mobile programs throughout the state at any given time. Each would remain in a needed area for no more than eight months. New England's homeless numbers dropped by twenty percent the first year, then thirty percent the second. America, it seemed, was too easy for her.

When she obtained her doctorate, she left the program for one of the most repressive regimes on the planet: Iran. Weeli spoke of the matter covertly, as if she worked for the CIA. With support from the U.S. government, Laura was operating under a program developed in the late seventies by the Carter Administration, which promoted the education and liberalization of Iran.

In the nineteen twenties, Reza Shah Pahlavi (then known as Reza Kahn) led a coup and crowned himself Supreme Ruler of Iran. Although he'd been a lifelong conservative militant, he began a wave of changes to free women and liberalize the kingdom. In the fifties, in an attempt to quell the communist movement, the United States and Great Britain replaced Reza Kahn with his son, and armed anti-communist Islamic extremists and militant zealots. They rolled back the clock on all human rights, especially for women. In the sixties, the Shah launched the 'White Revolution,' during which he tried to undo what the U.S. and extremists had done to Iran. Social and political reforms, designed to modernize Iran, were accompanied by rapid industrialization. While he attempted to liberate his own country in a progressive, democratic direction, the U.S. initiated a policy against him. The policy, known as *Iron Fist, Not Iron Curtain*, stated that extremists must be supported so that they could keep strict control of the country, thus keeping the Soviet Union and communism from taking over. By seventy-nine, the turmoil pushed the country to the brink of revolution. The Shah was forced out and the Ayatollah Khomeini left his comfortable home in Paris, France to impose one of the most dreadful and repressive regimes in human history. The Carter Hostage Crisis, Iran-Iraq War, Conservatives' Revolution, the reigning-in of women's rights, and rise of armed extremists all ensued.

How I came to know these things about Iran was all Laura's doing, unbeknownst to her. I spent a week of sleepless nights, of coffee and cigarettes, of smoking pot and dropping perks, obsessively searching the internet for everything there was to know about Iran. Oh, Iran, mysterious land where Laura dwelled. Night after night, cigarette after cigarette, joints, pills, coffee, with burning eyes and stiff fingers, I fell in love with the mystery of that exotic place and the idea of her.

Iran.

Voting age is fifteen.

Percentage of households owning illegal satellite dishes is forty-one.

Streets have two names almost everywhere.

Primary religion is Islam.

Primary language is Persian.

Primary resource is oil.

Iranians use oils for cosmetics, medicines, ointments, lubricants, glues, drinks, foods.

Iranians use herbs for cosmetics, medicines, ointments, lubricants, drinks, foods, highs.

Most Iranians are not militant.

'Iranian' and 'Terrorist' are not synonymous.

Salman Rushdie is not Iranian.

There are at least one thousand four hundred and fifty-one sites on the internet with information relevant to The Nation of Iran.

At least one human being has counted each and every one of these Iranian-related sites on one sleepless night.

# CHAPTER 8

# THE SECOND DREAM

*In a dream, in a vision of the night, when deep*
*sleep falleth upon men, in slumberings upon the*
*bed; Then he openeth the ears of men, and sealeth*
*their instruction.*

– [JOB 33:15-16]

Like the moonlit shadow of the hoodoo, premonition can be creepy, comforting, or both. Upon awakening I found my black cotton sleepers stained like I hadn't seen since freshmen year, when the last of my wet dreams vanished into memories of the good old days.

A soft fire warmed the large room, framed in thick oak. Two massive doorframes opened into the unknown. A group of entertainers and three young women sat with us.

An older lady came and went sporadically, occasionally followed by a small girl.

Weeli spoke of The Revolution with a comfortable, easy passion. On the floor, sitting with her feet stretched out and her beautiful head resting against my right knee, long brown hair hanging over my leg, was the girl who would cause that stain on my cotton trousers. She was brilliant, soft, and gentle. Enough to make tears come to my eyes just thinking of her now.

"You see," Weeli said, his face glowing in the flickering orange light, "there will always be the problem of the seemingly enlightened minds excusing themselves from personal responsibility under the guise of the restrictions of reality. There are no restrictions. The idea that others cannot understand, that The Revolution cannot be affected, is the restriction I speak of. It is the adult who directs the child, thus tainting the child. The intellectual is the adult who refuses to believe in the child's wisdom. They, and not the child, have been tainted by their experience. Thus, their perception of the restrictions has been predetermined."

The old lady appeared briefly. The young girl, of maybe seven years, followed behind, wrapping her arms around the torso of the older woman as if to hide behind her. Then her tiny innocent face poked out.

"All but one of you is tainted," the girl smiled. "The wisdom of a child is beyond your comprehension." She slipped away, following the old lady through the opening in the front of the room, disappearing in the shadow of the hallway.

"So, then, do you believe you are up for this?" the girl whose chin rested on my knee asked Weeli.

"I am," Weeli folded his hands in front of his face.

"You would lead this Revolution?" she whispered, pressing against my leg.

"I will," Weeli responded.

"I will," everyone said in unison. The woman at my knee grabbed my hand.

"You will," she said as she pressed her head into my thigh. I was aroused.

"I volunteered at a nursing home when I was little," Weeli continued.

"That's a lie," I interrupted. The woman pressed against me harder and shook her head at me as if to say, 'let him continue.' But it was my story.

"I would go in after my paper route and play checkers and chess with the old people. Now, besides the fact that even as a kid I enjoyed their war stories about life and their words of wisdom, the fact was, I went there for entirely selfish reasons. Some of the elderly whom I helped were bitter, demented, and angry, so much so that sometimes they would lash out verbally or physically. Even the people who had no good stories, no words of wisdom, and could barely keep the drool from spilling over onto me, I still played and talked with them. And when I was a kid, I thought of myself as the least selfish person on the planet, but the fact is, I did it for me. Frankly, it's a liberating thing to come to know that the most selfless acts I have ever committed were truly selfish. All good deeds are purely selfish. And," Weeli looked into me, "when someone dies for you, do not feel guilt. That is the most selfish act there is."

"And I," the woman said, pushing her right hand against my knee and raising herself up, "will partake in purely selfish deeds. Come," she told me.

We left the room through the dark wood-framed opening to the right, into a hallway, and then she was gone. Instead, I found the old lady who had disappeared earlier, standing with her back to me, staring dreamily out the window. Past her, through the window, a storm raged. I was nervous. Self-conscious. My apprehension was tempered by something else, something very strange. A sixth sense sort of thing, as though I could feel this lady's awareness of my energy, my anxiety.

"Don't be so nervous, young man," she said without turning around. "You want her, but you're not ready."

"I'm sorry?"

"Don't be," she continued. "After a hundred and three years on this planet, there are things you know. Some things are easier to recognize, you see? A man's lust is one of the easiest. Oh, you can almost smell it in the air. Men are so animalistic still...and how lovely a thing that is. A young man's lust has the power and the energy to divide a planet and you, my dear friend, no matter how hard you try, cannot escape that which you are, a man. You have lust on your mind. In your veins, lust. But you aren't worthy of her right now. Your lust is tempered like a wild wolf, wanting, but something won't let you. Tempered lust, my friend, is no good at all. Why yours is tempered, I don't know."

*Tempered lust?* I thought to myself. *If my lust was tempered, Sophia was to blame.*

"It is not this other woman who tempers you. You hear without listening. I am telling you now, you are the—"

"Mother," she interjected, walking around the corner, not yet in full view, "leave the young man alone. You'll terrify him." She swung her body around the doorway. She had changed her clothing and let down her hair. My mouth dropped open, wide and inviting. Tribes of flies could have laid their eggs on my tongue, fucked, and laid again for all I cared. I was beyond control. Her bare feet shone in the glow of the lamp at the entrance of the room. Her legs exposed, smooth. I couldn't help but want to suck on every inch of them. She wore thin black shorts like the shorts of a soccer player, but without the soccer. Her torso was covered with a sheer white t-shirt. There was nothing beneath the shorts or the shirt. The flies were lying away. As she stood there, knowing she was so wanted and wanting in return, I could feel her irresistible energy pulling me in.

"If you have something to say then speak up. Otherwise, please stop staring like that unless you really mean it. You don't really mean it. That wide-open mouth of yours wouldn't know what it means to mean it, even if it wanted to. Close your mouth and come to me."

I wondered why she humbled me before taking me. I said nothing. She closed in behind me, wrapped both arms around my torso, and pulled me to her. I leaned back, slowly pushing my head against her mouth, for the moment wanting nothing more but to savor the feeling of her lips against my neck and ear. Her hands wrapped tightly against my abdomen as she kissed my neck. She lifted her hands up to my head, pressing her fingers beneath my hair and thrusting her body against my backside. I wanted to come right then and there...I wanted to come into her...I wanted to hold her and hold her and hold her.

I wanted.

In an instant we were in her room, two soft candles burning on either side of her bed. I wanted to smell her, taste her, breathe her. We fell into each other in ways I'd never known possible. We fell into each other the way I had dreamed Sophia and I one day would, in the way that brings tears to the eyes of passionate lovers. We were like the wolves. Like the alpha pair, frolicking in bliss, indulging everything in our natural beings. Sure of ourselves, sure of each other, taking in as much of each other as is humanly possible. Even the wolves and coyotes would have been proud. She cupped my ass cheeks tightly, as I was about to come into her. Then a bright light, like the glow of paradise welcoming the resurrection, shone into the room. I thought it must be the sort of spiritual peak you could only read about in a novel, but it wasn't. The light came through the door as the old lady stepped into the room wearing a bright grin.

"It is time to go now."

The door slammed and I woke. I was alone in my bed, sweaty and stained. I held myself and laid my head back against my drool-drenched pillow. It was so real. I was lonely for her. She whose name I never knew.

# CHAPTER 9

# COMMUNICATING WITH ALIENS

*A man like me cannot live without a hobby*
*horse, a consuming passion – in Schiller's words,*
*a tyrant. I have found my tyrant, and in his*
*service, I know no limits.*

— SIGMUND FREUD
EXCERPT FROM A LETTER TO WILHELM FLIESS
MAY 25, 1895

Cody Hanson was a stout, jolly fellow who liked to give people shit for everyday things and share his shit by 'talking to aliens,' as he called it. He spoke to aliens in the language of flatulence.

He would walk into my Entipop office, communicate with the aliens, and then leave in a giggling hurry, closing the door behind him. He would do the same in the cubicles of his coworkers and sometimes the cubicles of my subordinates. One subordinate reported Cody to me, and wanted to know how I was going to discipline him. Unsatisfied with my response, she reported Cody to Human Resources for violating her worker's rights.

It was then that I learned the power of the company to protect management. Said subordinate was moved to another department. Cody carried right on spreading the good word of the aliens and I went right on to my next promotion, continuing the legacy of me, The Shit.

Cody spotted me outside the fishbowl.

"Back at it, aye?" Cody hollered across the courtyard where I stood smoking a cigarette with Josh Crenshaw, the Director of Network Services. Josh smoked like a chimney. Mostly, he smoked out of a state of chronic anxiety. He was entirely ignorant of technical matters, didn't know the difference between the old mainframe green screen technologies and the new Phairyway DB2 GUI-based applications. He couldn't map his own departmental drive on his computer or use the fancy Notes tools like Out-Of-Office Messaging, and didn't know any computer languages or even the difference between a language and an application.

I wondered why Josh didn't spend more of his smoking time meeting with his subordinates, forcing them to teach him what they knew so that he wouldn't be so goddamn nervous. Instead, choo-choo, like a steam train he puffed and smoked away. Cody's voice broke through the clouds of stale, slow-moving air.

"Back at it, aye?" he hollered again. I hadn't seen him in a week, enough time for me to have quit, and quit being a quitter. "I ain't moving in with your stinky ass," he called out. I had just agreed to rent a beach house with Cody once his lease ran out. At the time, I was temporarily living with Weeli's friend, K.C., in a plush condo in Newton. A few months prior, Weeli came to pick me up at my then humble abode in Brockton. It didn't take him long to figure out something was fishy. When he realized the blankets on the windows weren't just for shade, and that the house was in the process of being foreclosed on, he made other arrangements. That's how I found myself living with K.C. I was grateful, but knew it was temporary for all of our sakes. When Cody mentioned moving in together, it felt right. That the house was right on the water helped.

"I knew you couldn't quit," Cody shouted. "Talking to aliens smells better than that shit." With that, Cody was gone.

There I was, back at it, a full-time smoker all over again. The cigarette was such a close companion throughout my Entipop days it just felt natural. I missed my smelly smoke-break friends. Now I felt weak for letting something dangerous grip me so tightly. Forget the cancerous, sick feeling of a constant cold and fatigue that comes from smoking. Forget the tragic pain of quitting again. The 'canker cancer-causing wand of death,' as Frank called it, consumed me.

I would rationalize for myself. Now is not the right time. I will definitely quit, but only when the time is right. I must welcome it into my system fully to acknowledge its exorcism. You don't want to be a quitter. Etc., etc., etc.

I had quit smoking many times by reverting to what Frank called, 'the mouth-mangling king of gangrene gums,' or chewing tobacco. From Copenhagen to Kodiak, I was a spitting, swallowing, dripping, drooling fool. Talk about a turn-off.

Second-hand smoke was one thing, but no one ever forgets the first time you pass second-hand chew spew on them.

For a while, I was a full-time chewer at Entipop. Spittoon cups everywhere. I once walked into a board meeting to give a presentation with a half spittle-filled coffee cup and a wad of chew in my cheek. The dark, pasty, black leaves mixed with fiberglass, ammonia, and who knows what else were so familiar that I didn't notice I was spitting into a cup in front of the CEO, Mr. Garbway. As I pulled the cup from my mouth, I felt the warm, discharged saliva mixed with chew make contact with my bottom lip.

*Fuck!*

I pulled the cup away too soon. A stream of spit suspended from my mouth, one end holding strong to my bottom lip and the other end flinging away from the cup and dangling acrobatically, swinging downward with the form of a figure skater. I spun around as quickly as I could to hide it, but not fast enough to spare Jenny Bronske, who, on the sight of it, instantly began vomiting onto the oak table in front of her. Jenny and the only other woman in the room, Betty Shane, stormed out in disgust. I should have been terminated.

Fortunately, Garbway was an old-school sexist who said, "those two bitches aren't strong enough for a man's world," then proudly explained how he chewed tobacco back in his day. Once they realized Garbway was almost proud of my complete piggishness, the other managers laughed on cue.

Many times, I had tried to replace the cigarette with pen caps, fingernails, bubble gum, sunflower seeds, oak twigs, and even cigars. Aside from nicotine withdrawals, I had an insatiable oral fixation.

I was on one of my pre-Revolution quitting stints. They always ended with me deciding I didn't want to be a quitter. *Screw Cody,* I thought to myself, *I'll quit when I want to quit.* Weeli phoned soon after I returned to my office.

"I thought you finally did it, you pussy," he laughed at me, mocking a cough.

"Shouldn't you be giving someone a hand job in the men's room? I'm no quitter." Even I was tired of hearing myself spew that line.

"Things are moving, Herb," Weeli said with sudden urgency. "Movement is so fast the Concorde is sitting in a museum because it's too slow. You feeling me? News is instant. Revolutions occur at light speed. Overnight there's a new government in New Guinea. One market crashes, another's invented out of the blue. Egypt erupts, Syria's at peace. Got it? We need to catch up, get up to speed, get ready, Herb." He sounded like he was coked up.

"What the hell are you–" I tried to ask, but he was too fast for me.

"Listen, man. You're onto something with the energy stuff. Allen Davis, Herb. Listen to this. There is a constant electrical energy, which we are all a part of, as is everything in existence. Some have equated this energy to Karma and conscience. It is more like a cosmic electricity. With every action, thought, and emotion, we release a different charge. Sounds like the shit you were saying...no?" Weeli finished.

"Yeah, it does. So who–"

"You can find out tonight. Your place. K.C.'s away anyhow. Off on his hundredth European trek or some shit. I got some killer bud, too."

"Maybe we need to think about ditching the–"

"Maybe you can think about scratching my balls. Cut the shit. This ain't the time. Plus, it's really great stuff. Seattle, ten dead, seventy hospitalized, WTO. The Peace Corps, Greenpeace, the National Republican Committee, labor unions, environmentalists, the Gay and Lesbian Coalition, the Ku Klux Klan, teachers' unions, Black Panthers, Pink Panthers, and the Nation of Islam joined forces against one organization: the WTO. Shit's moving fast. Social media, technology. It's time to start a movement. It's real. Energies are shifting. I'll see you 'bout seven."

At a quarter to seven, springing up out of the clear blue, Sophia rang.

"Hey, you want to meet me at Crawley's Pub?" she asked.

"Hey," I said. "Holy crap. Hi, how are you? Aren't you supposed to be in Arizona or something?"

"Well, you know me. I'm here, but I fly out tomorrow so you want to meet before I go into town tonight?"

A rush of warm energy. Blood pressure spike. Weird feeling in my stomach. Before I could think, words came out.

"So, Weeli's supposed to be here at seven to watch some stupid video, do you want to–"

"Ah, that's too bad," she cut me off. "I've only got like half an hour and then I have to head into town to–"

"I can just tell him to come over later." I spat the words out as quickly as I could.

"No, that's all right. I'm just going to head into town. Next time. It's my fault. I'll give you more than five minutes' notice next time. Love you dearly. Bye."

She hung up before I could say goodbye. Before I said love. Before I cursed out Weeli to no one. Sophia would often pop up out of nowhere with no notice and only so much time. She was 'Spontaneous Jane' she would say. And after so many times, I should have known that no one is that spontaneous if it is important enough to them to make a plan, but such was the depth of my desperate love. Instead, I blamed Weeli for ruining my life, and continued believing that Sophia was dying to see me.

# CHAPTER 10

# R. A. DAVIS, ELECTRIC GOD

*__Revolution__ (rev-uh-*loo*-shuh n) [see 'revolve']*
*noun. 1. The movement of a body in an orbit. 2. A*
*turning around an axis; rotation. 3. A complete cycle*
*of events. 4. A complete change. 5. An overthrow of a*
*government, social system, etc.*

The music stopped. Bubba, the four-foot bong, slipped away. The larger-than-life digital image of Evan Bradley's face stared back at us. Bradley was one of my favorite hosts at a time in my life when I, too, reflected a glum seriousness and charismatic energy for life. A kinship Bradley knew nothing of.

The prior Sunday, Bradley opened with, "Sweepstakes and the lottery in the land of the brave. A fun and harmless pastime for consumers, or a societal nemesis taking advantage of America's elderly and poverty-stricken?"

*Dun...dun...daaaaaaah.*

The music of *Sunday Night Magazine* was just as dramatic as the host. He managed, as he did with any topic, to turn lottery winners and losers into a great American story full of tragedy and triumph, of hope and hopelessness, of lust and love, of life and death. According to Bradley, sixty-five percent of all lottery winners wind up dead, drug-addicted, or broke.

In a dimly-lit studio, soft colors glowing from behind, Bradley spoke straight to the camera. "Tonight the man a religious community has revered for years, R. Allen Davis, speaks to heaven and answers our questions. Davis has captivated and converted thousands of Americans with his self-proclaimed ability to translate for the Almighty. Tonight..."

Dramatic pause.

"...R. Allen Davis..."

Dramatic pause.

"Prophet or popular con artist? You decide as we bring you the real story."

*Dun-dun-daaaaaaah...*

The camera pulled away slowly. The image faded to a crowd of thousands waving hands in the air in an open field. Weeli sat upright, eyes wide, staring at the television intently.

The made-up face of R. Allen Davis came into focus, camera zooming in on his sharp yet gentle features. The screen then flashed back to the massive crowd, waving their hands in the air in a frenzy of holy worship.

"Thousands of people across America and even in other nations are now calling you the New Messiah," Bradley spoke over the celluloid images. "A prophet. An angel. Some have even called you the Return of Christ. The Second Coming.

So tell us, what is the phenomenon of R. Allen Davis?" A hard rain fell on the crowd while the voice of a minister shouted at the devil.

"This scene from the Protestant Power Movement, hosting a rally in Mississippi, shows thousands of fans and religious fanatics being moved by the message of that phenomenon. Mr. Davis, can we first start with who you are? Who is R. Allen Davis, and what has brought him to the status of prophet, Translator of the Heavens?"

R. Allen Davis folded his hands gently over his lap. His legs crossed in that effeminate way, thighs tight against each other that some men couldn't physically bring themselves to do. He spoke with that Midwestern-slash-Southern accent that had become so familiar to everyone since the phenomenon.

"I am not a prophet," he began, "nor have I ever claimed to be. I am certainly not the Second Coming of Christ. As for whatever other labels anyone has placed on me, I can only say I have made no claims to being anything different from you, Evan, or any other man or woman. Who am I? I am the son of two poor, hardworking farmers, James and Renati Davis. I spent many years working the fields. I studied at a number of universities with a focus on philosophy and religion."

Davis explained that his religious philosophy came from years of studying Eastern, Middle-Eastern, and Native-American religions and philosophies, along with the practice of his original religion, Pentecostalism. Through this process, God brought him to what would become known as the Protestant Power Movement. Davis answered another question.

"Sure I can talk to God. I can hear God, but so can you. What I hear comes from paying attention, being aware. Sure," Davis smiled. "As a matter of fact, right now I think I will ask him if he could help you come up with better questions for this interview."

"I would love to have him on my writing staff," Bradley quipped. "But you know what I'm asking you. Whether the question sounds asinine or not, there seems to be hundreds of thousands of followers who have been led to believe that you communicate with, and receive direction from, God. Is this a misunderstanding?"

"You say 'Him,'" Davis said, looking intently into the camera. "I guess you talk to Him more than I do because I am not sure He has any gender. Frankly, I'm not sure He has any form."

"It's common to refer to God as 'He,'" Bradley replied.

"It is," Davis smiled. "It's also very easy to just think of God as a great big male figure so as not to have to ponder or discover or feel the actual nature of what we call 'God.'"

"Well then," Bradley smiled back, "how do you refer to God? Who or what is God to you?"

"Our best scientists speak of the Big Bang. Their best science hypothesizes about what happened the moment of and after such an event, but can't fathom or explain where it came from. Meaning our three-dimensional, scientific minds can't fathom or explain how, from nothing, this." Davis extended his arms, raised his eyebrows, and smiled. "All of this.

"Our true nature, our origins, God, is not of three-dimensional form. And so to know God, to hear God, to feel God, the spirit of all we are, we cannot do with words and thoughts and science. How do I describe God? For lack of a better word, God is the formless origin, creator, and keeper of all that is."

"Is it true that you have spoken with the Virgin Mary?" Bradley asked.

Davis shook his head and maintained his gentle smile.

"Evan, don't you have a research staff? This must be the highest-rated Sunday night program. Where does the budget go? I have never said I speak to the Virgin Mary. I would never call her that. Do you truly believe Mary was a virgin?"

"So then," Bradley pressed, "what is it these people find so fascinating? Fascinating enough to refer to you as the Second Coming. Some people have said that you are the last shot at salvation this world has before it's all over."

"Evan, there is no end of the world in sight that I can see, or have ever spoken of. If I speak of a spiritual awakening, and people have fanciful ideas of the Mayan calendar or The Book of Revelations, and they put those things together as evidence of the great apocalypse, well, that is beyond me. When we rely so heavily on technology, it doesn't take a prophet to know there will be problems. A dramatic change in climate cycles, migration patterns of animals and humans, and a shift in energies will confuse, and is already confusing, all sentient beings. Entire flocks of sandpipers have fallen from our skies in places they have never been seen before. Great whites are washing up on shores from waters that have never been part of their migration patterns. Genetically-modified insects feeding from, and feeding genetically-modified vegetation. Now those mutations are in the animals, the air, and us. Good or bad, doesn't matter, but it all contributes to the confusion. In the century to come, well, you don't need me to tell you, humanity faces great challenges."

"So," Bradley leaned back, folding his arms in front of him, "what infinite wisdom might you impart on all of us? If things are so dire for the future, with millions of viewers watching you now, what would you tell us?"

"Well," Davis smiled, "I'm not sure I would impart anything, but," he paused. Crossed his legs. Held his hands in front of him like a praying mantis. The calmness in his face reminded me of my father. The familiarity brought memories of him rubbing the top of my head, calling me one of those foolish names he'd made up for me. Herby Shmerby. Herb the Blurb. "There's always a bright side to everything, Shmerby..."

"Both science and spiritual teachings tell us there is a constant energy that we and everything around us is a part of, which connects everything directly. Some equate energy to Chi, or God, or consciousness, but it is simply a very real, in human terms, almost electric, energy. With every action, thought, emotion, we release and receive. With everything we eat, drink, and breathe, we create a new charge. If we take notice, open ourselves to an awareness of our source, of God, of that which is not three-dimensional and obvious to us, but undeniably a part of us, it will heighten our awareness. Heightened awareness will not only result in each of us being truly good to each other and ourselves, but will bring about a greater intelligence, helping to guide us through the challenges ahead. A spiritual or cosmic common sense will arise. When God, as you would call Him or Her, guides us, I only know that it is guidance from the greatest energy of all. I don't know who or what it is. I only know that it is. When I speak to groups of people, I don't bother to try to convert them. If they hear me, truly hear me, then they will."

His jittery body, bouncing in his seat like a child, evidenced Weeli's excitement.

"You see?" Weeli exclaimed, barely able to control himself. He raised his arms in the air as if to question why my body wasn't bouncing in unison. "That's the same shit you've been talking about. Connected energy. The same shit that Susskind and the brightest physicists in the world are yapping about with string theory. This guy is trying to start his own revolution."

Weeli's tone was peculiar. Something about the way he said it made it sound like a competition, like somehow we needed to beat Davis to the revolutionary punch.

"I know," I said, disappointing Weeli with my tone and lack of emotion. In fact, I was mostly still upset with Weeli for ruining my chances to see Sophia, but was conscious enough to not make it obvious. "He's onto something, but why don't people get it?" I questioned. "Sounds a lot like what I've been saying, but he's convoluted the whole thing with God. Always the same shit. You saw those crowds, that's not it."

"Semantics," Weeli snarled, handing me the bong.

I wondered how this path might lead to any revolution. Two paths diverged, and we chose the lazy one for the time being. But even time, being the illusion that it was, even the thick clouds of marijuana mustard gas, even Bubba, could not stop The Revolution.

# CHAPTER 11

# FRIENDLY FIRE

## VSBO Statistical Page 11011111111101

＝⚬ ⚬＝

*Friendly Fire Casualties for the Year Nineteen Hundred and Seventy:*

*All casualties herein resulted directly from actions taken to further the cause of the United States Vietnam peacekeeping mission, sometimes referred to as a 'Conflict' and occasionally as a 'War.'*

*These statistics for a single year do not include non-American casualties, but only those soldiers who were children of the United States of America and killed by the gunfire of their own nation with bullets or bombs or shells paid for by their own tax dollars.*

*These statistics do not include the thousands of non-American soldiers, the innocent, friendly, Vietnamese nationals killed and wounded by friendly fire during the Incident in Vietnam.*

*These are the statistics of dead Americans killed by friendly fire during the year nineteen hundred and seventy.*

*These statistics do not include friendly fire casualties resulting from U.S. wars and military actions post-Vietnam, including: Dominican Republic Action of '65; Afghan Mission to Arm the Taliban of '76; Pro-Iraq Chemical Weapons Action of '79; Lebanon of '82; Grenada of '83; Panama of '89; Gulf I of '91; Somalia of '93; Bosnia of '94; Kosovo of '99; Afghanistan II of '01; Iraq II of '03; War on Terror of '01 – TBD.*

*These statistics, and others included on this page and all other pages of the VSBO, can be verified through the United States Department of Defense, The United States State Department, The VFW, VGA, VXP, DMV, and The United Nations Human Rights Coalition for Victims of War.*

*U.S. Soldiers Killed in the Year Nineteen Hundred and Seventy By U.S. Friendly Fire:*

*Feb – 467*
*Mar – 442*
*Apr – 428*
*May – 429*
*Jun – 415*
*Jul – 404*
*Aug – 400*
*Sep – 390*

*Oct – 374*
*Nov – 355*
*Dec – 356*

⇥ ⇤

— TEXT COPIED FROM THE OFFICIAL WEBSITE OF THE
VETERANS STRIKE BACK ORGANIZATION
@WWF.VSBO.SPBC.UFNC.WWW.MIT

I n the context of camping in Antarctica in the sun-forsaken midwinter months, fire may be referred to as 'friendly.' When stranded in the Rocky Mountains, hundreds of miles from anywhere, a fire set to signal rescue may be referred to as 'friendly.' In the context of war, there is no such thing as that fire which is 'friendly.' Nonetheless, deadly gunfire, falling bombs, missiles gone astray, and even tank shells were now being referred to as 'friendly fire.' Friendly fire pre-dates the Akkadian Empire. Since the time conscious humans have been able to identify fire and friendliness, they've put the two together.

At eight thirty this particular Sunday morning, as reported by the Channel Ninety-One Headline News, my old army buddy, Kenny Burdle, was killed by 'friendly fire.'

Sundays...

Sundays were supposed to be the carefree, lay-the-fuck-back, easy days. This Sunday morning was off to an unfriendly genesis. During the preceding months, Weeli and I were busy kissing the mighty green ass of a half-insane

CEO. Sundays were supposed to be a day of no Revolution, no Entipop, no bathroom philosophy, no nothing.

"Easy, easy like Sunday morning."

This easy-like morning was not what it was supposed to be.

The U.S. Army has a buddy system. Every soldier has what is called a 'battle buddy.' If you're out in the field constructing a lean-to that you both will sleep in, or digging a foxhole that you both will defend, or executing an assault, or in camp on cleanup duty or weapon maintenance, you are doing it with your battle buddy. It's an intense military marriage. During basic training, my battle buddy was Cosmo. Along with not being a particularly great soldier, he was also suspected of being gay by nearly everyone in my platoon, including me. On occasion, when we slept in the very close quarters of a lean-to on cold, snowy nights, Cosmo would comment on the benefits of body heat. I would ignore him. Out of earshot, some soldiers would refer to him as 'Ass Muncher,' 'Aids Bag,' 'Cock Smuggler.' At times, it led to them referring to me as the 'Fag-Loving Yankee.' Until the Army, I had no idea there was still a North-South divide. The Mason-Dixon Line was a term used in jokes, usually to refer to ignorant people, but it never meant much of anything to me until I was the Fag-Loving Yankee soldier.

Kenny Burdle was a decent soldier from Kansas. Kenny helped me through the many challenges of basic training with Cosmo. When the southern boys planned a 'pillow party' for Cosmo, Kenny gave me a heads up. At dinner, I found the chief redneck, Brandon Cooper, a fellow squad leader in the platoon.

"Pillow parties are serious," I told Private Cooper, who claimed to be a descendant of Confederate General Samuel Cooper and who liked to have his squad chant, "the South will rise again."

"You don't get to attack a soldier 'cause you don't like him. You're a fucking squad leader. Cosmo hasn't put anyone in danger and he hasn't fucked up in any way that's gotten the whole platoon in trouble. There's not going to be a pillow party."

"He's a goddamn homo," Cooper said, "you need to stay out of it."

"Listen to me," I told him, "if anyone even approaches Cosmo's bunk after lights out, I will fight so fucking loud the drill sergeants will come and you and I will be repeating this conversation to them."

"Good for you," Cooper said. He picked up his fork and went right on eating.

For the next week, I had Cosmo do as I did. Sleep in his hazmat suit, which had a thick lining and would soften any blows. We kept our gas masks and Kevlar helmets in our beds, but no one came.

As graduation approached, Kenny told me the southern boys were getting restless, that they were intent on ambushing and beating the gay and the Yankee out of both Cosmo and me.

"Well then," I told Kenny, "I guess we better beat them to the punch. I'll have to tell Cosmo that he's going to have to fight or take a beating, and then I'll challenge Cooper and whatever other hicks he's got waiting. What's the worst that can happen, right? It won't be the first beating I've ever taken."

"Yeah," Kenny said, "but you know there are a few guys who hate those boys, so why don't you give me a few minutes and see who I can round up."

"Round up?"

"You don't think I'm going to sit and watch, do you?" Kenny replied.

Once again, I found Cooper in the mess hall and told him I knew of his plans.

"You can be a big southern pussy and ambush us from behind, or you can round up your little rebel flag gang and meet us in the latrine after chow."

And so it came to a head in the head. Kenny had rounded up one guy. Cosmo turned out to be one hell of a scrapper and by the time the drill sergeants broke it up, things were pretty well settled. Neither Cooper nor I were squad leaders when we graduated basic training. Instead, we were paired up for KP (kitchen patrol and mopping floors) for the last week of our basic training, but I got the feeling faggot northerners gained a little respect down South that week.

Cosmo and I parted ways after basic training, when soldiers go on to what is called their MOS (military occupational specialty). Cosmo was off to military intelligence. Kenny Burdle's MOS was infantry, as was mine, so we went off to AIT together, battle buddies.

There are people you lose in life whose loss have a traumatic impact. Kenny was not one of these people. He was a close friend for a brief but intense period of my life. In this way, I was personally connected to the news this particular Sunday morning. Revolution was brewing in me, the news was broadcasting directly to me, and so a very common euphemism was suddenly driving me crazy.

*Friendly fire…friendly fire…*

The words bounced from synapse to synapse.

*Zing, zing, zing.* I changed the channel.

*Click.*

Friendly fire…friendly fire…

*Click.*

"Herb, your buddy Kenny was killed this morning. Herb, do you remember him? Yes, that's right, your buddy from Georgia…that's the one. Don't worry, it wasn't bad, it was just friendly fire…"

*Click.*

"Karmen Chad, renowned singer of U Forty-Seven finds himself in rehab once again and…"

*Click.*

"Zitorol may cause side effects including incontinence, blurry vision, and a decrease in blood pressure, which may counteract erectile function."

Zitorol wasn't an erectile dysfunction pill. It was the pill sixty percent of men taking erectile dysfunction medication needed to take to prevent blood clots caused by said erectile dysfunction medication. Zitorol, however, had a negative effect on kidney function in thirty-nine percent of test cases. 'Test cases' is the term used to refer to what used to be called 'people.' Lisinomax was the drug prescribed to those suffering from kidney failure caused by Zitorol, which was being used to reduce blood clotting caused by Ciagra and other erectile dysfunction drugs.

*Click.*

Friendly fire…friendly fire…friendly fire.

I did my sit-ups violently, as I recalled the good and bad times I'd shared with the late Kenny Burdle.

Crazy Frank said they called it 'friendly fire' when they 'sent three thousand of those poor unsuspecting souls right into the bomb site to practice securing the aftermath. Only thirty-two died that day, but the rest of those poor bastards didn't make it long after.'

*Click.*

Friendly fire...

I could feel my synapses burning away like pig-fat sizzling in a rusty frying pan. Even God called Sundays the day of rest. Even God recognized the necessity for a slow and easy Sunday morning.

Dr. Dahlia Gita, president of the Association of Mental Health and Good Living in nineteen ninety-one, published an essay in almost all of the major Sunday newspapers on the first Sunday of that year. His topic was the necessity of the 'easy-like' Sundays. He wrote:

*Stress is the primary cause of cancer, crime, depression, back pain, infection, suicide, drug addiction, alcoholism, animal cruelty, rudeness, and all things which affect any society negatively. In our nine-to-five society, where nine-to-five is truly five-to-nine, it is critical to the mental wellbeing of individuals, and the overall health of the society, that one day is set aside for absolutely nothing. Stress is rarely the result of boredom and relaxation. Programs such as the Watkins Method and Exercise Experiment have proven ineffective and unsustainable for daily life. We must return to the time-tested and long-forgotten remedy of our ancestors, the Sunday Method. All planned events, including church, ceremonies, family events, cookouts, and parties, must not be planned for Sundays if our society is to better*

*its existence. All work which is not absolutely critical to the
daily survival of the people must cease on this day, allowing
for a full, planned nothingness.*

Dr. Gita cited a government-sponsored study that demonstrated fewer suicides occur historically in the United States
of America on Sundays than on any other day of the week,
excluding Christmas Sundays. Gita was certain that a lay-
the-fuck-back Sunday was a necessity of life.

I concurred.

As my knees, then the screen, then the ceiling, went in
and out of view, an Oprah-wannabe announced, "mothers
who wanted their daughter to get makeovers, the theme of
today's show!" There was a war going on, my friend Kenny
Burdle was dead, and she was going to go right on with
her previously scheduled discussion about mothers who
want their daughters to get makeovers. The Revolution was
brewing.

*Click.*

"Damnation...Jesus said whosoever believeth in him
shall..."

*Click.*

"Jesus said my Father's house has many mansions, but
hell hath no refuge..."

*Click.*

"I don't think that just because my mother thinks I'm
ugly that..."

*Click.*

"Your attention, please. From now on, because of pressure from our sponsors and because the people of civilized
America just don't give a shit, we will not be televising the

major wars unless they are worldwide and affecting your immediate state, city, town, or neighborhood. All major and minor wars can be seen twenty-four hours a day on C-SPAN and Nickelodeon. You can listen to the latest wars on NPR. We'd like to assure our viewers that any gory scenes appearing to be rating snatchers that may arise from the war in the Middle East will be broadcast on primetime. Oh and, Herb, it's just friendly fire."

*Click.*

"God is on your side," the voice declared. "Slowly it is becoming clear, Greta," Chord Williams said, turning his head to the camera, "we are a backwards people, so far from truth and what matters. We are looking into a meaningless abyss. Vanity of vanities. America is on the verge of a revolution. People everywhere are giving up. A revolution is brewing right here in America, Greta."

*A revolution?* I paused.

"That's right, Greta," Williams continued, "a revolution. In the Book of Revelations of John the Divine…"

*Click.*

The phone rang. My slow and easy Sunday morning was shot to hell. Picking my buck-naked ass up off the cold wood floor, wheezing heavily, pressure building on my skull with every ring, I answered the phone.

"Yeah?"

"Yeah," Weeli replied.

"Yeah, Weeli. What's up?"

"Time for a vacation, Bubba." He was abrupt. "Things are happening. You know the other night we were talking about The Revolution, man? Time to prepare. We're going to head west. What do you think?"

"What do I think, man? About a goddamn vacation? Are you kidding me?"

"Huh?" Weeli grunted, "Don't be a Gum Cuddler."

"What do I think? I think I woke up to air raid sirens and my dead battle buddy on TV. Good morning to you, too."

"Huh?" Weeli grunted again. I paused. Took a breath. Wondered if I had the energy or interest to even bother.

"My friend, Kenny Burdle, is dead," I said, "killed by friendly fire. Your sister's in fucking Iran, man. No one cares. Shit is going down and all you can do is call me to ask about a vacation?"

Weeli said nothing. For a brief moment, silence ensued.

"You know what? I thought I'd be sitting here on a nice quiet Sunday morning waiting for the football game to come on. That's all I thought, you know? It's Sunday."

"No shit?"

"No shit."

Silence.

I assumed Weeli was checking the news, but he could have been picking his ass for all I knew.

"I think they said it's over," he said. "I'm, uh, sorry to... you knew him, huh? This guy here?"

"Burdle."

"No shit?"

"No shit."

"Were you close?" Weeli asked.

"Not like family, but friends, you know?"

"No shit?"

"No shit."

"That's messed up."

"Yup. He's the guy I was telling you about. You know, the gas chamber and all."

"That's him, huh?"

"That's him."

Silence.

"So what the hell are you talking about a vacation? Did you really call me this early on a Sunday morning to ask about vacation?"

"Yup," Weeli said plainly. "No, really," he said, his tone making it painfully obvious that he had fulfilled his obligation to be cordial to me in my moment of loss and was now moving on to his original intent, vacation. He started in giving no care whatsoever to the fact that I was angry and frustrated. "I'm very serious. We need to go out west soon. It's time."

"Weeli, I haven't planned a vacation. I'm not planning a vacation. I'm busy as hell at work, plus, when I do take a vacation, I have no idea where I want to go, man. I haven't even thought about it."

"Listen, H, it's all about The Revolution, I swear. It's time to give up the laziness, stop the monkey crap, and start preparing."

"A vacation is your way of getting serious? I'm hanging up, Weeli."

"No. I'm serious."

"I'm serious, too. I'm hanging up on you now."

"Fine," Weeli shouted over the phone as I began to pull it away from my ear. As usual, I kept it close enough to hear the remainder of what he was saying. "I'll be over in a little bit."

*Click.*

Weeli was gone. I slammed down the phone as if some-how expressing my anger to the inanimate object would help. I needed a back-up plan. I needed to put on clothes. My 'easy-like' was going to hell 'fast-like.' I didn't want my slow, meaningless Sunday to become anything meaning-ful, like a philosophical discussion about The Revolution and why going west would be a great thing. Weeli and I had started something with our talk about his mother's ideas, his sister's ideas, and The Revolution. And I believed in it, but I knew it was much too early. I didn't want to fill in the time between with psychobabble or half-hearted actions.

Weeli could talk about not being lazy, but I knew what he meant. This was his idea of not being lazy. As long as we were talking about The Revolution and planning for preparation three times removed from any real action, then somehow we weren't being lazy.

It was nearly a straight year of whoring the world of Entipop, and it was tiring. Nearly a year of Garbway and his insanity.

"Nothing matters," Garbway told me earlier that week. "I didn't like how much paper towel we were wasting. It's bad for the environment. But look what happens when you try to fix things. As it turns out, we waste more paper with automatic hand dryers than with paper towels. Goes to god-damn show you, doesn't it?"

"Huh?" I mumbled.

"Now," Garbway went on, "everyone rips toilet seat cov-ers out to dry their hands. You know how many of those things it takes? What a waste. And they make a goddamn mess, too. I'm telling you, nothing works no matter what you do. So forget what I told you, do whatever you want."

A year was a long time.

Maybe Weeli was on to something. It was time for a vacation, Revolution or not.

⤙ ⤚

Weeli smiled west.

⤙ ⤚

I had never been out West. I wasn't sure I wanted to be.

*Crack.*

My first beer had come much earlier than I had planned. Weeli, the great storyteller, arrived seducing me with mysterious tales of the Wild West and The Revolution. If he possessed the desire, Weeli could sell anyone on the idea that touring a ripe, overused outhouse on a sweltering summer afternoon in ninety percent humidity is a necessary experience, charge a dollar a head, and make a million bucks.

# CHAPTER 12

# THE LAST KNOWN BUFFALO BEARER

### *Amazing Grace*

*Amazing Grace, how sweet the sound,*
*That saved a wretch like me.*
*I once was lost, but now I'm found,*
*Was blind, but now I see.*
*'Twas Grace that taught my heart to fear*
*And grace, my fears relieved.*
*How precious did that Grace appear,*
*The hour I first believed?*

*Through many dangers, toils and snares,*
*I have already come.*
*'Tis Grace that brought me safe thus far,*
*And Grace will lead me home.*
*When we've been here ten thousand years,*
*Bright shining as the sun,*

*We've no less days to sing God's praise,*
*Than when we've first begun.*

— JOHN NEWTON,
MAYBE A LITTLE WILLIAM COOPER

Some sang it in the Negro spiritual style, some in the eerie Appalachian shape-note form, some in key, all obsessed, possessed, infested with the spirit. With arms flailing wildly, Pentecostals sang it like the black Baptists, bursting with emotion. From west to east, people continue to be brought to tears by a song written by a British slave-trading sea captain turned minister for the Lord God Almighty under the Church of England.

Even my mother, who was moved more by the bottle and a cigarette than she ever was by God, was moved to tears nearly every time she heard the song. It was her favorite. That is not what drove me to learn everything I could about it, though. Sophia was my inspiration.

Fear of death and torture kept some blacks from coming out for voter registration in Mississippi in nineteen sixty-four. Crazy Frank was there. Accounts, not just Frank's, tell of moments when tension could have bred violence and, instead, the sound of Amazing Grace. To imagine a wretched slave-trading sea captain would write the hymn that would touch and move slaves and descendants of slaves is something even Nostradamus wouldn't have dared. The energy was undeniable.

"How industriously is Satan served," John Newton wrote. "I was formerly one of his active under-tempters...and, had my influence been equal to my wishes, I would have carried all the human race with me...'Oh to grace, how great a debtor!' A common drunkard or profligate is a petty sinner to what I was. I had the ambition of a Caesar or an Alexander, and wanted to rank in wickedness among the foremost of the human race."

I sent those words to Sophia from my oversized office, prodding her to guess who the author was. "Would you ever guess," I asked her, "that these words came from the same man who wrote, 'How precious did that grace appear, in the hour I first believed?'"

Newton obtained his first job at sea by the doings of his father, a long-time seaman. He pioneered the slave trade for the British Empire. Raised from the sludge of evil and darkness, born again into godly ministry, the good slave trader became a God-fearing minister. From the wretched pit of evil to the revered pulpit he rose. Having once commanded a Napoleonic reputation, he was now leading a parish in the name of God Almighty.

Inspired, Sophia found her own sources and bits of information. And so ensued our off and on intellectual foreplay. I invited her over to watch a biography on John Newton.

Newton's slow transition...

One day in the Mid-Atlantic, the slave-ship he captained seemed to be sinking. After exhausting all options, when nothing seemed to work, he crumbled in fear and repentance. He looked up to the heavens and said, "If nothing can be done, Lord have mercy on us." The ship was not wrecked. They survived, but Newton was a changed man. According to his own accounts, it was on that day that he realized the existence of the true God and God's grace, and slowly began to change. He didn't give up his trade right away but began a gradual evolution. Crazy Frank equated it to music.

"He got a taste of the good stuff," Frank said, pointing his thick index finger toward the sky. "Once you get a taste of that shit then you're hooked. It's like with music, you know? When you're playing an instrument or singing, and you get it. When I hit those first few notes, when the sax actually sounded like I felt, like I wanted to feel, like I wanted to say I felt, I mean, it was euphoric."

Newton's evolution culminated when he finally gave up his ship and pursued the cloth. In seventeen sixty-four, he became a minister for the parish of Olney in the county of Buckinghamshire. It was later, after beginning a weekly prayer meeting with poet William Cooper, that Newton wrote, likely with the help of Cooper, Amazing Grace.

Sophia believed it was possible that Cooper was conspired against, and that he was likely the author of Amazing Grace. She refused to believe any of Crazy Frank's money interest conspiracy theories, but she had no problem believing in a song credit conspiracy. She also believed that Shakespeare had never actually written a word, and might not have even been a real person.

She emailed me one morning in the midst of our three-month obsession as I sat in my new office staring at the refresh button in the corner of my Lotus Notes email screen. Whenever Sophia emailed, a mix of emotions beat on me. My stomach sank.

*H,*

*JN quotes/writings.*

*Enjoy,*
*S*

'*Monday, the seventh of January, seventeen fifty-one. This morning, went on board Captain Coburn, he having told me that he had eight slaves to change with me for teeth and wood, according to our agreement at the Bonanas, but could not take them upon his terms, which were sixty bars per head round, though there were but three sizable and two of the remaining five under three foot, six inches. Sent the steward to the shore again in the yawl to purchase the woman slave, and brought her up in the evening, number forty-six. She cost sixty-three bars, though she had a very bad mouth.*'

'*Usually, about two-thirds of a cargo of slaves is males. When a hundred and fifty or two hundred stout men, torn from their native land, and who often bring with them an apprehension they are bought to be eaten, I say, when thus circumstanced, it is not to be expected that they will tamely resign themselves to their situation. It is always taken for granted that they will attempt to*

*gain their liberty, if possible. Accordingly, as we dare
not trust them, we receive them on board from the first,
as enemies.'*

*'Thoughts upon the African slave trade, seventeen eighty-
eight. I hope it will always be a subject of humiliating reflection to me that I was once an active instrument in a
business at which my heart now shudders. I first saw the
coast of Guinea in the year seventeen forty-five, and took
my last leave of it in seventeen fifty-four. I fitted out for a
fourth voyage and was upon the point of sailing when I
was arrested by a sudden illness, and I resigned the ship
to another captain. Thus, I was unexpectedly freed from
this disagreeable service. Disagreeable I had long found
it, but I think I should have quitted it sooner had I considered it, as I do now, to be unlawful and wrong, but I
never had a scruple upon this head at the time, nor was
such a thought once suggested to me by any friend. What I
did, I did ignorantly, considering it is a line of life, which
divine providence had allotted me and having no concern
in point of conscience but to treat the slaves, while under
my care, with as much humanity as a regard to my own
safety would admit.'*

*'With our ships, the great object is to be full. The cargo of
a vessel of a hundred tons or little more is calculated to
purchase from two hundred and twenty to two hundred
and fifty slaves, for the slaves lie in two rows, one above
the other, on each side of the ship, close to each other, like
books upon a shelf. I have known them so close that the
shelf would not easily contain one more, and I have known*

*a white man sent down among the men to lay them in these rows to the greatest advantage, so that as little space as possible might be lost. I write from memory, after an interval of more than thirty years, but at the same time I believe many things, which I saw, heard, and felt upon the coast of Africa are so deeply engraven in my memory that I can hardly forget, or greatly mistake them.'*

═══◆◆═══

*Thou shalt remember that thou wast a bondsman<br>
in the land of Egypt, and the Lord thy God<br>
redeemed thee.*

– [Deuteronomy 15:15]

═══◆◆═══

*'To be engraven upon my death:<br>
John Newton, Clerk.<br>
Once an infidel and libertine,<br>
A servant of slaves in Africa,<br>
Was, by the rich mercy of our Lord and Saviour<br>
Jesus Christ<br>
Restored, pardoned, and appointed to preach<br>
The Gospel, which he had long laboured to<br>
destroy.'*

I, of course, had mixed emotions after reading the email. Thrilled to read Newton's writings and hurt to read, re-read, and re-read Sophia's only words to me, which were so impersonal, but words nonetheless. How many times could I read, "H, JN quotes/writings. Enjoy, S?"

*H, JN quotes/writings. Enjoy, S.*

Five times.

So few words.

*H, JN quotes/writings. Enjoy, S.*

I tried to explain the relationship of Amazing Grace to the energies of all things, but Sophia did not understand, or maybe I didn't understand well enough to explain it succinctly. She thought Weeli and I chatted too much while stoned. She could ramble on with psychobabble with the best of them, but when she was sober, she had no time for nonsense. To her, the connected energies of all things, The Revolution, was nonsense. In response to her email, I sent her the following in hopes she would come to understand my theory. To get her interest, I began with a native female piece.

*Sophia,*

*Let me begin by saying, if I were nearly as thoughtful as you, I would take the enormous amount of time and energy required to write so thoughtfully as demonstrated by:*

*H – read below – S*

*So, once again, very nice. So personal, so interesting, and so from the bottom of my heart, from H to S, let me say, thanx. No really,*

*H Thanx U 4 Eva S.*

*Any who, I know you enjoyed the shit I sent you about the wolves and the Chiricahua, so here is something you might find interesting as well. Written by the father of the only known living Buffalo Bearer of the Western Navajo Nations.*

'*No more than I can understand why a child is born king or the boy Buddha, can I explain why I was born to be the Buffalo Bearer. I am blessed and burdened with being the only Buffalo Bearer of the Sioux Nation and maybe of all nations. I will tell you truths, as I have no respect for secrecy, and value not this notion that our native ways must remain secret if they are to remain sacred. Secrets and lies. These are the thieves in the night that sweep in with a cold chill to steal our souls one feather at a time.*

*The Buffalo fed my peoples for many generations, and accompanied my ancestors in ancient times, many cosmic cycles ago. The Buffalo keeps the light of the Great Spirit here on Earth. I bear the burden of keeping that Buffalo alive for the sake of all humanity. The new world has not made it easy for my predecessors, or me. Now I fear for her, the young girl to whom I must pass the torch before my own passing, my daughter Jasmine.*'

*Soph, even the natives believed that all things are connected. I mean, think of it, this one girl is responsible for keeping the Buffalo, for the sake of all humanity. Amazing Grace, written by a slave trader, has had as much impact on slaves as anyone. The energy is universal. It connects.*

*Everything is connected, my friend.*

*Cheers,*
*H*

I hit refresh, but nothing. As far as I can recall, there was never a response to that particular email. Sophia would do that sometimes. Infuriating. For a short time, whenever I heard the song, I thought only of Sophia and cried for all the wrong reasons.

# CHAPTER 13
# CRAZY FRANK'S ORANGE SUNSHINE

*Where am I? You ask.*
*I am here. Here in the belly of the pig.*
*A monkey in the bowels of corporate America,*
*And the wastelands of humanity. I am there.*
*My aura, my being, mostly my odor, is there with*
*you in Arizona.*
*Crossing through the universal cosmic connection*
*of electricity and matter,*
*Colliding with everything and all of you, making*
*us one. I am.*
*I am everywhere. Thanks for asking… take care.*

— A LETTER FOR SOPHIA

**Mindfuck** (mīnd-fuhk)
*verb. 1. To experience enhanced brain function. 2. To*
*cause enhanced usage of the brain or functions of the*
*brain in one's self or another.*

*noun. 1. Slang, sometimes used to refer to that place one theoretically arrives at on some spiritual level, causing one to use the brain or functions of the brain in an enhanced capacity.*

A good mindfuck may cleanse the mind of the fuckee, removing limitations encouraged by sensory perception, illuminating consciousness, and eliminating self-consciousness.

A tremendous mindfuck may cause enlightenment or insanity. Similar experiences of varying degrees can be recognized through meditation, deprivation of food and water, and extreme mental or physical conditions.

By the turn of the millennium, renowned cosmologist, Dr. Skip Bater, explained thusly, "as we come to now know that all unifying theories of physics are only possible in a multi-universe state, in light of repeated evidence of random, anomalistic behavior of bosons within our perceived universe, we can presume that the dimensions the human mind exist within are far more infinite than our senses perceive. It can also be presumed that the seemingly random, anomalistic behavior of bosons is at work within the human brain, in a constant state of creation. It is most rational to presume there are no random or anomalistic behaviors, however, and that these behaviors only seem random within our perceivable universe."

"It is obvious," according to Bater's article in *The Journal of Science and Evolution*, "that human beings are using only a small portion of their brains. In fact, it is likely that only eight percent of the brain is being used to capacity on a day-to-day basis."

"Don't need a rocket scientist to tell me that," Weeli said. "I hang out with you every day. Eight percent is a stretch."

Though Weeli and I found ourselves using the word 'Revolution' more and more, the bond that truly tied us in the early days was our common passion to understand and experience the true nature of Us, and the whole kit and caboodle cosmos.

Homework required. We studied the forefathers, pioneers in the field. Thompson, Vonnegut, Muhammad, Buddha, Freud, Burroughs, Cheech, Chong, Jesus, and Dr. Leary. While some of these pioneers left writing, videos, clues, and artwork, Frank said he was with Dr. Leary when the good doctor recorded evidence of mind-expansion experiments. Devoted to our research, Weeli and I watched one of these videos for hours on end.

We had made what we would call 'breakthroughs' in our research through various forms of meditation and fasting. I was a terrible faster. Faster and faster I wanted to eat, and before any tremendous mindfucking occurred, I would gain ten pounds and my fasting venture would end in a food orgy. Weeli, on the other hand, was no good at meditation, but could go days in a state of deprivation. We built on each other's practices and experiences to lay the foundation on which we could build the ultimate temple, The Church of the Great Mindfuck.

After months of too much time and effort spent trying to concentrate on nothing, I experienced something amazing while meditating in my bedroom.

"I sat in the middle of my room as I had done before, na-ked of course…" I paused to roll my eyes and allow Weeli his adolescent reaction to the word 'naked.' "It's best to medi-tate naked. I'm not going to explain it again."

Weeli just puckered his lips and nodded his head as if to say, 'Sure, man. Sure.'

"Anyway," I continued, "I did the whole atmosphere thing and all that. Then, after an hour or so, I decided, fuck it. The candles and incense were just distracting me. I blew them out, shut off the lights, and basically spent the next two hours keeping my mind as wide awake as possible, and that was it. I didn't bother to try to focus on anything, but I also stopped trying to not focus. That's what was fuck-ing me up, man. When Steve Chu, the Kung Fu guy, was trying to make a Buddha out of me, he'd always tell me to concentrate on clearing your mind and thinking about absolutely nothing. I'd be so busy concentrating on trying to think about absolutely nothing that every thought would freak me out. So instead, if a thought popped in, I just let it be as long as it wanted, 'till it wasn't anymore.

"I became aware of the mind from outside the mind. It's a funny place, the brain. I could feel the movement of air, blood, the workings of my veins and my cells, which was pretty fucking neat, but also distracting. I just let it be until it wasn't anymore. Eventually, I started feeling really light, you know, like weightless. I felt a sort of cosmic frequency that we all exist on."

I paused to suck in a hit and make sure Weeli was still listening.

"I only call it cosmic frequency 'cause I've got no better word for it. It's a way of feeling all of the energy around you, and the energy you are putting out, and the frequency it is all connected on. Every emotion, every action, every odor, everything puts out or affects a particular energy.

"I was terrified," I told him as I rubbed my head. "I told you I started feeling weightless, and I swear to God I felt like I was about to go somewhere that I couldn't turn back from, man. I was fucking terrified. As weird as that sounds, the weightlessness, the connection, the energy…it felt mathematic or electric or something, and I got scared. I opened my eyes, jumped up, and turned on the light. I was frightened by the verve of the cosmos ('Verve' is a word Sophia introduced to me. She defined it as the nerve and the vibe of a thing). It was like I wasn't anywhere or anyone."

Weeli badgered me to expound. When I wouldn't, couldn't really, he moved onto his favorite activity, talking about Weeli.

"I was ravenous. I starved myself to the point of famishment," he explained. Weeli could be explaining the death of a close relative and still do it with a smile that was contagious.

"I not only began to hallucinate and see visions of the inside of my mind, but I was able to project the hallucinations." He took the pipe from me, raising his eyebrows, shining like a child with excitement. "And what a peculiar thing to be able to do. It was as if my brain was a movie projector, and as long as it was in there, really in there, I could project it and physically see it right there before me. At first, I had no control and it was frightening. Every insecurity, every fear projected before me like holograms beyond my control. But then, a comforting sensation. So when you tell me you don't know how to explain it all, I understand because I can't explain that sensation. What it is—"

"What did you see?" I interrupted, entirely interested in what his most minute fears and insecurities were.

"Not important, Herb," Weeli told me and continued on. "The important thing is, when I could control it, Herb, the brain...the brain has powers that we don't tap into."

Back and forth during smoke breaks or over lunch, we inspired each other with our experiences, setting the foundation for our new order, The Church of the Great Mindfuck.

Every church has its backsliders. The worst of those were nearly always the leaders. Catholic priests molesting children while vowing celibacy. TV evangelists soliciting gay prostitution while selling damnation for sinners. Rabbis sending money to spread rabies to Palestine. Imam clerics funding terrorism while preaching the word of Muhammad. Every church has its backsliders. The Church of the Great Mindfuck was no different.

The paradigm of a great mindfuck, or any mindfuck for that matter, is that by its nature it is nearly impossible to remember in standard sensory memory fashion. The episode itself, much like the experience of an intense dream state, is all too often lost somewhere between the moment of fucking and the moment of the mind inhaling, comprehending, and translating the harsh conditions of reality. Sometimes, mindfucks are like that half-awake, half-asleep, death-is-coming dream except you can't wake yourself. Unlike the dream, the risk of the mindfuck is the inability to wake up, sometimes resulting in a person remaining in that state of mind until death. Sometimes, death is the result of a mind-fuck. It is not risk-free.

⇒⋅ ⋅⇐

K.C. was dark-skinned, as polished and educated as Weeli and, despite his African descent, the 'whitest' kid in the house, according to Weeli. Weeli had introduced me to K.C. shortly after I started at Entipop.

"My friend needs a roommate," Weeli said to me after seeing where I had been staying at the time. "He's a great guy and his place has curtains instead of blankets on the windows. Plus, it's ten minutes from The Dugout so you'll be much closer to work." That was Weeli's way of looking out for me. So K.C. and I became roommates for a time.

K.C.'s folks had an estate in Vermont. His parents were off to France for the weekend and it was decided the estate would be our temple for The Great Mindfuck. We decided on a Wednesday, and that Friday Weeli and I were on the road heading north. We met K.C. and his farmhand, Crazy Frank, at The Riverboat, a small café in the west end of Putney, Vermont.

Crazy Frank.

"You wouldn't believe it unless you saw this shit with your own fucking eyes, my friends," Frank said waving his massive, leather-skinned hands in front of his face. The Riverboat seemed too small to accommodate Frank and his big giant being-ness.

"She had...I mean...I'm goddamn tellin' ya," he continued much too boisterously, stretching his arms and cupping his hands out in front of his torso as if he were holding two large bags of popcorn or big fat water balloons. "I'm goddamn tellin' ya, she had a big double fucking D kinda smile, man, if you know what I'm saying. You boys ever see a goddamn smile like this? You sure would remember it. Sure as shit, man. Big double goddamn D kinda smile," Frank repeated as he licked his chapped lips and rubbed his musclebound fingers together.

"Frank," K.C. snapped, "not so loud," his voice calm and collected, his left hand stretching forward in a pumping motion as if to cool Frank down. "You're going to freak someone out...and lay off the cursing."

"Sorry," Frank said loudly enough to be apologizing to the entire place. "But," he proceeded just as exuberantly, "one thing's for sure. Anyone with a double D kinda smile is somewhat oblivious. That's not a bad thing, it's just a thing. Oblivious to the whole charade," he said looking down at the menu. "They always talk about a strong middle class. That's the grabber there. Everyone thinks they are middle class even when they ain't anywhere near the center of it. And when the middle class gets too comfortable, too close, they manufacture a reset. The Cold War was brilliant. Can't get too comfy when you're terrified of frying in a mushroom cloud. Now it's terrorism. Be afraid."

"Hey, K.C.," Weeli said quietly, apparently attempting to change the tone of the conversation, "are there any other black people in this whole fucking town, man? I haven't seen one."

"We're it, man," K.C. replied proudly. "One black family probably for the three surrounding towns."

"Is that tough?" Weeli asked.

"No, it's not like we live in the Live Free or Die state. It's actually pretty liberal. Mostly lesbians. Besides, just like everywhere else, money rules all. You can buy enlightenment apparently, 'cause a few dollars seems to make a person forget they're racist for a while. Vermont is full of people who are out to prove just how open-minded they are."

"Damn, Frank," Weeli said. Frank was dumping packets of crackers into his soup before the waitress could finish putting the food down.

"For the love of God, man," Weeli went on smiling at Frank, "how many crackers you need?"

"I'm often thinking the same thing," K.C. smiled.

"How 'bout a bit a soup with your crackers there?" Weeli suggested. The crackers continued to drop, overflowing until there was no sign of broth.

"Y'eva getta bad fuckin' bowla soup, man?" Frank managed to blurt out mouthfuls of words in between bites and slurpy chomps of soup. "Ya know," he continued, as his tongue made its way around the full reach of the outside of his mouth, wiping clean his slopper. "Too f'in..."

*Gulp.*

"...watery. No goddamn flavor. No big, fat chunks of substance, you know? I mean fat, meaty, double D kinda substance." He went on scooping heaps of chowder onto his spoon then into his mouth. "Ya know, like them bowls of thin blood bullshit you git in New York. Red tide, menstrual-cycle looking. Manhattan clam bullshit."

Frank had developed a rhythm and incredible speed for inhaling his chowder and water. Four massive mouthfuls of chowder to every one great big gulp of water. In between, somehow he managed to breathe and ramble on. It was a spectacle.

"Frank," K.C. snapped again, quietly, like a parent trying to control a child without hurting its feelings.

"Nobody fucks up crackers, man," Frank reiterated. "Oyster crackers are fucking oyster crackers, you know? You can't count on the goddamn soup. It's the Cracker Solution."

"The final Cracker Solution," K.C. mumbled.

"What if you don't like crackers?" Weeli asked with a smirk.

"Take it from me," K.C. said, "you just pretend. It's easy."

"That's ridiculous," Frank snapped, "everyone likes crackers."

Frank's hands looked like thick leather gloves, disproportionate to his body. He stood about five foot eleven, but his hands were almost twice the size of mine. Frank's arms were like Robin Williams's in the role of Popeye. His forearms were almost as large as his shoulders and biceps. He wore a dirty, red sweatshirt over brown, long underwear. At his neck, it was clear he had at least one t-shirt on under both of those. Above all of that, he wore a jumpsuit. He looked like a man who belonged up there in those mountains, more so than any of the three of us. Frank was a veteran of the Vietnam War and when the gentleman on the other side of the counter commented about his son fighting in the war, Frank's demeanor changed dramatically, along with his volume and tone. He was respectful and reverent, quiet and sad.

We left the café and headed south, passing a large factory, oddly placed amidst the vast spread of evergreens and horse farms. We took a left heading up a long private drive.

"I live right up here," K.C. said as we pulled into a brilliant piece of land based at the foot of Mount Spirit. As we drove up, K.C. pointed out stables off in the distance which, as it turned out, were Frank's home.

"We have the place to ourselves this weekend, boys," K.C. said as we pulled into the semicircular driveway.

"Fucking A," I shouted out, getting a good look at the mansion. "I've never even been on a piece of property like this."

"Glad you like it, H. Wait 'till you see the inside," K.C. said, "it's pretty fucking sweet."

"Pretty sweet?" I asked. "Sweet, my ass. This is mad, man. Absolutely mad. I can't believe this is where we're staying." Weeli, of course, was used to mansions and money, estates and freedom.

We settled in quickly. The size of the mansion was overwhelming. Every room seemed at least half the size, if not all the size, of a normal house. Wood, brass, gold, glass, and crystal-framed pictures decorated the entire place. These weren't Bev Doolittle pieces. These were the types of work that get loaned out to the Museum of Fine Arts. We exited through a glass door after only covering three rooms, headed for Frank's abode. He was excited for us to see it.

Beneath a moonlit sky, we made our way to the stables. Around the large, brown barn, there was very little noise. Frank went ahead to prepare the wolves, horses, and whatever else was living in there with him. Weeli and I made our way over to the double-wide barn door.

As Frank pulled the door open, my jaw must have been hanging wide open, waiting for the flies. The glow behind Frank was bright, emanating from a huge lantern and several candles. Brilliant feathers hung above the entrance. The flickering light reflected the many colors. The feathers did not appear trimmed or cleaned like the ones you find in commercial dreamcatchers or feather fans. Some of them were over a foot and a half long and maybe four inches wide. Most were dark gray with speckles of white, like the cold Vermont mountains in wintertime. Others seemed to encompass the entire spectrum of the rainbow.

Behind a brown, reclining, leather chair three quiet beasts paced in the shadows, their breathing slow and heavy.

Wolves.

A small stove half-covered in a blanket sat above the fire pit. The dull, blank screen of what looked like an old black and white television occupied a milk crate in front of the recliner. Frank would explain that the wolves like to watch the television. They didn't mind black and white, as that was how they saw the world anyway. Past the shadows of the wolves were two hand-carved wooden chairs.

Frank called them the Royal Rockers. They were not rocking chairs. A king and queen carved meticulously out of solid dark wood, with incredibly detailed and lifelike features. The crown of the king's chair must have stood about six feet tall and the queen's head about five ten. The details of the crown, the jewels, and the robes were astonishingly real and somehow, even though all the same color wood, shone a brightness and royalty. Every adornment, including anklets, bracelets, and rings, were eerily lifelike.

The facial features of the king were so intricate that you could see his strength, wisdom, and kindness in the wood itself. It was the face of a man who was comfortable with, and aware of, the power he had, but kind enough to show mercy and humility.

I stood gaping, waiting for the flies to land, hatch their eggs, fuck, and hatch again, but this time the flies actually came. They were abuzz in the stable and welcome members of Frank's kingdom. I awed with a closed mouth.

As we stepped into his living area, there was no avoiding the pungent aroma of ammonia. Sharp enough to taste. Wolf urine, bird shit, horse manure, moldy wood, dusty hay, and Frank's distinct body odor all mixed together.

Beneath an old wool army blanket, which covered the cages, were three birds. One spoke repetitious English and another whistled.

"Where'd these chairs come from?" Weeli asked. "They're incredible."

"Fuck the chairs," Frank said grinning wildly, "that's just goddamn wood. Those birds, though, they are the amazing things." He pointed up toward the doorway, nowhere near the wool blanket covering the large birdcages.

"What birds?" Weeli asked turning his head up and around. Frank pointed up toward heaven, from which the great big feathers fell, hanging like a dreamcatcher in the entranceway.

"Those goddamn birds saved my life. God fucking bless them, man," Frank said with reverence. He tilted his long, square face to the heavens and closed his eyes briefly. "Every one of those fucking feathers means another piece of my ass saved, man. Those things aren't up there for looks, you know. For God's sakes, they sure aren't just pretty little feathers," he said, shaking his head back and forth and beginning to pace.

"Those fuckers saved my life through an entire winter up in those goddamn mountains, man." Frank pointed north toward those goddamn mountains. "I never thought I was coming out. At least not alive, but those fuckers saved my life, man. God bless them." He stroked the feathers like royalty, wept, and went on to tell us the long, exhausting story of the man we'd come to know and love as Crazy Frank.

He showed us his antique nineteen fifty-nine Volkswagen Bug, formally introduced us to his three birds, and gave us a tour of an old horse trailer that he was converting into an 'animal farm on goddamn wheels,' as he put it.

He spoke of survival in Vermont and Vietnam as if they were synonymous. He spoke of playing with Janis Joplin's band. "She wasn't there at the time. It was a Holding Company show. You know, Big Brother and The Holding Company?"

A descendant of Noah. He kept two stallions (one spotted white, the other pitch black), three wolves, two of which were wild Canadian wolves, the other, half-tame, rescued from the mountains, five exotic birds (three in the cages and two in the horse trailer/animal farm on goddamn wheels), one not-so-exotic turkey, and a cat he called Magic.

"Have you ever heard of the Lapsit Exillis, Mr. Weeli? I have the stone. One day I will show it to you."

"I think it's actually supposed to be a chalice, isn't it?" Weeli smiled.

"A lot of things are supposed to be," Frank said with a smile, dismissing the entire thing out of hand. "But," he finished, "it belongs to the aliens."

"What's that?" I asked.

"Lapsit Exillis," Weeli said, "is the Holy Grail."

"Let's get this show started," K.C. said from outside the barn. "Come on, let's head in."

⇐ ⇒

The Great Mindfuck.

Terrible nausea came over me after we overdosed our bodies with one of just about everything in K.C.'s portable medicine cabinet. We drank the pain away.

"Gentleman, we...and you, too, Frank," K.C. announced, raising a glass of wine to his lips, "are in for the mindfuck of all time." K.C. had no appreciation for The Revolution. He heard us ramble and occasionally even joined in, but he had no personal investment. It was all bullshit to him. A mindfuck, however, was something he did believe in.

Things shifted quickly. I sat down on the couch, trying to hold down whatever was crawling up my throat, rising from my gut. Frank was shouting nonsense. It felt like things were spinning, but everything except Crazy Frank was still. His voice was deep and loud. I was in pain, surely about to vomit. A familiar feeling accompanied by a familiar question was quickly upon me. *Why did I do this to myself? Why not just meditate?*

*Why the...ugh...my stomach.*

But like the times before, energies shifted and it all began to change. Some indeterminable amount of time passed neither quickly nor slowly, just sort of lingered around and meandered by.

"White carpet, white tiles, a white goddamn tab...it's f'in hopeless," I heard someone say. Sound was blurred, bubbly, warped into a slow, underwater gargling. A simple name like Herb might sound something like a slow, stretched out 'ah-hoo-ah-rab.' A name like K.C. could easily morph into 'cuh-rashing-sea' or 'cuh-rushing-me.' Communication could be dangerous and volatile. But it was still early, and even through the carpets-in-a-fishbowl sounds, I could make out the words clearly. A white tab of acid had been lost on a white carpet. A dangerous thing for a property with many animals. *God forbid they make their way inside and accidentally...fuck, what about the insects? The poor ant that mistakes that fucker for sugar?* No one else seemed overly concerned.

*Maybe it never fell onto the carpet. Maybe the tab wasn't missing at all?*

*Fuck.*

My brain was being taken over by a warm, radioactive blanket of mushy shit, a dull pain, and an unnatural, internal itchiness. Very few words were spoken. Pre-trip paranoia set in.

The room was aglow, shimmering with shadow and light. Energies shifted back and forth between a warm-and-cozy and a cold-and-shivering sensation.

*My breathing? Was I doing it? In, out, in, out. Let nature take her course. Things breathe.* No use. I wondered if everyone in the room heard me wondering, or panting loudly. I wondered if my paranoia was broadcasting through some sort of megaphone of energies. *Did I drink enough water? Should I be drinking this beer?*

A dull pain. *Fuck.* This time much lower and to the left. *Was I really feeling my heart? Fuck. Not my goddamn heart.* I wasn't even sure what a pain in the heart would feel like. *Maybe it was the lack of oxygen?* It was my breathing. Now it was having a chain reaction, slowly shutting down my system. I was sure of it. Then I wasn't. Then I was sure I was just being paranoid. Then I was sure I was going to die. *What the fuck?* Deep breaths. I stretched my neck to bring it back to life and in touch with the rest of my body.

*Thump. Thump.*

A rolling bass penetrated my overly sensitive ears.

"Sowum funa...coooodeelic if you do...wann mind... boys," came K.C.'s burbled voice.

*Fuck.*

*Zam. Zap. Zoop.*

*Hold on.*

Just like that, my brain became electric soup. Forget the anticipation, the nerves, the apprehension. None of that mattered. It was much too late for all that. I was in the shit. Within the tingly confines of my skull, my brain seemed to compress and shrink until there was no more awareness of the brain.

Sharp images, brilliant and colorful, shifted mysteriously. The room became a checkerboard of parallel lines, colors, light beams, sparkles. The cushions on the couch were so well defined I could almost count each stitch.

"Cahagoso...felosaha..." Weeli said. Burbled and slow.

"Huh?" K.C. mumbled.

"Algohohol," Weeli said. "I thuh-ink I fee-ow sick. Cah-heen I get a beer?"

I heard the word 'sick.' That's all it took. So fragile. I felt rigor mortis in my own stomach. I'd seen the way waves of thoughts and emotions spread over the fragile minds of drug-induced companions before. One person is cold, they throw on their jacket shivering, and then another is cold.

It doesn't matter if it's a hundred and ten degrees. Sure enough, the tripping banshees follow.

"Oh God, I'm cold, too. Wow, man, it's like my sweat is just freezing right on my body."

The worst is the wildfire of bad feelings.

I had seen entire groups lay down on the ground thinking they were sick after eating mushrooms. Then someone would come over and say something simple like, "Hey, you guys want to go check out the lake, the sun's about to go down?" And, as if nothing was ever wrong, the whole group would get up and have a terrific time watching the sunset. I once used the power of suggestion to convince my younger brother that we were standing in a field of dog shit. In reality, it was early winter, the ground was covered with snow, but the snow was speckled with fallen leaves, mostly brown. The suggestion made its way to my brain and we both ran in the house and took off our shoes.

"This is the shit, man," Frank said. I noticed my ability to hear, or their ability to talk, was mysteriously returning. "This is definitely the shit," Frank repeated. "The goddamn shit that grinds into the long and short nerves that connect our thoughts and...and our thoughts and words and everything, man. There's something here." He held out his arms as if feeling the fabric of air itself. He stepped slowly around in a circle.

"Can you see it, man? If I could connect these nerves, yeah, then the thoughts and words would...you...yeah... yeah, man...do you see?" he asked, forming lines and trails with his fingers in the air. "They would all come together perfectly," he said, as if he'd just discovered how to put words and thoughts together. "It's like they can be one... yeah...one, man."

We said nothing, but that didn't stop him.

"You see, man, if this connection was never molested by this shit the world feeds you, it'd be perfectly one and… entirely unbroken…and one and the same."

*Fuck.*

There was talk of the hospital on the other side of the room. K.C. was doing his best to talk Weeli down. He wasn't getting over that sick feeling as quickly as the rest of us.

"You're just feeling a little queasy, man, it's expected. You'll be all right." Weeli looked at K.C. like he was some sort of monster. K.C. looked at Weeli like he might have to shoot him and end the bullshit.

Energies shifting.

"You listen to me," K.C. instructed Weeli. K.C. rubbed his head with both hands as if trying to push something out from the inside. "You wanted this, now grow up. You're not going to die and you're not going to the hospital." He stood up in front of Weeli. "Snap out of it, man. Go take a walk or something."

Everything went silent. K.C. left the room. Weeli looked like he wanted to cry. I felt mostly helpless but offered what I could.

"You want some water?" I asked him.

"A beer, please," Weeli replied. He stood up, grabbed ahold of the back of his neck, and rubbed it desperately. A metallic taste had invaded my mouth. Tin in my throat and copper on my tongue, but thank God, my breathing and my heart were coming around. A beer sounded nasty to me at the time, but what the hell? These were fragile times. Getting the beer, I brushed past K.C. as he was splashing cold water on his face.

With his beer in hand and a desperate look on his face, Weeli disappeared out the front door. On his way out, I tried to ask if he needed company, but nothing came out of my metallic mouth. I was grateful my heart and lungs were working. What more could I ask for? Frank had been shouting. There was something about the French government and a woman named Jacqueline.

The gritty teeth, tight chin, racing-head shit was replacing other bad things. Frank passed by me in a flash, his arms spread out like the wings of an eagle. My heart no longer felt like it might explode, but paranoia set in again. *Would I ever come out of this?*

"Do ah...you ahblear me?" Frank shouted as he passed, leaving a lingering trail of sizzling colors behind him. "I blush at all of you! My color fades into the falseness that is all of you...all of us. I...will not shy away! Look at me! Don't shy away." Frank moved almost without use of arms or legs. He seemed to glide across the room.

"Tonight," Frank continued to shout. A lyrical rhythm to his words. "Gentleman," he leaped onto the bar, "tonight we are most alive. Running high in rivers wild. Burning 'neath the night sky, drowning 'neath her smile. Alive, boys. Burn your skin and run.

"Fuck her," Frank said, a pillow gyrating violently in his crotch. "You gotta fuck the shit outta life, man...argh. Argh," he moaned as he ground with the pillow.

"Hey, ah...K.C.?" I could barely hear Weeli as he spoke, returning to the house seemingly out of nowhere. He sounded like he was talking through a tin can phone. "K.C.," he called out a second time, "I think he's ah, going to um, ah, kill that pillow, man."

"Who is the Pillowman? Why are you killing him?"

"Who is Frank killing, man?" K.C. mumbled. Somehow, he'd ended up on the floor in the prone position. Frank stood above K.C. He stopped fucking the pillow and looked down at him.

The beast had all of us. Church was in session.

⋯⋯

"Kill," Frank said. His expression was a strange one. He bolted to the bar, leaped up, both feet at once, landing like King Kong. He was much too large a man to be standing on the oak bar.

"Yes!" Frank hollered, while pounding his right fist against his chest. "Sure, I've killed a man. Probably killed more men than I'll ever know about. Maybe I'll even kill again...yes...yes...I've killed!" Frank screamed.

K.C. rolled over.

"I'll fucking kill again if I have to...uroooh...rghh," Frank growled like a man-beast, a werewolf with supernatural evils roaring out from the depths of his tortured soul. "Yes, I'd kill again if I had to!"

Weeli was crawling around on the floor with a large, shiny knife. Frank remained on the bar. K.C. remained on his back on the floor. I was the only one sitting normally on the couch. I felt like a creep. Something must have been wrong with me. *Why didn't I have a knife? Why wasn't I on the floor? Why wasn't I ranting about killing? What the fuck?*

I had an urge to run out of the house. I was freaking out. I played it cool. I didn't want to freak any of them out.

"Kill, you say?" Frank continued yelling.

*Fuck.* I was too fragile for that kind of crazy talk.

"A broken spirit," he screamed, arms flailing wildly. "That's what I'd kill for. Fuck, they broke my spirit, didn't they? I'd kill a man for breaking a horse's spirit. When you see a broken horse, it'll make you cry...make you want to kill. Fucking kill."

I was done for. His words morphed into absolute nonsense. I walked out of the room. For a time, I melted into the glass lining the entire length of the kitchen wall. I stared through the glass, both arms fully pressed against it. For a moment, layers and layers of glass unwrapped before me as I stared deeply into the wall. I rolled against it like K.C. did the carpet. Everything morphed into mush, then complete clarity, then mush again.

Hours passed. A hazy memory of inspecting a bathroom. A long session washing my arms. Staring at a painting. Touching a fluffy carpet. A horse stall? Strange times.

I was lying in a horse stall buck-naked with a horse named Sky, rubbing her. My heart beat with hers. I melted into oneness with her.

Then I ran. I ran like a wild horse. Then...*Jesus Christ. Fuck.* I found myself lying naked in a large pile of horse manure. I rolled around spreading it on my body as if baptizing myself, cleansing myself. It was soft and comfortable. The smell was good and natural. Soon, Frank was there pulling me out of the pile. He showed me to the water spigot.

I headed inside for a hot shower. I could handle it at that point, I thought, and goddamn, it sounded like a good idea. Through the glass door attached to the glass wall I went. Weeli stopped me, made some vague comment about my lack of clothing then told me to stick out my tongue. It was some sort of pill.

"Well-uh-cuhum...tohoo church," he said. I swallowed and continued on. I showered for what seemed to be an hour or so. The water felt good, then painful, then great, then hurt again. The droplets looked beautiful, morphing into white butterflies, then naked women, and then water again. Time passed. When I came out, everything had changed.

The long, wide hall was a round tunnel like two half-pipes that a skateboarder or skier or snowboarder could have a field day with. A Monet was in constant motion, following me around as if computer intelligence was at work. The hallway was lined with lights, which were throwing smaller splashes of light all over the place. The carpet had an oceanic design and gave an illusion of waves rolling past.

*"Rrnt...errnt...errnt...rahernt..."*

*Tanks?*

*What the?*

Tanks. Clear as day, or at least as clear as anything was at the time, I heard tanks coming from somewhere. They were closing in.

*"Rrnt...errnt...errnt...rahernt..."*

Silence.

A piano. Beautiful voices. "...Always hoped that I'd be an apostle, knew that I would make it if I tried. Then when we retire, we can write the gospels, so they'll talk about us when we've died...what's that in the bread? It's gone to my head, 'till this morning is this evening, life is fine."

There was no tank. Only *Jesus Christ Superstar.*

"I must be mad," Jesus said as I set out to find the source of the music, "I must be out of my head."

K.C. had an IMAX theater in his house. The half-shell screen encompassed the entire room with the exception of the floor. The sound and screen were designed to give the audience the sense that they were right there within the movie.

I found myself in the middle of the desert where Jesus pleaded with God, "...Take this cup away from me. For I don't want to taste its poison." Tears streamed down my face as I sang my heart out, eyes opened so wide, I caught every angle of the screen surrounding me. I reached out to Christ himself. I danced. I sang. I cried.

I found myself dancing jubilantly, inspired by the voice of Judas calling from the afterlife. He looked like an angel in a white robe, his voice strong and powerful.

"Why'd you choose such a backward time? And such a strange land?" The deep bass and heavy groove of Andrew Lloyd Webber's score pounded into me.

Exhilarating.

In between that moment and the ones I actually remember next, I'm positive I came to many understandings, moments of clarity, states of enlightenment. However, because of the state itself, I have no recollection of them.

I woke up lying naked in the kitchen. My head stung in a way I'd never experienced before. I thought I was too young, too much The Shit to feel such a thing, but the feeling was there. Undeniable. Areas of my body that had never felt pain before felt like they were burning or ripping apart, or both. Somewhere just south of my heart and above my ribs, there was a warm fire that felt as though it was slowly trying to burn itself out, but couldn't quite extinguish. Just above my testicles, in a region of my body that never before had any distinct sensation, between the phallus and sack, there was a strange, dull pain. My ears were ringing. My eyes were dry. My bones hurt. I stood up and realized two things. Weeli was lying on the floor in front of me. I wasn't wearing pants. Just then, just as pre-piss dribble was falling from the tip of my dick, Weeli woke.

Frank came in carrying a bucket and a mop.

"You got no clothes on, you know?" he informed me, placing the bucket down and beginning to mop. "Ain't got much time," he said as I tried to pass quietly to the staircase, which would hopefully lead me to my clothes.

"Huh?" I mumbled to him. "We've got 'till Tuesday, man, don't we?" K.C. had told us his folks would not be back until Tuesday. It was a long weekend. That should give us at least a day, if not more.

"Tuesday is about seven hours away. They'll probably be early, too, they ain't late very often," he said.

*Seven hours.*

*Fuck.*

We arrived on Friday. I thought it was Sunday morning. I thought we had another full day of mindfucking, of recovery, of a weekend, before we even considered clean-up, wrap-up, et-fucking-cetera. It was Tuesday.

The cleaning frenzy would occupy the next six hours as we tried to make the house somewhat recognizable to K.C.'s parents. We broke a few things in our frenzy. As we were winding down, the phone rang. The answering machine picked up.

"K.C.? Frank? K.C.? Pick up if you're there, honey," came his mother's voice. K.C. did not pick up.

"Hope all is well, Son," his father said.

"We decided to stay a couple of days longer. Hope you're having a good time. We should be back by week's end. Love you. Bye."

*Click.*

Weeli and I plopped right down, planting our tired asses on the floor. Frank kept on sweeping like a good soldier.

"Hey, guys, I got one piece of stable fence in the bathroom here...any ideas?" K.C. called.

"Hey, Frank," Weeli said rubbing his eyes, "who are these folks you told us about? They for real?"

There was talk of taking over capitals. Talk of important people, leftovers from the sixties who were now in government. Not just American officials, but throughout the world. Frank got angry with Weeli and me for not remembering.

"How the fuck are you going to lead a goddamn thing?" Frank asked Weeli. "You guys don't even pay attention to the shit right in front of you."

"Come on, Frank, are you kidding? I remember some of it, but the Elders? What was all that about?"

"Right," I said as pieces dribbled back into my cranium, "Princess Jasmine, the Elders. The West?"

"You will come around," Frank told Weeli then looked at me. I shrugged my shoulders. "You will come around. Jasmine is sort of a go-between. She will help point you in the direction of the people you need to see when you are there. She will likely not even know them, but she will know how to guide you. She's a bit crazy, but who isn't? She is a princess with the Paiute peoples, though she is likely to tell you she is Navajo. I believe she is shacked up with a Crow medicine man these days."

"I don't get it," Weeli said.

"Let me show you something," Frank said. It was clear that neither K.C. nor I were invited to join them. As they left the house, the phone rang again. The machine picked up.

"Oh, K.C., honey. Since we're not going to be back 'till later, we wanted to give you the good news. The doctor says there's no real threat. If you decide to keep the testicle, that's fine, but if you'd like to have it removed, he can do it next week. Love you, honey. See you soon."

# CHAPTER 14

# CORPORATE DRIVE

### A Plymouth Night Howl

*Whistling mysterious songs, the mighty wind howls,*
*Chimes, eerie sounds scatter 'cross rooftops like*
*gypsy fairies.*
*The horizon, dazzling the charmed night sky,*
*captures with her hypnotic yellow glow*
*Sparkling light, dancing stars, fireflies bounce*
*'round them all.*
*Like Pentecostals speak to God, in a language of*
*tongues without words, she speaks.*
*Intimidated, frightened, timid, fighting, I cannot*
*reciprocate.*
*Pillow side Lions roar as kittens purr pressed*
*pleasantly against my head.*
*Heart beats in rhythm. Soul sighs, 'Throne resigned.'*
*I will race my newfound friend.*
*I will beat her to her own morning.*

*On this, most clear and humid of nights, the*
*mighty wind howls.*

– POOR JOHN, 1997

A t Entipop, rumors abound. The latest predicted that Weeli or I would be promoted to manage the technology division. We were traveling to Jersey on business, as the entire project team was asked to fly out on Monday morning to attend a three-day seminar.

Weeli and I would be missing a half-day of those sessions to accompany Garbway, and deliver a presentation to the board of directors in New York. The intent was to give them some level of comfort surrounding the cost overruns and overall progress. I was to demonstrate what the test effort would consist of for both technical and business users, what the requirements for acceptance would be, how performance testing would be conducted, and how we'd measure success or failure, so the directors could make an informed decision before accepting the system on behalf of Entipop. Acceptance of the system had financial consequences. We would begin paying Nacroya immediately after accepting the first iteration. Weeli would present his plan for converting all existing businesses to the new system. We were both half-full of shit and still three-quarters of a lap ahead of everyone around us. Rather than fly out on Monday morning with everyone else, Weeli and I decided to drive out Sunday morning, and meet some friends in the city.

When Sunday morning came, I volunteered to drive my car. I was a born volunteer. Amnesty International, Civil Air Patrol, Civil Defense, U.S. Army, etc. I liked to be in control. My car, a ninety-one BMW Five Twenty-Eight E series, was more comfortable for the long ride than Weeli's new Mercedes. The Beamer was the first decent car I'd ever owned so I was pretty much happy to drive it anywhere, even Jersey City. Weeli didn't much mind. Taking a vehicle like that was his form of 'roughing it.' We would rough our way to Jersey City.

The feedlot...

You can smell a feedlot well before you actually get to it. You can feel the stench burn the nose hairs, scrambling for shelter in your nostrils before you even step out of the car. Like the smell of an unattended, overused outhouse on a sweltering hot day, the stench of a feedlot is nasty, sharp, and unnatural. Feedlots, where cattle learn to feed from tubs instead of grazing in open fields, are now more common than grazing farms. In the refuse of hundreds, sometimes thousands, of other cattle, the beasts are injected with hormones and crammed together in disgusting pens, fighting to access the synthetic tubs which will be their only source of food for the rest of their unnatural lives. As far as the eye can see, pens and tubs stretch across the horizon, broken up only by the fog of toxic stench surrounding the rectangular, city-like, lagoon of waste, manure, nitrogen, and toxic pharmaceuticals. I do love a good steak.

Before Hoboken was the artsy hipster community that it became, and before the Newport waterfront was redone,

Jersey City had the smell and feel of a feedlot. At the time, Jersey City was within wind proximity of the largest waste dumpsite in the Unites States. You could taste it.

Stench or no, we had to make our way there. We left before sunrise. It was a brisk fall morning. The sun was no-where in sight as we loaded all our goods into my four-door yuppie-has-been-mobile. The New England winds were whipping the chilling rain at a slant.

"Fuck," Weeli said to me as he stepped out onto the driveway. I was at the rear of my Beamer, loading the trunk. "You might be right about the weather."

"Yup," I said to him, yawning, eyes half-shut. "I told you I heard it the other night. We may be timing this perfectly to pick up the remnants of Hurricane Barty."

"Fuck," Weeli repeated. Sometimes he was a man of few words. Often, those words were profanity. A few 'fucks' lat-er, and we were on our way.

I tuned into the local public radio station, Ninety-Point-Nine, WNPR. There it was, like they were just waiting for us to turn on the radio.

"The National Weather Service says to expect strong winds in the Mid-Atlantic and Northeastern Corridors. The eye of Hurricane Barty is just below South Carolina, moving at a speed of twenty-two miles per hour. The storm was expected to move out to sea last night, and not make landfall. The National Weather Service projects the storm to continue making its way northeast and out to sea."

Weeli slept.

I drove into the cold wind and rain.

"The time is five twenty a.m., Eastern Standard. This is Ninety-Point-Nine, WNPR Boston. The size of Barty has surprised experts as the cloud mass extends as far south as the Florida Keys. Hurricane Barty has blanketed the East Coast with gray sky, winds, and heavy rain. The eye of the storm remains just south of the Carolinas. A state of emergency has been declared as far north as Maryland."

As I found my way to Route Ninety-Five, having cut over from Twenty-Four North to hit Three North (otherwise known in the mess of Massachusetts highways as Ninety-Five South), I began to think about what the week would bring, aside from heavy winds and rain. Somewhere in the back of my mind, I knew I wanted to make a really good impression with the board. Not so much to secure my future at Entipop, because that seemed pretty secure, but more because these guys had a corporate headquarters in the heart of Manhattan and a satellite office in Asia. I wanted to secure my possibilities, really. If the rumors were true, if Weeli or I were about to take the big job at Entipop, then this presentation could be the deciding factor.

It wasn't even six a.m. and I was already exhausted. Something about driving in the wind and rain, the dull gray of the sky and air, put me into a sleepy trance. That sort of driving took the fun out of a road trip.

I passed the 'Welcome to Connecticut' sign and reached the stretch of Ninety-Five that was lined with nothing but trees on both sides for about eighty miles. Just as I began to relax, just as WNPR repeated "...may be downgraded to a tropical storm by day's end," the wind blew a large branch across the interstate and right under my car.

*Clunk.*

*Crunch.*

*Slam.*

"Fuck!" I screamed.

The impact was instant. So was the familiar, uneven thump of a blown tire. The wind pushed, and the weight of the steel box pulled toward the dead wheel. I pulled on the steering wheel. Futile. There was no give. I pulled the other way and yanked the wheel to the left and, like a good bus driver, set the car into a spin.

"Oh, shit!"

We spun once, full around.

Weeli was jarred awake. Wide awake, and instantly screaming like a petrified baby. He slid straight into me, and pressed hard against my right side. The stick shift jammed into my knee somewhere between his leg and mine. My head slammed against the driver's side window. The car hydroplaned sideways right toward the guardrail.

*Slam.*

A dead stop, but no crash. The guardrail ended just before we hit the side of the road. We missed it by inches and were stopped by the rocky ground at the edge of the highway, which had caught the sharp rim of the rear tire. I held up my hand to Weeli, shaking my head, imploring him not to say a word, to not even look at me for a moment. He understood. My nerves had reached the point of no immediate return. Hands shaking, blood pressure exploding, heart racing like a souped-up nineteen sixty-five Harley on acid. I took a moment to enjoy being alive. Way in the back of my mind, somewhere next to questions about whether or not I packed enough underwear for the trip, there was a thought about what a pain in the ass it was going to be to get out in this shit weather and change the tire. Mostly, I didn't give a fuck about the tire. I was ecstatic to be alive.

As I was calming down, as I was reveling in life itself, Weeli decided enough time had passed.

"What the fuck, man?"

*Stay calm,* I thought to myself.

My peripheral vision made it all too obvious that he was staring at me. His head hadn't moved. I didn't turn to meet his stare.

*Fuck. Couldn't he just give me a goddamn minute?* No, that was apparently not possible.

"What the fuck?" he said again. His angry eyes still fixed on me, he continued, "did you fall asleep or something?"

*Zing, zing, zing* it went from synapse to synapse. *Did you fall asleep or something?*

How dare he?

*Did you fall asleep or something?*

*Zing, zing, zing.*

A violent anger rose up from beneath my testicles and shot right up into my cranium. I felt like Crazy Frank at that moment, like maybe I could kill a man. Maybe I would. *That motherfucker.*

I was no longer talking myself down. There was no more 'calm down' running through my mind. Instead, I tried desperately to just contain myself, not react, to just take a–

"I should have fucking drove. What'dya fall asleep?" The words bore into my skull.

Without even looking in Weeli's direction, I thrust my fist into his jaw. I'd lost it. I pushed my hand into him, grabbing his neck and chin, pressing his face against the passenger window.

"Shut the fuck up," I growled as I tightened my grip. "You were sleeping, you fuck…not me…I was driving when we almost fucking died, you lucky piece of shit."

Weeli's hands were instantly against my face as he fought back. Pressing my cheeks with his hands and pushing me back into my seat, he shouted, "get the fuck off of me, you psycho bastard!"

My grip tightened. So did his. His other hand came up and whacked my chin. I tried to catch it with my teeth.

"Get the fuck out of my car!" I screamed at him. "Get the fuck out! Don't fucking touch me, you little fuck. Get out!"

"Grow up, Herb!" Weeli screamed back. It was the first time Weeli or I had ever gotten violent with the other. I wanted to pound the fuck out of him. Pound him for being so ignorant. Pound him for being so rich. Pound him for being so spoiled. Of course, he'd just pound right back. Nonetheless, it seemed worth it. There had been a tension building between us that meant a primitive, bull-like test of will and physical strength would eventually have to happen.

"You ignorant fuck!" I hollered. "Did you have a good time fucking sleeping, you prick?"

"Grow the fuck up, Herb!" he yelled back.

"I said, get the fuck out of my car, you little fuck. Get out." My left fist was clenched, my teeth gritted together, and though I knew very well that I should grow the fuck up just as Weeli said, I didn't want to. At that moment, I wanted to bite a chunk of flesh out of his dumb-ass skull.

"You don't want to do this, Herb," Weeli warned. "I'm telling you. I'll beat the living shit out of you like…"

Rage!

"You're going to beat…? Get the fuck out of my car!" I screamed. I slammed his head back against the headrest. I have no idea what harm I expected a leather-cushioned headrest to do, but what the hell, I wasn't really thinking. I reached for my door handle. In a raging instant of stupidity, I was out of the car on Weeli's side, ripping open his door. I would pull the rat fucker out of the car and pound the living shit out of him. I would whirl my fists furiously like the hurricane winds and the cold rain bashing against my face.

Weeli decided to help me out. As I pulled at his door, he pushed the door with great force right into me, knocking me on my ass and onto the cold, muddy ground. I thought for sure he'd be on top of me in a second, but instead, he slammed the door shut.

As I heard the lock latch, I ran to get back to the driver's side before he could lock me out of my own car. I ran around the front of the car, in clear view of Weeli, when my right foot slipped in the mud. I crashed down, my chin catching the steel. My hands didn't have time to attempt to break my fall and, in an instant, I was face down in a puddle of mud and stone and chunks of road. I was a total mess, a raging bull of anger with nowhere to go, completely humiliated.

"Are you all right?" Weeli asked. He was genuinely concerned as he leaped out of the car to give me a hand. That angered me even more. The frustration built. After all that, he was going to be the bigger man. *Motherfucker.* It was all his fault. *How dare he ask me if I was all right?* I needed to crush his skull. *Would that still be acceptable, though, now that he had come to rescue me?*

"No, man, I'm not fucking all right. Look at me, for God's sake."

"I got a towel in my bag. It's in the trunk. I'll grab it. Is your head okay, man? Look at me...oh man, you're fucking bleeding."

"I'm okay." I wiped my chin to find there was a little more blood than I expected. "I'm not okay. I'm a fucking retard."

Little was said as we changed the tire, except for a few mumblings of "just our luck," "isn't this the way it fucking goes?" and "who else does this shit happen to?" As soon as the tire was secured, we jumped in the car, me in the driver's seat. I pulled on the shift to make sure it was in neutral.

*Fuck.*

During our fight, the pushing and shoving had knocked the shift out of whack. Without a second thought, I ripped the leather casing off.

"What are you doing?" Weeli asked. I continued ripping from the bottom up.

"It's broken," I informed him.

"What?" he responded, shaking his head in disbelief. I pulled from the top until the entire piece came out.

"What good is that now?" He paused, hands tightly folded together in front of his face, fingertips meeting his lips in some weird form of thoughtful meditation.

For more than an hour, we tried in vain to jimmy the gearbox so we could shift. In and out of the trunk, under the seats, in the creases of the leather, and even along the side of the road, we searched for strange-shaped articles that might assist us. We pondered our options.

"What did you say earlier about push-starting this fucker?" Weeli asked.

"Yeah, we can try that, but I don't even know what gear it's stuck in, if it's even in gear. And if we get it going, you may have to get out and push every time we stop."

There we were, pushing a dull gray light through the sheets of water pouring down on I-Ninety-Five. I sat in the driver's seat, scooting with my left foot like Fred Flintstone. Weeli pushed. His first attempt brought my first good moment all morning. In the rearview mirror, I saw his head disappear behind the car as he slipped and fell. My first smile of the day. I hadn't even wondered if he was okay. I saw his arm come up in a frenzied motion. He stood up, waving frantically. Another car approached. Two cars passed by with no sign of interest. Weeli was muddy and wet. All was right in the world again.

Energies shifted.

I got out to help Weeli push the car out of the mud. Back into the trunk we went, and dropped the tire jack behind the passenger rear wheel. Then into the woods along the road to find a cold, wet branch long enough to hold the clutch in while resting against the driver's seat. Then we pushed, slipped, and pushed some more. I fell, and then Weeli fell, until finally, the car was on the road. We landed on the interstate at an awkward angle. I managed to pop it into gear.

Maybe third gear? Weeli was outside the car now, jack in hand, trying to keep up. Stopping might have stalled the car. He slammed the side of my car with the tire jack. I pressed the clutch in with one foot and the brake with the other. Weeli jumped in. Stalled. Out he went again. A few attempts later, we were on our way.

—:— —:—

A few hours behind, at nearly nine a.m., we found Pep Wrecks Auto. Right off the highway across from Betty Jones's Truckin' Biscuits and Breakfast. Six hours later, the tire was replaced, the clutch and the gearbox fixed, and we were on our way again.

"...Hurricane Barty has picked up speed," the radio warned. "Severe weather warnings are in effect for the entire East Coast. Landfall is expected in the D.C. area by this evening, and possibly as early as this afternoon. The eye of the storm, initially expected to land somewhere in the Carolinas tonight, pushes north, propelled by the high-pressure front. Flooding continues along the East Coast."

"Food," Weeli said.

"Yeah, I'm fucking tired. Maybe we'll be all right," I said, trying to put some mental effort into sticking to the plan. We're halfway through Connecticut. It'll only take us another two or three hours if–"

"In this shit? It'll take us much longer to get there, *if* we get there. And no offense, but you've nearly killed us twice already, so maybe crashing for the night is a good idea, in a hotel as opposed to a car."

*Skid.*

*Swerve.*

"Fuck!" Weeli exclaimed. I panicked. It was just a little branch.

"I'm ready to stop."

"Yup, I think so."

After another twenty minutes or so of slow and uneasy Sunday driving, I pulled off the highway into a town called Exeter. WNPR continued with their monotone alarmist broadcast.

Evacuations.

Downbursts.

Death.

Exeter was a quaint, one-traffic-light town. Likely due to the weather, it also appeared to be a ghost town. We stopped at the first occupied building, the Exeter Police Station, which had the appearance of a small post office with old brick walls and two large rectangular windows in the front. Inside, we found two people. A woman who appeared to be about fifty or so, and a young girl, neither of whom resembled cops. The small, gray-haired woman seemed to be the dispatcher. The young girl was strangely familiar to me. The way she looked was too familiar, too mature, too knowing for a small child. Weeli explained our predicament.

There is one small bed and breakfast in town, or," the lady explained, we could "go to the Holiday Inn two towns over." The little girl gave us only one option.

"You can't go to the Holiday Inn," she explained, looking straight into me. "No, no, no, that just won't do. You can see the storm from the top of the mountain at Jeri's. That's where you go."

*Where did I know her from?*

"Come now, Sarah, the boys can make up their own minds, I'm sure." The déjà vu was making me uneasy.

*Why did she seem so familiar? Sarah? My dream?*

"She's right, you know," the woman said to Weeli, who stood there smiling at the girl politely. "Best place in the world to watch a storm like this...best place in the world, just about. Probably beat my Aunt Clara's cliff-side, ocean-front estate in Pote-lane, Maine. Yes, indeed, but we ain't in Pote-lane so the next best place is, without a doubt, Jeri's little bed and breakfast." The woman slowed her speech and looked up. She fixed her wrinkled eyes on me. "Yip, she sure is restless today. You boys look like the type that enjoys watching a storm like this come over these here hills."

It was decided.

The violent rains continued. I struggled with the driving while Weeli chanted like a native banshee, mimicking the old woman, "Looky here at them there skies open up wide-eyed and bushy-tailed like. Yes, she is a-pissed. She is a fuck-ane peessed."

The left-hand turn the lady instructed us to take came up quickly. The house sat atop a hill on the backside of a cliff which dropped straight into the Atlantic.

A small man held a flashlight, motioning for us to pull up and park by the barn. The roar of waves crashing against rock, rain pounding against everything, wind blowing along with the howling thunder, was powerful. A voice called to us through the roar.

"You must be the boys. You come for a place to stay, yes?" a woman's voice called from the doorway through the rain. "Come on, get out of the rain."

We ran to the porch where she held the door open. For a moment, everything stopped. She was magic. I wondered if this was what Castaneda had in mind when he said "stop the world." It was as if everything else had vanished.

"I'm Heidi," she said inviting us in. "You two really lucked out today, you know?"

"I was thinking the same thing," Weeli said raising his brow.

"Well, I guess maybe it's about time. Our day hasn't exactly been made up of good luck," I said.

"Well, you're in luck now," Heidi assured us. "You'd never guess who got stranded in the storm on the way to their show in Boston."

She paused.

No guesses.

"U Forty-Seven. They're right in the living room watching the news if you want to go say hello."

"No shit," I said. "U Forty-Seven."

"You like them?" Weeli asked.

"Don't be silly," she said, "but it's quite a novelty to have them drop in. We're not exactly five-star, VIP, but we'll let them hang out. Some pictures for our Wall of Fame."

U Forty-Seven was the biggest pop band for teen girls at the time. '...Take a strange dog off the street...' Their latest radio hit started going through my mind. 'Smile and greet... her with love da dada da da...' It was another number one.

Heidi and déjà vu occupied me completely.

She led us down a wide, hardwood hallway lined with two paintings, one framed in gold, the other in glass, three brass candleholders on each side of the paintings, a thick, rust-colored carpet, and an antique-looking oak table holding one of those ancient, original phones that Thomas Edison built himself.

We made our way through an arch and down a wide hallway lined with woodcarvings, leading into the dining room.

Familiar.

We came to the large living room where the boy band and their entourage lounged.

Heidi interrupted them to introduce us. Weeli began the bullshit procedure of telling them how good they were, and rattling off the names of a few of their songs. He was careful, though, to compliment their success and not their music. As I looked around the room, it was easy to pick out the five members of the band. They didn't look nearly as young as they did in their videos. One of them, Karmen, a short kid with dyed brown hair, blond streaks, and a goatee, looked shy and out of place. He drank his beer slowly, and only looked up to nod when introduced. It wasn't the sort of nod that says, 'I'm too good for you,' or 'Don't waste my time,' but rather just a modest gesture. He looked to be the youngest one in the group.

The oldest one, Shawn, had an almost embarrassed look on his face when Heidi introduced him. He politely said hello and even reached out to shake my hand, then Weeli's, but all the while his thoughts seemed to be somewhere else, absorbed by whatever things occupy the mind of a man who just turned thirty and finds himself idolized by ten- and eleven-year-old girls.

Next to him, sitting on a brown, leather ottoman, was a young brunette who everyone called Heather. Her unfazed smile and comfortable demeanor gave me the impression she might be a girlfriend or groupie.

The two older men in the room were the road manager, The Hammer, and a fella named Charlie.

The Hammer sported a ZZ Top beard. He looked like one of those hardcore hippies, the kind of peace-loving hippy who might have kicked some ass with the Hell's Angels, maybe even killed someone back in the days of Ken Kesey, Timothy Leary, Hunter S. Thompson, and all of it. The sort of hippy you don't fuck with. Takes his drugs and his guns seriously.

Heidi sat Indian-style on a carpet in front of the couch facing us. Smiling up at me with inviting eyes, she asked, "where were you headed?"

"New York," I answered. "Well, Jersey, really." I wasn't sure if she'd heard me over Weeli.

"The way you dance that part and sing the whole..." Weeli was carrying on loudly next to me until Jack Longfoot Carrigan, otherwise known as The Hammer, cut him off.

"Weeli, is it?" he asked, stepping in close to us. "If you could stop kissing these pretty little boys' asses for a second, I'd appreciate it. I was in the middle of explaining something tremendously important here."

"I'm sorry...I didn't–" Weeli started apologizing.

"Don't need to fucking apologize, just shut the fuck up for a second so I can tell my story and I'll know you're sorry." He was an intimidating fuck. Neither Weeli nor Heidi seemed bothered by him, though.

"You curse a lot," Heidi pointed out, looking up at the Hammer. "An awful lot."

"Sorry 'bout that, honey," he replied.

"It's okay, but if my grandmother comes in and hears that, it won't matter who you're with or how popular they are, she'll...well, as you'd say...kick your ass."

"Sorry 'bout that, honey," The Hammer repeated, turning back toward Weeli. "I was simply trying to make a point to my dear friend Heather. The fact is…the fact is, the good Lord, the Holy Bible God himself, is just a straight-out sexist tool, you see? Do you see that?"

"I couldn't agree with you more," I told him.

The Hammer paused, waved his finger around the room as if counting, then looked straight at me.

"All these other people in the room," he said, "all eight of them, they've managed to listen and not interrupt each other. These aren't great thinkers, mind you. Just ordinary superstars. And you two have only been here four minutes and–"

"Just get on with it, Jack," Sajoo, another member of the band, urged.

"The thing is, if you ever really read the Bible you'd know it. If you listen to the churches, you'd know it. It's all ignorant, sexist bullshit. The Bible Belt of sexist bullsh…bologna is what it is. If you eat so much sexist bologna bullshit, your body expands. So you just use the next loophole on the belt. The f'in paradigm here is, we only need the belt 'cause we're so f'in gluttonous with bullshit. It's like all the computers, you know? We'll keep buying the newest, latest software, making us forever computer dependent when, in fact, we never needed computers. It's a man's belt. The Bible is a sexist way for men to keep control and how you as a woman don't–"

"What's wrong with being sexy?" Weeli interrupted, putting on his best British accent. The reference was lost.

"Not true," Heather snapped.

"Twelve apostles," The Hammer continued, "all men. Not one woman. Eve tempted Adam. Then the whole damn thing went to shit. Delilah stole Sampson's hair.

Even the Mother Mary. Hell, if men could've found a way to make her a man they would have. She couldn't have sex. Only thing Mother Mary could do was have a child. Sound familiar? The ideal woman? And the other fucking Mary, the second most popular bitch in the Bible, is a whore."

They'd been smoking freely and were happy to share.

Pass the pipe.

Inhale.

Another round.

"Mary couldn't even attend the last fucking supper. And it's not just sexist. How about sadistic?" He stood up, animated, arms stretched upward in a 'V.'

"Abraham was called to the mountaintop by God himself," he said leaning back. "God said to Abraham in a deep voice, 'Abraham, if you love me you'll knock off your little boy there.'

'You mean kill him, God?' Abraham replied.

'No, you stupid shit. I mean I want you to knock him off his pedestal. Of course I mean kill him, you moron.'

'But, God,' Abraham questioned the Almighty, 'why would you want me to kill my only son?'

'Yours is not to question now, is it? Are you questioning me, your God?'

'No, God, I guess not,' Abraham mumbled like a little bitch. Then Abraham told his son what God needed to be done, and his son took off like a terrified jackrabbit.

'Well, God, I was going to, but he's just too fast for me,' Abraham told the Lord.

'Then, Abraham, I will give you the speed of the cheetah. Now go run and catch that little punk, and bring him back up here so you can tie his scrawny little ass up and give him the horribly painful, torturous death that I so need to see to know that you believe in me.'

'Okay, God,' Abraham said.

He ran as fast as he possibly could to catch his only son, Isaac. Isaac threw his body on the ground at the base of a large tree and pleaded, 'Please, Father, please don't kill me up on the mountain. I'm scared. That hurts, Father. Don't you love me at all?

'No, Father...please no,' Isaac cried out as his tiny little hands attempted futilely to cling to the massive roots at the base of the tree. 'Father, how come I didn't hear God say that? Are you sure, Father? Why would God want to hurt me and kill me, Father? Why? Why?' he continued to cry, as Abraham carried his tiny body up the mountain.

'Father?'

'Yes, my child?' Abraham said, in a voice that was quivering and cracking.

'Why do you want to do this to me?'

'Son.' Abraham began to weep. 'Son, I don't want to do this to you...I don't want to at all. I know you won't believe this, but it is harder for me to watch you suffer than it is for you, Son, because I love you that much.'

'You're right, Dad, I don't believe you. Why? Why would God be so cruel, Father? I have never done anything wrong. Are you sure it was God?'

'Yes, I'm sure.'

'How come I didn't hear Him?'

'One day, you, too will hear Him, Son, and then you'll know.'

Isaac began to panic. His arms and legs were slamming against the aging body of Abraham as his father tied him to the altar for sacrifice.

'Why, God? Why must I do this?' Abraham screamed out.

Abraham pulled out a long knife from the sheath on his belt. He raised it up, tears streaming down his face, his hands quivering and his heart breaking. With all his might, he thrust the knife toward Isaac.

But his arms froze. Halfway between his shoulders and the body of his son, there seemed to be a wall. A wall so strong that he couldn't push through it.

'Ahhhh! No!' Isaac screamed as he clenched his eyes closed.

'Abraham.'

'God,' Abraham replied.

'Abraham, you have proven your faith and trust in me and, for that, I have spared your son. Now bring me your daughter.'"

For a moment, everyone was silent. No one seemed to know what to make of The Hammer's tale.

"You're messed up," Sajoo said. "I was really curious how the hell you were going to tie that into God being sexist."

"Yeah," Weeli said, "not to mention that Abraham didn't even have a daughter."

"Who knows?" The Hammer said, "He probably had ten wives."

"Well," Heidi said, looking up at Weeli and me, "I bet you two didn't expect this at all, did you? I'll tell you what, sure isn't what I expected when I got up this morning."

*Déjà vu.*

Her smile was familiar.

Her voice was familiar.

Thunder in the background.

"Do you have a porch or something?" I asked. "Someplace we could watch the storm coming across?"

"Yes. Do you all need to get anything out of your cars before you get settled in?"

We made our way through the driving rain, Heidi leading us to the car to grab our things, then back to the house. There was one room for Weeli and me to share. We dropped our things and she brought us out to 'no better place to watch a storm coming over the water.'

The view was astonishing. The patio was all glass.

Heidi sat down on the floor just to the right of my leg. Sometimes, two seeming strangers, with very few words and a certain faith, feel a comfort between each other that neither questions. When Heidi leaned back and rested her head on my knee, I knew this to be true. I could feel it.

The Hammer growled at Charlie to "roll a fatty." We were stoned off our rockers in no time. The conversation meandered in and out of intelligibility.

After some time, my hand naturally found its way to Heidi's hair.

"Do you guys really like the music you make?" Weeli asked out of the cold-stoned blue.

"Huh?" Shawn mumbled.

I felt Heidi's hand press on mine. *My God.* Warm. Comforting. *Familiar.*

The thing about Weeli was, even when he pulled shit like this there was always something magnetic and inviting about him.

"You know," Weeli continued, "do you like the words, the sound, the music. Like, if you didn't make it yourself, the music, is it something you'd listen to?"

"What kind of shit is that?" Jace, another band member, said.

"Shut up, Jace," Shawn cut in. "The short answer for me is no. No, I wouldn't listen to it if it wasn't my own, but it is, so what do you want? Fuck," he went on, "I can't help but listen to it almost obsessively."

"Maybe if you sang like you gave a damn," Jace said, "maybe you, maybe we'd all like the shit a little more."

Shawn broke into tune. "She's so fine. She's so fine. She's so fine like the hard body of an iron side. She's so smooth. She's so smooth even her lies are telling the truth. She's not just hot. Hot. Hot. Hot. Her skin burns like a four-wheel pick–"

"Fuck you," Jace snapped poking his finger into Shawn's chest. "Fuck you, man. Then quit."

The Hammer spoke.

"Hey, it's a fair question. As fair as asking a politician if they love passing bullshit laws to open loopholes for the money hounds whose asses they gotta kiss. Or asking a cop if he loves arresting two-bit, mentally ill, poor motherfuckers while they watch the mayor and the DA swap favors." He passed me the joint. "It's like...like an old girlfriend. You just can't figure out why you dated, but it made sense at the time. These guys, some are in love with the girl, some with the idea of a girlfriend, and some just need to get laid. You know what I'm saying?"

"Huh?" Weeli said.

"Well, what do you guys do?" The Hammer asked.

"Yeah, it's hard to explain," Weeli replied.

"Huh?" I mumbled. Stoned. "Hard to explain? It's fucking lollipops."

"It's not fucking lollipops," Weeli insisted.

Heidi pressed my hand and leaned back into my leg.

"Lollipops," I mumbled again.

"So," The Hammer said, "money."

For a moment, it was quiet again. Then Weeli said this.

"The Revolution. That's what we're doing." He took another hit.

At the moment, neither lollipops nor revolutions mattered to me. I was floating in the light air of faith, the substance of things hoped for, the evidence of things not seen. I could taste her she was so close. Our fingers moved.

"Well," Charlie said, "I believe Mr. Weeli was about to tell us about this Revolution."

As I melted deeper into Heidi and Heidi into me, Weeli embarked on giving our Revolution form by putting it into words.

The Revolution, Weeli to U Forty-Seven:

*"These truths, evidenced by the energy of all things, exist for those living deliberately. Communicated so directly are these things that only the billions of microscopic entities, which exist in what appears to be open air, stand in the way of verbatim translation.*

*The true virtue of selfishness can only be realized through the absolute understanding and practice of selfishness itself.*

*Through this realization, humanity will evolve and possibly survive the struggle that evolution presents.*

*As all things exist connected by universally shared energies, the good of the singular, the individual, must always prevail.*

*The good of all things, by this path, can be recognized. The singular understanding of masses of individuals will thus lead to the common good. This common good is a necessity dictated by evolution and our only hope for survival as a species.*

*The aim of The Revolution, survival of the human species, can only be arrived at through the individual. Truth can only be known by the individual. The root of all problems within human reach, and all potential causes of the demise of human existence, stem from the individual, and therefore can only be alleviated by the individual.*

*Thus, the aim of The Revolution, survival of the human species, can only be arrived at through the individual once the individual, bound by truths, successfully pursues pure selfishness.*

*To simplify, if it feels good, do it. Feeling good must be understood from an enlightened, connected state of selfishness.*

*In this way, The Revolution can be recognized."*

Weeli wrapped up his eloquent soliloquy. The words were too familiar to me. As if they were mine, as if I'd lived this entire thing already.

*Déjà vu.*

I knew it was more than what it seemed. In this way, and in more intense, almost magical ways to follow, The Revolution became a very real and spiritual experience. As I had already seen in my dream, Heidi was calling to me. Her eyes bright and sure, her smile wide-awake and comfortably confident. It was as if she had already seen this night in her mind's eye, and she knew that I was aware of what was about to happen. Soon, I would be inside of her. While Heidi and I passionately fulfilled the prophecy, Weeli occupied his time gathering information and making arrangements unknown to me, but critical to The Revolution.

# CHAPTER 15

# THE DEPARTURE

### *Capital Hill*

*The self-interested pursuit of wealth may not
satisfy the individual.
Coupled with capitalism's predisposition to barter,
to sell,
Free market mastering is, for the one, dire and
trivial.
Complete with coarse competition, what kills the
one makes the many well.*

– J.P. MILO
FORMER CHAIRMAN
OF THE FEDERAL RESERVE INSTITUTE
OF THE UNITED STATES OF AMERICA

L ogan International Airport, Boston, Massachusetts. Weeli's sexy tales of Big Sky Country adventures, peyote, and Revolution were too seductive to turn down. My bags were being tossed and fondled along the conveyor belt as I wondered if I was headed toward a destination or embarking on a departure, leaving something, maybe leaving everything I ever thought I knew behind. I stood in the terminal, waiting for Weeli to return.

Behind the glass, plastering the walls, were countless images of an unnaturally thin woman whose features screamed the praises of the gods of the day: plastic, silicone, Botox. I watched a child's innocence start the slippery slide, oozing out of her as she stared curiously. *Capitalist porn*, I thought to myself.

A young man, head shaved glistening clean, gold loop earring dangling, a salmon-colored shirt sticking to his fashionably sunken chest and skinny-jean, high-water trousers hugging his waist, reached for her hand. Her hair was slicked back, tight like a thin-skinned turtle shell. It looked painful for her. *Is it democracy or capitalism*, I wondered, *that leads to this?*

The stores, restaurants, advertisements, and crowds seemed endless, loud, and offensive. *The Shoe Shine Masseuse* offered 'free massage with every shoeshine,' and 'free shoeshine with every massage.' *The Mini-Golf Martini Bar* offered waitress caddies in miniskirts and waiter caddies in skinny-jean shorts. *Oralmadic* offered dental and cosmetic services. *Law and Spirits* offered legal and religious services, including marriage, divorce, Shiva, and Mass. From sushi to deep-fried chocolate-covered crawfish, from *Macaca Monkey Shakes* to *Brazilian Swampsnake Moonshine*, there seemed to be a restaurant or shop for every kind of food or beverage imaginable. People, it seemed, needed all sorts of things between flights. *Democracy, capitalism or something else?*

"Now boarding first class," was broadcast over the loudspeaker.

"Class-free society, my ass," Weeli said, snapping me out of my haze. We boarded.

"The plastic bag will not fully inflate," the flight attendant proclaimed cheerfully over the PA system. A psychic palm reader sat to my right. "Passengers with children," the flight attendant continued, "should fasten their own mask and ensure it is secure and functioning, taking three full breaths, prior to fastening their children's. We'd like to welcome all children aboard and say thank you for flying the friendly skies."

"Do you know," Maria, my new palm-reading friend, said, introducing herself to me as the plane began picking up speed on Logan's runway, "it is a much better life for a woman to be a palm reader." She smiled. *Weird,* I thought, *but intriguing.*

"Hmmm?" I mumbled.

"You know why?" she asked.

I squished my lips together, shook my head, and said, "no."

"Because I can predict my future and please myself with the same finger."

*I must have one of those faces,* I thought to myself, *one of those harmless, you-can-say-anything-to-me, faces.* Here's the thing with this Maria woman. She was probably nearly thirty years my senior. Her skin was dry and worn, with that look a person gets from spending years in the company of the sun, sand, salt, and sea breeze. Maybe it was the proximity of her gleaming green eyes and wily spirit that made her very attractive up close.

She was born in the year of the Tiger, she told me, more Yang than Yin, heading east, northeast. Tiger meant courageous, bold, vibrant. She held out her hand and showed me her life line, which stretched along above the Mount of Venus and below the head line, explaining that it tells nothing about the length of one's life, but rather reflects one's energy health level. The important one, she explained, was the heart line, which runs along the top of the palm just below the base of the fingers, for that determined emotions, feelings of love, hate, apathy, and all of the things that make a life anything or nothing.

We could fuck, but I could not be her friend as I was born in the year of the Ox. The Ox was not her foe, however, and shared seasons with the Tiger, so maybe we could be lovers for an unforgettable winter. She was friends with more Dogs, intimate with more Horses. Some of the best sex she'd ever had, though, was with an Ox. As she said that, her finger gently glided along my heart line.

My heading was north, northeast, my element was Earth, my Yin and Yang were balanced and, like another Ox, Napoleon, I was born to lead, for better or worse. My heart line was long and solid, which made her horny.

"What I could do with this," she said, pressing her thumb against the center of my wrist, feeling my pulse.

She said my life line was hard to translate, that the energy was the strongest she'd ever seen, but that she didn't know what it meant for my health and longevity. For that reason, she pointed out, I should do everything I was born to do now.

"You are on a mission," she said.

"Huh?"

"That's not in your palm," she smiled, "I can feel it."

"I guess, kind of," I replied.

"No," she said looking into me, "whether you know it or not, you are on a mission."

She lifted her fingers from my palm and turned her head, looking out the window into the blue abyss. The rhythm of the plane rocked me to sleep. I woke to my first glimpse of the great big American West from two thousand feet above the planet. Still, the vast magnificence of raw stone mountain and deep swallows of canyon and craters inspired me. We had arrived.

"I have no idea what to expect," Weeli said to me as we waited for our bags. "Frank didn't tell me much more than he told you. Her name's Jasmine. She's an Indian princess or something, and the guy is a witchdoctor or a shaman."

"No, he's not," Jasmine, our Frank connection, said from behind us. "He's a warrior who likes to fancy himself a shaman."

She had long, straight, brown hair and suspicious brown eyes. Her dress was beige, plain. She introduced herself with boisterous hugs and a volume of fast-spoken words. Somewhere in between disconnected Frank references,

Jasmine explained that the ranch was just outside of Cedar Mountain so we were in for a four-hour ride.

"Crazy Frank," she said, as we made our way down Interstate Fifteen, "I'm pretty sure that's how he knew who his friends were, back when keeping track of your real friends could mean life or death, and anyone could be an informer, what with so many transients, wannabes, and hanger-ons. It wasn't easy. Yup...I'm pretty sure he always figured who his friends were by knowing who just called him Frank. If you didn't know him as Crazy, you weren't his friend." It seemed as though she didn't pause between syllables.

"You know," she carried on like a firecracker, "I believe I even have some newspaper clippings that refer to him as the Hippy Leader, Crazy Frank. I guess they weren't really his friends, though, those so-called journalists. I'd do anything for him, you know? He did more for me, back when we were all crazy and confused and trying to find our way. He broke some cats out of jail. He went to jail for Leonard once." She took a rare pause.

"Leonard Peltier?" Weeli asked.

"Yeah, Leonard."

"Frank's the only one who kept The Revolution alive, really. At least for us. There were others, we hear, but not on the grid, you know? Phantoms almost."

The crisp air of the wide-open Utah desert blessed my face. It tasted better than any air I'd ever tasted.

"I'm Indian, if you ain't guessed," she said. "Arikawa tribe, but most people consider us Sioux or Chippewa because of where we come from. You know what Dakota means?"

She left no time for pause or response. "Friendly," she said. "Probably no coincidence you've come on the night of our quarterly miigi dance. Well, of course it isn't. There are no coincidences. People think miigi came from the Ojibwe, but that's 'cause they know nothing of Arikawa or miigi. They probably think Site Four keeps the miigi and Area Fifty-One has the God Ship." She let out a laugh. Jasmine spoke so quickly about so many disconnected things, alluding to connections without so much as taking a breath for the entire ride. I was becoming convinced that Jasmine was right. There are no coincidences. Even her nonstop banter was likely by design. We came to a long road, which turned west toward Cedar Mountain. That road led to dirt. Dirt led to Jasmine's ranch.

Massive, intimidating peaks of sharp stone formed a panorama of magnificent beauty. Shadows stretched across the eastern edge of the mountains, with hues of dark red and orange. Prickly pear cactus, Indian grass, fireweed, sagebrush, and juniper filled the vast open landscape. The trees twisted, turned up and down, reaching for something, struggling for life, striving for survival, maybe for water in the barren desert, maybe air, maybe for things I couldn't perceive. Eternity and wisdom seemed to possess the earth and sky.

The place felt like home. Spiritual.

'Spiritual' is what Jasmine called the ceremony we were about to partake in.

"You're just in time," Joe said, his tone and body language making it clear that Weeli and I were not going to have time to settle in, recover from jetlag, or get to know these two before the ceremonies. "Drop your bags in the front room here and drain the tanks. Sun will be going down soon."

Joe would lead the ceremonies. When I'd finally come down from my spiritual experience, I found Joe and Jasmine crying like children in each other's arms. They had willingly given their strength, their defenses, themselves, over entirely to their love. It was a dangerous thing that I hoped to experience with Sophia. Instead, Weeli and I were about to take that same dangerous step for The Revolution.

# CHAPTER 16

# THE DESTINATION

*...And so, the spontaneous hallucinations took hold,
slowly sanding away the rough edges of reality. Visions
brought about by leftover Lophophorine and a hung-over,
exhausted brain gripped him like the dark and terrible
flashbacks of the Tsoa Mi Vietnamese POW camp his
father survived. Flashbacks, however, which he was not
strong enough to live with. Now, he wondered if he would
be damned to fulfill the destiny of a father-like-son life.
He struggled with an urge to forgive his father now,
for the unthinkable act of abandoning his family, his
children, his son. He sympathized now, with the man
who he believed a coward for taking the coward's way
out. He chose to be his father's son, and one more cactus
tragedy waned into forgotten memory.*

— Excerpt from
*Waning Tragedies of
Cactaceae Lophophora Williamsii*
By Dr. Majica Perez Muhatuk

D eath, delivered to us in the form of Coyote Peyote, seemed certain. Sophia and I had spent days talking about the wisdom of shaman and how we would one day share an amazing peyote experience. Instead, I lost my Coyote Peyote virginity with Weeli.

Other drugs could be vomited up and thrown right out of the body. If, for instance, you told yourself that you were on a spiritual journey and happened to drink one too many bottles of Robitussin in hopes of discovering the nature of the cosmos via a Robotrip, then you could stick your finger down your throat and vomit it out before it shut your system down. Peyote was different. You could not vomit it out. It made you vomit. Vomiting was the method by which the coyote kicked other shit out of its way so it could mindfuck you properly. It was on its way to properly kicking the shit out of me.

A wrenching pain grew, climbing from what felt like my nuts, then my bowels, right up into my throat. Then...

*Wham!*

Just like that, a thick flow of rancid vomit was pouring out of me in a steady stream.

Violent.

There was a pain in my back. I tried to walk it off. I tried to walk. I was disoriented. Time lost relevance quickly, or maybe not. Impossible to know. The pain in my body subsided. Recollections of crouching by a rock. Holding my gut. Lying on rock. Staring at sky. Little more.

Time lapsed.

I rose. My body light, comfortable. From agonizing pain to an ethereal, floating euphoria.

As the Utah desert slid away from my sandals...*too good... too something.* The mescaline from the peyote cactus was taking control of my nervous system and sensory functions. I watched grains of sand float, then fall gently into place, one by one on the ground. I saw each individual grain take its place among the other grains in the air, and then slowly descend.

Individual grains.

One by one.

Everything shifted. Sound warbled and morphed. Grains of sand passing through space made a slow *whoosh* sound. Befogged by auditory sensations, I stared into the sand, wondered if I was hearing the sand moving through the air, crashing gently, scraping away from my toes, and falling to the earth. Much too focused on the sand. I looked up to get my bearings. My bearings were nowhere to be found. I heard Weeli blurt out something to the effect of, "you'll find your palace ear," in a bubble-sounding voice as he flew by, riding bareback on a brown horse with white spotted wings. The *swoosh* of the sand kicked up by the horse rang past my ears. I had wandered a little too far in hopes of walking this thing off.

Weeli and the white-winged horse disappeared as quickly as they appeared. Having lost any ability to gauge time, I hadn't a clue how quickly. It could have been days passing for all I knew, complete with sunrises, sunsets, and flash floods. The terrain was unfamiliar. The cactus grew larger, stretching shadows. The Rockies rose like beasts. A juniper with leaves as thick as buffalo rawhide.

Everything shifted.

Warped.

*Fuck.*

This thing had me.

A web-footed bird, exhaling green gas from its gills, swam through the sky. In the distance, a rhinoceros-like creature with beady eyes stood on two legs, laughing hysterically. Slimy-looking reptiles, a cross between alligator and swamp snake, the size of a seventy-five Fleetwood, crept gently across the desert floor. They seemed to be approaching. *Better move.* Behind me, seeming to come from over the large rock, I could hear a muffled, underwater, rumbling sound. I moved toward the sound. I climbed with unnatural ease, feet and hands barely seeming to touch the ground.

*Vwhoomf...vwhoomf...*

The sound got louder. Weeli. He was in a ravine at the base of the mountain. He smiled up at me, revving the gargoyle beast he was riding. The sand cloud sparkled as Weeli drove off. Through the cloud, the web-footed creature emerged, flying right at me. It rose out of the ravine, up the rock wall, landing in front of me. It turned its monstrous head slowly, then looked straight through me. I couldn't look away. The massive, round, white eyeballs surrounding shiny black circles grew larger, closing in on me until the world shrank into them. The eyes grew until I saw my own, larger-than-life-sized reflection staring back at me. At first, I tried to be amused, to ignore the terrific nature of the thing. Then my reflection took on its own movement, its own being, and any chance of amusement ceased. My reflection had a life of its own.

*Fuck.*

I was terrified of myself. I blinked. Nothing. He's still there. I closed my eyes. Wiped my face.

Still there.

*Fuck.*

"You," the larger, grotesque me said, looking down and into me. "You," the voice repeated. This sound was not burbly or muffled like everything else. His voice was crystal clear. More disturbing, even, it was clearly my own.

"You do get it now, don't you?" my voice came back at me. How eerie it was to hear myself say that, knowing exactly what I, this other version of me, meant. *Of course I got it,* I thought, *but,* I wondered, *can't I escape it, make it go away, if it's just me, my trip?*

"Come on, now, look at me…you certainly can't fool me," the voice said. "Can't I stop myself then?" he said, mocking my thought in my voice, looking straight into me with a grin more devious, eviler than I knew I could muster.

*Fuck.*

"Can't I, though?" he said, again. "It's just me. Can't I stop myself?" he, I, mocked. Even in my state of mind, I knew I must have brought it on myself. All my overthinking about my own motives, questioning myself, wondering what one moment of pure honesty with myself would reveal. I knew I had talked myself into this. But I didn't want this, not this way, not in such a fragile state. I closed my eyes again, hands to my face, wishing myself away, rubbing my eyes, hoping, hoping, but my voice carried on.

"But," he said in my whiniest tone, "not in a fragile state. Not now. Who the fuck are you kidding? When aren't you in a fragile state, you pathetic child? No, you can't just make me go away because I frighten you. Do you know what you'd be doing to yourself if you could just wish the truth away every time it frightened you? Do you?"

The thing about peyote is that when it's got you, there is no wishing it away. Even knowing that things may not be real doesn't help because there's always an overwhelming awareness that everything going on at the time is real and entirely inescapable, at least for the moment. There is always the fear that you might never come out of it. That maybe you did discover the true reality and, even if you don't like it, you are stuck there for eternity.

"It is time," the larger me spoke again as I opened my eyes. "We will kill the shit that clutters our soul, that torments our thoughts...the us that isn't really us. I am here. Sandy and the accident, Uncle Ray, the fish market, we know the truth. All the people you have judged and ridiculed while you envied their actions in secret. I am there. I know. I know we steal, I know we cheat, I know we lie, but I don't deny any of it. And now you can't. What's worse?" the larger me accused as I saw his reflection in the reflection of my own eyes in his.

*Worse?*

My thoughts were scrambled in the dreadful mess. I didn't want to think of any of it. I was young, then, and could forgive myself.

*What could be worse?* I thought to myself.

Unfortunately, I was there to answer.

"What's worse is that you still don't get it. You come all the way here." He stretched out his arms. "You come all the way here and you still don't get it. Maybe you don't want to get it. Maybe it is just another part that you'd like to lie to yourself about. Enlightenment...Revolution...blah, blah, fucking blah. You can babble your way through the world, but you can't talk yourself around yourself, around me. You can't lie to yourself forever." His eyes, which held reflections of my own and which, except for their size, were identical to my own, opened wider.

"Don't try to wish me away!" he barked. A hard, loud command. His tone shifted. His voice, my voice, grew more hostile. An ominous tone I rarely used, and only in very serious moments of anger, desperation, or rage. It was a tone reserved for those I cared so desperately about, loved so hopelessly, that I could not control my emotions. It was a tone that frightened me even when it came from my small and usual self, never mind this most disgusting and disturbing version of me. I closed my eyes. I wanted out.

"Don't!" he growled with the roar of the earth opening up.

Angry.

Desperate.

"Don't!" he screamed. My eyes flashed open. "Don't you dare," he roared, lips quivering like mine might on the verge of tears. "Don't you dare try to wish me away." I turned my head away, looked down to the ground terrified.

"Don't you dare try to wish yourself away, the truth away. This is your only chance. You will have made me another one of your lies to yourself, about yourself, about everything." The large and terrifying me took a deep, heavy breath, and lowered his tone.

"It is time for the baptism, for you to face the truth, to take the journey. We will not be the diluted, pitiful, human soul that is a lie. I won't," he told me. "The Revolution, Herb. You run away from me now, from yourself when, finally, you've reached far enough to find me, then you are doomed."

He reached his hand out and motioned to me.

"It is time."

He gestured for me to walk with him. I did. I stepped forward until we stood above a natural pothole, which deepened and widened as we looked into it. A terrible scene unfolded. My sister Jenna held her womb, bleeding.

"I hate you! I hate you! Why do you do this to me? My little girl...my little girl," she screamed. The little girl she held was her daughter, my niece, Leah.

"I didn't do anything to you," I tried to scream, but nothing came out. Her little girl was the love of her life. Her little girl called me her favorite uncle. *What had I done? Was it my niece in her womb?* My little brother was there, trying to break away from chains, rats gnawing on his limbs. He struggled. My sister's blood fell onto him as he kicked and screamed. There was a large man with a dirty, balding head and hairy arms, holding the back of Jenna's neck. She was begging the man not to hurt our little brother. My brother cried, pleading for my sister. I shouted, but they didn't hear me. The dirty, bald man in the pit turned around so that I could see his face.

"Hello, Herb."

My heart sank into whatever remained of my soul. The man I'd revered in life, looked to for hope and validation, the man who'd been kinder, more thoughtful than anyone I'd ever known, my father, now dead for five years, stared me straight in the eye with an evil smile. I was mortified. I had longed to see him nearly every day since his death, dreamt of seeing him, but this?

"Hello, you pitifully weak child. Can you remember, Herb...can you remember?" So angry. So evil. I saw myself, a child at the bottom of the pit, cowering, head between my knees.

"No, no, please no," the child version of myself wailed from the bottom of the hellish pit. Then the child rose and picked his head up, smiling at me.

"Herb," the child said, "everything is fine, Herb. Remember?" He walked over to my father and sat on his knee.

"Everything's fine, Herb," they all said in unison, smiling up at me. The pools of blood turned to emerald green. The pit began to close, slowly filling with liquid sandstone.

"No!" I shouted, "No! Dad!" I had come this far. I wasn't turning away. *What was happening?* I wanted to know why I was seeing this. The scene morphed back into the sandstone pothole.

Everything shifted. My stomach wrenched. It felt like a large fish was swimming around my gut. A zinging sensation rose from gut to brain. A rush of heat. I tore off my shirt.

"Where did you go?" I shouted to the desert air, as the grotesque version of me vanished. I felt the desert air against my bare skin. It felt so good, tantalizing, that I took off the rest of my clothes and lay on the stone. Just then, the *verhoom* sound returned.

"Whoblatoo ouryouhoodi," a voice said in slow, bubbly fashion. It was Weeli. His face shifted with lines of blue, making him look older and colder than I had ever noticed.

"Whohot...ehire...hib?" It was a question, for sure, but I could not make out the words. I stood.

"Speal...lek...eee...gnlishhh." I tried desperately to speak normally.

*Fuck.*

It wasn't just Weeli. I rubbed my lips, hoping it would help. Weeli kept trying. He had a strange look on his face.

"Whurahurt yollubading?" he asked again.

*Fuck.*

I stretched my head back and touched the back of my neck, which had a synthetic, metallic feel to it.

"Huh?" It was the best I could do for the moment.

"You fub da rog?" he asked in a matter-of-fact sort of tone. The tone was easier than the words. "Oh gay?" he mumbled. "You o gay?"

*Fuck,* I thought to myself, *of course I'm not okay.*

"You?" I nodded back to him.

"You fubin dahha rog," he said...again? "You o gay?"

I struggled to tell him, "I think so," but I wasn't sure if I thought I was okay or not. I shook my head rather than trying to explain the rock episode. I pushed aside the urge to let him know his face was now melting into the rest of his body, which was in turn melting into the rock. As he slowly melted away, I tried to gain control. I tried to focus in and grasp what was going on. *He couldn't disappear right in front of me, could he?* Then his slurred words became frightening and uncomfortable.

"Dole...do...you hear me...sto...stop this thing," he said slowly, sounding like a cassette tape played at half speed. "Stop this...this...thing...I'm...melting into the...Herb." Weeli slowly dripped away into the stone. I heard his burbled voice behind me.

"Maybe you should be alone," my own voice came at me. The face was that of Weeli's and my own meshed together. Unlike Weeli's burble, my voice spoke to me in clear, articulate English.

"I thought you were ready for this," he said.

"Weeli?" I whimpered, my heart racing and my eyes shifting over his shoulders to see just how out of control this had all become. I was unable to concentrate on the scenery behind him. Instead, I focused intently on his face, which grew more and more into my own.

"I thought you were ready, but you're not," my own voice said.

"What?" I screamed at him. "I'm here."

"Sablop yublin ab moo," I heard, but this time it was Weeli's burbled voice again. He dropped to his knees and covered his face. The yelling had frightened him.

"Weeli," I said, suddenly conscious of my nakedness. A few more steps and I would be standing with my dick in his face. As fucked up as I was, somehow I knew that might not be a comfortable thing. "I'm sororry," I tried to say.

Weeli's expression changed.

He looked amused. He looked up at my naked body. His expression of concern and apprehension had shifted to something more menacing. He laughed hysterically and rose to his feet.

"Look at you," he said, but his voice was crystal clear now. His laughter was evil. "Arg ahaharg." The laugh morphed into my own.

*Fuck.*

"If they could see you now, you foolish, foolish child," my voice said from Weeli's lips.

I caught a glimpse of Weeli and he looked terrified. I struggled to know if it was Weeli or the beast in front of me. The beast or Weeli pushed me away, with anger and fear. Weeli or the beast was now yelling for me to get away.

Confused, I walked. I walked in no particular direction until I was in unfamiliar country, with no sense of direction and no clothes.

━┿ ┿━

Some unknown amount of time passed. The beast was gone. As I wandered through the desert night, I walked in heightened awareness of everything. Energy, like electricity, passed through the air, my body, the stone. I was the connected energy of all things. When, exactly, the peyote wore off, I don't know, but as I came out of the drug haze, I remained in a hung-over state of awareness. I touched the tip of the iceberg. The iceberg was larger than the Milky Way, larger than the cumulative spaces of all known universes. The iceberg was melting into the waters of my Revolution.

I woke to the sun peeking her squinting, yellow eye over the Rockies.

# CHAPTER 17

# THE MORNING AFTER

*He after honour hunts, I after love:*
*He leaves his friends to dignify them more,*
*I leave myself, my friends and all, for love.*

— WILLIAM SHAKESPEARE
EXCERPT FROM *TWO GENTLEMEN FROM VERONA*

Lena was the daughter of the great Bedonkohe Apache Chief Geronimo. Geronimo met her briefly, four years after her birth, in the custody of the United States government during his fourth voluntary surrender to General Miles. The U.S. Army shipped her off to school to break her of her 'Injun-ness,' educate her in English, both language and culture, and 'civilize' her along with hundreds of other natives and 'Negros.' The school was unsanitary, infested with malaria and other diseases. She died one year later.

In her honor, a sacred trail was named 'Lena's Passage.' There were no white-man signs reading 'Lena's Passage.' We would make our way to that sacred trail.

"You scared the shit outta me," Joe said across the picnic table, filling his mouth with potatoes that had been roasted over the burning coals. "You really did, you know? Christ, to picture this," he went on, looking over to Weeli then panning across the picnic table to Wolfy and Carol. "Herb jist comes a-walking up to me. Looks like he's coming right in fer us. Well, I have to explain first," Joe said raising his hand to his mouth as if to contain his laughter. "So Jasmine and I are laying on the ground together. Probably looked like we were in the middle of something sexy, but we wasn't. We were actually balling our eyes out. That's another story. Herb comes walking up and I'm still half-tripping so it's to me like he's making a perfect b-line for us. Killer is, he's buck fucking nekid, man. Buck nekid."

Laughter.

"He's buck fucking nekid. Dick dangling in the breeze. I don't know what kind of shape he's in, so I start to get up, jist kind a-wondering like, 'what he's planning on doing?' and how to handle this whole thing. And Herb ha-ha...oh, God...ha, he looks so pitiful...ah, God...and he says...he says..." He could barely speak through his laughter.

"I just want to find some clothes," I cut in, as Joe couldn't speak without laughing. Hysterical laughter cut through the peyote hangover haze.

"Then, oh my God, he gets this really sad and desperate look on his face like a little bitty kid, you know? No, no... more like a puppy dog, lost and confused, you know, and he jist says...huh...he jist says..." Joe took a break to slam his slaphappy hand hard against the table as if that was all that kept him from rolling over onto the ground. He continued. "Oh...huh...ah...the pitiful look on his kid face. And he says...um..." Joe went on mimicking me, "he says...'I jist...I jist um...I jist need to find my clothes.'"

"Yeah," Weeli said, "my God, that's right. You were fucking a rock when I saw you. I had just finished digging a hole and you were looking down at me, then you tore off your clothes or something. I remember, then you started screaming at me, and I was in no condition to handle that."

My mind wandered deep into the backcountry of my peyote experience. The voices faded out as I wondered what I had gained from this, how this would lead to The Revolution. Then there was nothing. Without any effort, I had slipped into a Zen state of meditation, consciousness. The sound of Weeli's voice brought me back to the conversation.

"Did you hear that, Herb?" Weeli asked again.

"What's that?" I asked.

"Joe was just saying this coyote peyote isn't done with us yet," Weeli explained, eyebrows raised with a childlike, mischievous smile.

"What I said," Joe looked at me, "is that a lotta times, not always, the true vision of a coyote quest comes days after your trip."

"Like a flashback?" I asked.

"I guess you could say that, but not really. A flashback is in the brain, sorta like remnants of acid messing with your synapses. No, with the coyote they say it's the Great Spirit waitin' 'till you're ready to receive."

"What do we make of what we've already seen?" I asked.

"Considering we've seen you bare naked," Jasmine smiled, "what do you propose we make of what *we've* seen?"

"I'm serious," I replied shaking my head. "I can remember bits and pieces, and one of them was really intense. I was facing off with myself and I saw—"

"Stop," Joe said calmly. "This ain't for you to share with us. A spiritual journey is yours and the Great Spirit's, and the rest of us experience it through you, but don't taint it. In fact, it's best you don't even think on it much. What you was meant to get out of it you already did or you already didn't, but treat it as sacred either way. Only a spirit warrior, a shaman, should speak of their visions. And even they only do so sparingly."

"We are in a funny time," Jasmine said. "A time of great change, a shift in cosmic energy. This is why Frank sent you here. I don't know exactly why. I don't know what you are going to find when you get to where you're going, but I do know Frank. You'll find something, and I look forward to hearing about it when you get back."

"Right," Weeli said, "I guess we should probably start making our way, then."

"You'll take our car," Joe said.

"We were actually hoping you could just bring us to pick up a rental," Weeli smiled.

"No, really," Jasmine said, "we insist. No need to pay for a rental. Besides, not to be rude, but the closest place to pick up a rental out here is two hours out. It runs fine. It's a convertible anyway. Best way to see the big country."

The convertible was an old, rusty, red two-seater.

"There're a few routes you could take," Joe explained, "but this here's the one you need to take," handing Weeli a piece of cardboard with directions scribbled out.

On paper, the directions didn't make much sense. We would take an unmarked road known as Lena's Passage south of Zion National Park, then make our way back around, headed northeast. I was beginning to accept that everything had a purpose, a design, even if that purpose was beyond me. Lena's Passage led straight to Route Nine. Nine led into Zion National Park, through it, then to Eighty-Nine. Eighty-Nine would take us to Route Twelve. Twelve would take us into Bryce Canyon National Park.

As we hit the road, vivid layers of red, brown, beige, granite, and orange shades reminded me of the Atlantic. Those waters tend to be layered horizontally as a storm floats by from west to east, coming off the mainland over the ocean. Each layer distinguishable in its splendid color. As clouds move in, the waters closest to land darken. Plush shades of green and gray mix together to form a color made only in ocean waters. A dark, translucent, ocean green. Further out, the ocean is lighter, more of a blue-gray. The blue-gray is the area of water just below the front of the storm. Finally, in waters most mysterious and distant, where clouds have not yet tinted the sunlight, the true ocean blue, sparkling with white bubbles, remains. As the storm passes, the shades mix, morphing the layers, shades, and colors, frolicking with each other until it is all gone, never to be seen exactly the same again.

Like the Atlantic, the layers of colors in stone and sky were in constant metamorphosis. Unique, majestic. As the sun sank on the southern tip of Utah, the layers shifted faster. We could see the front coming in from miles away. An ominous gray ceiling approached. A dark wall of water fell like a curtain from the sky to the ground. We stopped the car, stepped out, and gawked in awe for what seemed like hours.

We carried on. The road was lined with Native American, capitalistic, entrepreneurial endeavors. The large signs and rickety shacks cast shadows across the highway in front of us. First, *Indian Artifacts and Gifts*. Then, *Geronimo's Last Gift Stand*. Then, *Apache Artifacts and Gifts, Native Nativities and Pleasantries, Shop of the Big Chief,* and *Chief Running Wolf's Handmade Crafts*. They continued on for miles until we hit Route Nine.

The sun was setting as we approached the entrance to Zion. We passed through a long, manmade tunnel. Emerging from the tunnel, we found ourselves on a narrow, winding, red-clay road with a steep drop-off on one side into the deep canyon. No Jersey barriers, no guardrails. The clouds had caught up with us, or us with them. A torrential rain dropped like a curtain. Darkness began to descend.

"This is the main highway?" I asked Weeli.

"Yeah, no shit, huh?" Weeli said, shaking his head.

"Slow down, man. We could go right off the side," I warned.

"I told you, man," Weeli smiled.

"Told me what?"

"Water. Water's gonna get me."

"Just slow down."

The downpour grew stronger. Sand and small stones began to wash onto the narrow road and down into the abyss. Weeli slowed to a crawling ten miles an hour.

Radio off.

Windows up.

Rain pounded.

Soon, small bits of debris slammed against the car.

Nervousness begat fear, fear begat anger, and anger, hysteria.

"Look out!" I screamed. There was nothing there.

"Fuck! Fuck!" Weeli articulated thoughtfully. His right hand held tight to the steering wheel. He stopped the car in the middle of the narrow road. With a drop on one side and the canyon wall on the other, there was no good pull-off. The pounding wind and rain shook the car. Weeli turned on the radio.

"Let's see if we can get the weather out here. One of those signs said tune to some AM station for park weather. Maybe this is a flash flood and will pass."

"Before or after it washes us into the abyss?" I asked.

"The Taliban claims responsibility for two recent killings of U.S. soldiers in Kansas City–"

"How about the weather, Weeli?"

A gust of wind hit the car. It rattled in protest.

"It'll come, for Christ's sakes. Give it a second."

"...The peacekeeping mission in Sierra Leone has hit major hurdles, according to State Department spokesperson, Mary Claire. Freetown, Sierra Leone seems to be in a state of anarchy as all British peacekeepers have abandoned their posts, and foreign embassies have been evacuated.

"Backed by the U.S. Defense Department, the military establishment in Egypt has once again taken control of Cairo and all government functions."

A new voice.

"Now for the weather. The Northeast remains, for the most part, under cloud cover for the next two days. Severe thunderstorms in the Southeast, Florida, Georgia, and the islands. The Midwest is mostly clear. As is normal for this time of year, the western part of the country can expect flash flooding through the end of the month..."

A new voice.

"The United Nations protests the United States anti-environmental–"

"That's fucking it?" Weeli demanded.

*Clank.*

*Crack.*

We got out of the car to see what hit us. A juniper branch.

"Look at this," I said to Weeli.

"What's that?"

"It's only like fifteen feet to the switchback below. It looks so scary from the car."

"Funny. It'd still suck. Twenty feet could kill us, don't kid yourself," he said. Just then, the rain subsided.

"Plenty of room to turn around, too," he pointed out.

"Yeah."

"I told you."

"What? You told me what?"

"Flash floods. Flash storms. Get 'em all the time out here, just passing over. This was just passing over, man," he said, with a straight face, as if he were sure and confident, not panicked at all, as if his hands hadn't been trembling against the steering wheel, as if I had not been with him for the last hour watching his psyche deteriorate before my very eyes. The anger begat rage. After all that, he summed it up as an 'I told you so.' As quickly as the flash floods came and went, so did thoughts of me throwing Weeli off the cliff into the dark, black-hole abyss of the canyon. As quickly as the rains came and went, so did thoughts of Weeli's body crashing against rock after rock on his way down. Visions of painfully smashing his head open were replacing the peyote post-trip haze that had gripped my brain. Those visions vanished with what we saw next.

*Fuck.*

Weeli saw the terror in my wide-open eyes. I looked straight past him, to It.

"Turn around, Weeli," I said nervously. Weeli turned and saw.

A naked man.

Dripping wet.

Dark-skinned.

Thin.

Maybe five foot seven.

Long hair.

Comfortable.

Confident.

He made eye contact with me, studying, then leaped up, disappearing into the canyon wall as if into a secret passage, or maybe just into the dark. Aghast, confused, frightened, we stood in silence.

Suddenly, I felt very far from home.

"What the fuck?" Weeli broke the silence.

We looked at each other. There were no words. We got back in the car. With the rain behind us, we continued toward a dim light at the bottom of the road, presuming it was the campground. Many 'What the fucks?' were mumbled along the way, but not much conversation. There wasn't much point. Neither of us had any clue what to make of what we'd seen. The tiny light came into view. The ranger station, with what looked like a reading light on inside, was just ahead.

"This feels like a horror movie. If there's no one in there, I'm driving as fast as I can the hell out of here," Weeli said. I said nothing. The ranger station wasn't empty.

"Is there a lodge around?" Weeli asked as we pulled up to the window of the ranger shack.

"A lodge?" the young female ranger replied. "Are you staying in the park? You'll need to purchase a pass."

"Ma'am," Weeli said as calmly as he could, "we are lucky to be alive. We'll pay for a pass. We just...is there a...um..."

"You fellas okay?" she asked.

"Well, besides the rain almost washing us off the road uh...um, the naked aborigine...I guess we're fine," Weeli said.

She laughed.

"I'm fucking serious," Weeli said, "there's like a naked aborigine or some shit..."

"Naked aborigine, huh?" she questioned smiling. "Come all the way from Australia just to visit our beautiful park, maybe?"

"I'm telling you, there was some crazy, naked fuck out there. Buck fucking naked. Just ran right in front of us."

"Are you just trying to avoid a fifteen-dollar fee?" she joked.

"We're serious." Weeli pulled cash out of his pocket and handed it to her. "We're serious. A naked fucking Indian. Is there a place we can stay tonight?"

"So, naked Indians, you say?" She took the money and handed him five dollars back.

"Just one," Weeli explained in a calm and serious tone. "One was plenty though. Naked, just running up the mountainside. Straight up the rock like some sort of animal. Herb saw him just standing there."

"Have you ever heard of anything like that?" I asked.

"Hmmm," she grinned, appearing to ponder her response. "There are lodges outside the park. Zion's lodge is full."

"Naked Indians just running through your park, you'd think we'd get a free pass for that and a place to stay." He looked at me. "Maybe it's Crazy Frank's group. The Elders or some shit."

"A group?" she asked.

"Yeah," Weeli told her, "a friend of ours, Apache, told us about a group hiding out here, somewhere along the Northern Arizona, Utah border. Ever hear of that?"

"Friend of yours, huh?" she said curiously. She shook her head at us, then looked up at the truck pulling in.

"Well, that's my relief." She paused for a moment to think.

"Pull up over there," she pointed off to the right, past the shack. "I'll be right with you." After sorting things out with her relief, she pulled up next to us in her truck. "You guys need a place to stay. The lodge is full. Follow me."

"What do you think?" Weeli asked me.

"Fucking confused," I said. "We staying at her place? I mean, 'follow me?' Weird."

"Yeah, weird," Weeli confirmed. "This is all very weird."

We followed her down a dirt road marked 'Employees Only' to what appeared to be something between an old army barracks and a strip mall motel.

"Hang here for a second," she said, "just gonna check in with my roommate. I'll be right back." She returned so quickly we barely had time to mumble to each other. "Well, how 'bout you guys crash here tonight with us since there aren't any rooms available."

"Really?" Weeli asked.

"Yeah. Got someone who wants to meet you. Lynn," she said, reaching out to shake my hand, "and this is Rusty, our most famous interpretive ranger. I'm going to leave you with Rusty while I go change."

"How 'bout a beer?" Rusty offered. We sat on a stiff wicker couch in the small room. "So," Rusty said, as he handed us each a can of Utah Natural Light. In Utah, even regular beer was light. The laws of Mormon country forced every beer maker to manufacture a lower alcohol content beer to sell in Utah. So, unless we were staying at a military post, fake beer it was.

"The objects," Rusty went on, "these objects, UFOs, lights, whatever, just about anyone who works out here long enough will see them once or twice anyway. Don't know what they are. Your Injuns though, that's a different story. Almost no one ever sees them. I got my thoughts about them. I was twelve first time I saw one."

"He says he's got a friend," Lynn shouted from her room, "an Apache who told him about a hidden group out here. Right, Weeli?"

"Yeah," Weeli answered.

"Apache, huh?" Rusty asked.

"Apache."

Rusty looked at me for confirmation. I shrugged my shoulders. If Frank or The Hammer were Apache, it was news to me. A lot of shit Weeli came up with was news to me.

"Interesting," Rusty said. "Well, my theory is that it's that hidden civilization that you saw tonight. At least one of them, anyhow. But I've never heard anything from the Apache. The Apache have always seemed to discredit this, historically, that's why I'm curious to find that your friend, an Apache, believes they exist."

"Maybe he's not Apache," I said, knowing damn well that Frank never mentioned being Apache. He once mentioned Massasoit and Iroquois, but even that heritage he wasn't sure of.

"No," Weeli corrected, "Apache for sure. He told me."

"The ancient Puebloan peoples of the Third Nation and the Navajo both have stories," Rusty explained, "which are very rarely shared with white men. They tell of an advanced civilization pre-dating the ancient Egyptians and the Anasazi. Like your friend has told you, these stories claim that their historical dwelling place lay somewhere along the Utah-Arizona border. They are a wise people. They're descendants of Taklishim, who believe that Chief Mahko of the Bedonkohe tribe was born in that secret place. That would place it closer to Southern Arizona, or Mexico, even. This is why Geronimo was so elusive. Whites never caught him. He was only taken into custody when he chose to surrender. Anyway, these people are supposedly the wisest of the wise," he said, as if speaking of something he knew for sure. "Evolved unlike any peoples on Earth, they use senses we don't. They move effortlessly. They speak without actually speaking, through thoughts and emotions. They are said to understand, feel, and affect the energy of all things, not just earthly, but all things. I believe they exist. I think this is who they are, who you saw. I don't know why they wander out during storms without clothes. But I'll tell you this. They're something special, no matter what you make of them. No one's ever caught them. Most people never see them. They can outrun a jeep and blend into the rock."

"You try to catch them?" Weeli asked.

"They used to try," Rusty explained. "Not that long ago either. Just fifty years ago they were still trying. During the Injun wars, they tried and tried. Drove the whites insane, too. To think they'd cleared the area, eradicated the natives, and then, right through the camp, one would go running by. Never caught a-one. I tried to follow one once, but that's frowned upon 'round here. But if you believed what I believe, then you couldn't help but want to find them."

Rusty described in romantic detail how the past ten years of his life had been devoted to finding the place, the people. That was the reason Lynn invited us back, he explained. He wanted desperately for us to put him in touch with Crazy Frank. It was a spiritual quest to find 'the Shiners,' as Rusty called them.

"What do you think about Bryce?" Weeli asked Rusty.

"Astonishing," he said. "One of the best places on the planet–"

"No," Weeli interrupted, "what do you think our chances of finding that place in Bryce Canyon are?"

"Seriously?"

"Seriously."

"I've been looking for the past twelve years, anyway, and I'll tell you this. Not there. Besides, prescribed burnings are still going on there, last I knew."

"They do that during hiking season?" I asked.

"Hell, they'll do it in the winter if they need the money," Rusty replied.

"The money?"

"Yup," Lynn confirmed, "need to meet their quota, spend every penny in their fire-fighting budget so they don't lose the money next year. That's how they decide how many prescribed burns are needed."

"No shit?"

"The system, you know?"

"Too far north, for sure, anyway," Rusty continued. "I'm telling you, that ain't where they are. Besides that, I've personally been through every nook, hoodoo, canyon, and cranny in that entire park. Is that why you're going there? To find this group? 'Cause that ain't it. Tell you this though, wherever you go, you gotta promise to let me know if you find or see anything, yeah?"

"Sure," Weeli said.

"And I think I need to know this Crazy Frank cat."

"Can do," Weeli assured him.

"Bryce? Really?" Rusty asked.

"Bryce."

"Why there?"

"Not sure."

"What do you mean?"

Weeli looked at me. "Frank was adamant that we go to Bryce. 'The Revolution will find you there,' he kept saying, remember?"

It was another thing I did not remember. Maybe in Vermont he said something, but that was all a blur.

"The Revolution?" Lynn asked.

## The Revolution, Weeli to Rusty and Lynn:

*"These truths, evidenced by the connected energy of all things, communicated so directly that only the billions of microscopic entities, which exist in what appears to be open air, stand in the way of verbatim translation.*

*The true virtue of selfishness can only be realized through the absolute understanding and practice of selfishness itself. Selfishness must be seen through the lens of the connected energy of all things. It is the connected energy of all things that dictates the evolution and survival of humanity.*

*The good of all things will be realized by the selfish pursuit of the good of the individual. Thus, the aim of The Revolution is to bring about the realization of pure selfishness within the human conscience, affecting humanity's survival and the positive evolution of the connected energy of all things.*

*To simplify, if it feels good, do it, only suffices once the individual has achieved a true understanding of what 'feeling good' means in respect to the connected energy of all things.*

*The Revolution will affect this end."*

# CHAPTER 18

# BRYCE CANYON

**_Hoodoo_** (hōō-dōō)
   _verb. To cast a spell._
   _noun. A pillar of sandstone shaped and formed by erosion._
   _noun – alternate def. Natural, colorful stone skyscrapers, lively in form and shape, as if human. Capable of absorbing and transforming light into fiery, glowing hues, always eroding, evolving, and shifting, the pinnacles are in constant transformation._

   *– Poor John's Dictionary of Spectacles, 2004*

The ascending sun enlightened towering stone silhouettes, rising like Wall Street skyscrapers from deep within the canyon. We climbed a road thick with ponderosa pine, juniper tree, small oak, claret cactus, and Indian grass until we arrived at our destination, Bryce Canyon.

My first hoodoo.

Burning away the dew, the liquid gold rays of the morning sun illuminated armies of massive stone sculptures, burning like candles, reaching with all their spirit to the wide-open western sky. Hoodoos. The spell was cast.

Like the ponderosa pines, they stretched to the heavens in mass formations, each unlike the other, each unlike anything else. Sublime. Some were orange and red at the top with shades of white and yellow in the middle, and orange again at the base. It appeared as though, out of nowhere, the earth had placed an ancient army to watch over the landscape. Some appeared to defy gravity. Thick, crown-shaped peaks, maybe twenty feet wide, stood firm atop a column only five or six feet wide, giving the illusion of a thin soldier holding an entire planet on his head. The sand, stone, earth, everything. Breathing.

Spiraling trees clung precariously to the edges of the canyon, peppering the landscape with life where it would seem life could not exist. Out of sandstone and desert sprang life. Utah junipers, Douglas firs, silver aspen, ponderosa pines, bladder sage, and Indian paintbrush. These, along with the Utah prairie dog, burrowing owl, golden eagle, short-horned lizard, mule deer, mountain lion, black bear, Cooper's hawk, and others, occupied the seemingly dead desert terrain.

When I sent Sophia a letter telling her how spiritual and moving the hoodoos of Bryce were, she emailed me these facts with a header that read, 'Geology, Herb, it's science.'

According to her 'research,' fifty million years ago, the Colorado Plateau, including the area known as Bryce, began uplifting. The oxidation of minerals accounts for the astonishing colors, while iron and manganese oxides create the most vivid hues. Iron, the reds and yellows, manganese, the purples and blues. The off-whites, oranges, grays, and beiges come from the natural colors of the various sand and stone. The erosion, which played such a large part in creating the natural beauty of Bryce, is estimated to reduce the outer rim of the canyon by nearly two feet every hundred years.

It was more than geology. It was magic. The spell had me as I stood at the canyon edge.

A silent reverence.

The sensation of being home, finally. Déjà vu. This was a land familiar to me, calling to me, missing me, and I it. The scent of the post-rain desert tickled my nose hairs. The taste of the air, distinct, crisp, familiar, delicious. The sweet vanilla aroma of the ponderosa pine permeated my being. Concealing the canyon's secret beauty was a forest of juniper, pinion, bellflower, yarrow, firs, ash, Mormon tea, rabbit brush, sagebrush, skunk brush, rice grass, silver beard grass, and mountain mahogany. Away from the rat race of corporate America, away from the stenching sewerage piling up in the city streets and flushed oceans, beneath the pavement and paint, away from the manmade bullshit, I felt most at home. There was a difference out west. Pack rats, unlike the rats racing back east, served as patient historians and preservationists.

Weeli said something about seeing a mountain lion. Maybe he saw a bobcat, antelope, bighorn sheep, coyote, gray fox, black-tailed jackrabbit, desert cottontail, or antelope squirrel. He could have. Maybe I missed it. Maybe it was a white-tailed squirrel, kangaroo rat, or the walking garter snake. Perhaps just a gopher snake, a rattler, or a whip snake. Whatever it was, I missed it. For a barren desert, there was much to see. Eagles, vultures, doves, falcons, hummingbirds, bluebirds, tanagers, jays, swallows, ravens, wren, leopard lizards, whiptail lizards, blotched lizards, fence lizards, collared lizards, fairy shrimp, tadpole shrimp, frogs of all sorts, and thousands of varieties of insects flourished in the lifeless badlands of Southern Utah.

I stepped to the edge of the canyon and sat on a rock, which hung over the nearly thousand-foot drop into Bryce Canyon. Everything came together. I felt myself, alive and right. There, on that stone, was a wide-awake, full-of-life-and-energy moment, not for the past or future, but a moment just for the moment, virtuous in and of itself. I was most alive. Something larger than me, larger than anything I'd known, had me. The energy of all things had me.

"The faces of the rock were believed to be the faces of ancient peoples," Weeli explained. "A spell was cast on them, their souls frozen in stone, doomed to stand guard for eternity. It doesn't seem like forever in this place is any kind of curse. All natural, H. Incredible, isn't it?" His voice sounded older and wiser. "Let's go find our spot."

Our site was just below the South Rim. We set up camp then ventured out for supplies. We would need an overnight permit, Weeli told me, and some overnight supplies. He had it planned. As it turned out, his plan was not so good. Bryce didn't give out overnight permits.

"You can see it in the daytime," the ranger told us. "Portable radio? A radio is good for weather broadcasts.

Never know when the flash floods are coming. Folks come out here and think we don't get rain in the desert. Surprised when they get washed up." He had no idea what we'd just been through.

"You won't see most the animals out there 'cause they'll have spotted you first, but," he paused, raising his thick, gray eyebrows and ensuring he had our full attention, "should you run into a problem, a mountain lion or bob-cat or something that you may have accidentally stumbled across or cornered...it doesn't happen often here. If the thing is finding a way out, just let it go. Don't do a damn thing. But if it's cornered or looks like it's going for you... well, that's a different story. Panic as loud, big, and mean as you can, but don't run. Stick together. Raise up your arms," he said, stretching his ranger jacket up from the pits till the seams looked like they might burst. "Look as big and mean as you can. Scream holy hell. If the animal is frightened, it'll find its way out."

"And if not?" Weeli asked him.

"Then you're in for the fight of your life, kid. Don't wor-ry 'bout all that. Chances are you won't see a damn thing," he said with a wink. "Just have yourselves a good time."

"Right on," Weeli said, giving me one of those looks like, 'let's get the fuck out of here.'

Ignoring most of what we'd heard, we headed into the canyon early that evening. The hike down the canyon was a slow and easy one. We reminisced about the past two days as we made our way down the steep trail. It didn't take long before The Revolution dominated the conversa-tion. According to Weeli, during our mindfuck adventure, Crazy Frank made it clear that here at Bryce, we would meet our most important connection. During this conversation, Weeli made it clear that he believed fully, as fully as a Pentecostal believes in tongues, that he, Weeli, would lead The Revolution. I was so overwhelmed, or comfortable, or at home, that I found myself less impacted by the details. Bryce, the energy in the stone, the air, the sky, somehow made it clear to me that everything would happen just as it was meant to.

The hoodoos were in constant metamorphosis, the light and shadows shifting. As the sun set, the shadows took on their own character, as full of life as the hoodoos themselves. For every stone pillar grew a shadow, which continued to move and grow until they would all disappear into the black canvas of evening. Sounds of dry cracklings, rocks sliding, creatures crawling, were quiet but present. We hiked without flashlights so we wouldn't impair our night vision. The stars took over the night sky. Like nightlights, one by one, then many by many, they popped on, lighting up a deep, mysterious, black sky.

"Should we find a place to set up?" I asked Weeli.

"You know what? Let's just keep hiking. We've got the headlamps if we need them, right? You know, Herb, it all makes sense to me now. Where I came from. The opportunities, the education. Everything really was just leading to the moment when – what the?" he shouted, looking over my shoulder. His eyes were huge. I could almost see the stars reflecting. Maybe it was the whites of his eyeballs.

"Fuck!" I screamed. I didn't see anything yet, but half expected to see a naked crazy standing behind me. I don't really know what I expected when I turned around, but I saw nothing.

"Some light or something shot up into the sky."

We stood like hoodoos.

"You didn't fucking see that? Are you serious?" Weeli demanded.

"What?"

"A fucking light, man. Just shot right up into the...fuck, well, something just shot up into the sky."

Then I saw. A sphere of solid white light, an orb, hovered unnaturally above the horizon of the canyon wall and the starlit sky north of us. The way it hovered was peculiar. Just a massive light, spherical, hanging. Not hovering like a helicopter. Certainly not flying as a plane would. It shifted from side to side effortlessly and quickly. We watched it drop in an instant into the canyon and out of view. Before we could say a word it was in view again, hovering.

"What the fuck?"

The sphere sprang straight up as if it were propelled by a cannon or a rocket or...or something. Too fast and too high for any manmade object. In a matter of a second or two, the sphere shot high enough to leave the atmosphere and then drop back down. It shifted right and dropped out of view again. Two solid balls of light hovered together, just a small distance from one another in about the same position we had seen the first. Just as the first had done, the two sprang up into space, almost disappearing into the mysterious realm of the stars, and again were back down in view, a bit south of their original position. As the second two returned, the first sphere rose up from the canyon. Three orbs hovered.

*Fuck.*

Curiosity.

*Fuck.*

*UFOs?*

*Fuck.*

"Do you see that, man? There are three of them," Weeli whispered.

"Yeah, I see it," I whispered back. We had instinctively dropped our voices as if whatever it was could hear us from way up there. "Look at that." The lights shifted east and west, parallel to the canyon floor, without losing or gaining altitude. They appeared to be playing, bouncing around in all cardinal directions with great ease and speed.

"Gotta be UFOs," Weeli said.

"UFOs," I mumbled.

First, a fear, then a warm courage, and a sense of purpose.

"Let's climb. See if we can find these things. See them better from the rim." Weeli needed no convincing.

"Yeah," he agreed, swinging his bag around his right shoulder, grabbing the back with his left hand, and feeling for the waist strap. "Let's. Maybe they'll find us."

As we ascended the canyon rim, the three spheres danced in the sky, for just a second nearly touching the canyon floor, floating, and then escaping beyond the atmosphere. They were gone.

"Shit," Weeli exclaimed. He crouched down low, motioning for me to do the same.

"What? What?" I dropped into the prone position.

"Shhh," he shushed me, nodding his head to his right.

"I saw them," I told him.

"No," he nodded again.

"What?"

"Shhh. There's someone out there."

My heart raced like the Dead playing an early version of Mexicali Blues. I reached for a stone.

"What? Someone out here?"

"I just saw him running over there."

Flashbacks of Fort Benning live fire training.

Flashbacks of hand-to-hand combat.

The rush of being slammed upside the head and going back for more.

The stone was steady in my right hand. Weeli looked at me as if I were a stranger.

"He ran across the fucking canyon, right up there." He pointed west. "He was cruising."

I surveyed the area. A ten-foot drop then a climb up the canyon wall would put me in perfect position to see what was on the other side of the rim. I tossed my pack next to Weeli, handed him the rock, lifted myself, and darted out into the night. I reached the other side of the rim and dropped back down again.

Nothing.

Brush, rock, shadows, but nothing moving. I put my fingers to my forehead and motioned for Weeli to come. As he approached, I heard the rustling of dirt in front of me. Still, I saw nothing. Weeli stood beside me. I put my finger to my mouth. He was silent. Only the sound of crushing leaves, but it was not autumn in New England. There were no leaves.

"I hear it," Weeli whispered.

I took my backpack from Weeli. In it was a small ax, the kind used for breaking firewood into kindling. It was a good weapon. Weeli looked petrified. I handed him my knife, removed the ax from its case, and stood silently.

Another rustling sound. Longer. More constant. Rapid steps. I spun around.

"Someone's running toward us," Weeli stammered. There was evident fear in his voice.

"Relax," I told him. I was not relaxed. "Get a handful of dirt."

"Dirt?"

"Just pick up a handful of dirt." He saw me do it and followed suit. "If anyone gets close to you, throw it in their face then do what you have to do."

I scared Weeli when I screamed, "Who's out here?"

Nothing. No response. Another rustling, this time, behind us.

"Fuck," Weeli shouted, "warn me next time."

"Shhh," I whispered.

"Shush nothing," he said, "you think they didn't hear you scream?"

"Shhh." The rustling got louder. It was behind us. I spun around, pulling the ax back by my right shoulder. Weeli turned instinctively.

Nothing. No one.

It was behind us again. This time closer. I whipped around, leading with my left hand, releasing the dirt with full force.

*Fuck.*

Standing directly in our line of sight, but just too far for the dirt to reach his eyes, was a native man, naked, like the one we'd seen before. He didn't flinch. I reached my left hand out as if to protect myself from something, keeping the ax cocked. He studied us. His energy was entirely benevolent. He meant no harm.

"I think you should drop the ax," Weeli said.

"You think? Why haven't you dropped my knife?" I asked him. "Did you hear that?"

"What, H?"

"He said something about Frank."

"He didn't say shit. Don't freak out here."

*Frank sent you.*

"You didn't hear anything?" I asked again.

"Herb, cut the shit." The man knew what I heard.

"Did you say Frank sent us?" I asked the stranger.

He said nothing.

"Herb," Weeli whined.

*Weeli.* The stranger looked Weeli dead in the eye.

*Fuck,* I thought to myself, *what the fuck?*

"I can't believe it," Weeli said, "Frank said we'd know them by their clothes."

"Frank didn't tell me shit."

"Herb, please," Weeli pleaded, "don't worry about it, we're here now. That's why. Now is why. Do you know what this means?"

"I have some idea."

"Kareen," the man said from a distance. "Quick, we must—"

"Hey," I interrupted him as I noticed the light again. A single sphere returned over Kareen's shoulder. "There it is again," I pointed up to the sky. Kareen immediately pulled my arm down. I hadn't noticed he'd crossed the distance between us.

"Please. Quick."

"What is that in the—" Weeli started to ask, but Kareen was on the move.

He ran. We followed. We were running as much from as toward something, moving at a good pace. I wheezed, releasing smoke that had built up for two solid years in my lungs. Kareen seemed to glide over stones, barely making contact. His steps were swift and smooth. He ran straight ahead, toward the canyon wall, just off of the dried-up riverbed, aiming for what appeared to be solid stone. He disappeared into the rock. We followed. It was a natural illusion. One rock hung over the ravine just above another, which stretched up into the canyon leaning outward toward us, creating the appearance of a solid stone wall. We followed. Again, just a minute or so later, as we began a slight incline, Kareen seemed to be running into the solid base of a large hoodoo, so wide that I could not see the other end. He ran straight into it and disappeared. Weeli followed, then me. It was a cave. The entrance was invisible to the eye at night. Two large stones leaned into each other, hiding the natural tunnel. We emerged from the hoodoo on the opposite side and ran northwest, up the canyon wall.

"Stay," Kareen instructed, holding his left hand out in front of him, directing us not to follow.

"No problem," I said, collapsing onto a stone, desperate to catch my breath. Weeli remained standing, panting like a dog in heat.

Laying my head back, I stared up at the night sky. Something was strange. It was pitch black. *Pitch* black. No stars, no planes, no lights, no nothing. Black abyss. It didn't look as though clouds had moved in. It just looked black, like a black curtain had been placed over our sky.

By the sound of Kareen's steps, as light as they were, I figured he ran a circle around the perimeter of our location. Then, almost as quickly as he had gone, he was back, not short of breath nor showing fatigue. He sat down, folded his hands together and bowed to Weeli and me as if we were gods.

"Well done," he said. "You ran well."

"What now?" Weeli asked.

"Rest," Kareen answered.

"What about the lights?" I asked. "The spheres, what were they? What…"

He grinned at us, brought his face to his folded hands, looked up, and said nothing.

"What are they?" Weeli pressed.

"I am a runner," Kareen told us. "I am just a runner."

"Yes, but what are those hovering lights?" Weeli's impatience was insatiable.

"A good distraction," Kareen said, looking up.

"A distraction?"

"A distraction. As they hovered in front of you, what else were you looking at? We runners use them like we use the weather, the rain, the floods. To move unnoticed.

"Follow," Kareen spoke aloud, and again was on the run. This time less hurried, and for barely a minute before stopping. We seemed to run in a circle around a large stone formation. The black abyss was no longer above us. Stars, once again visible. Kareen had given us a brief glimpse of one of their places before returning us to the canyon floor.

"Now I must go." Kareen said.

"Go?" Weeli's voice cracked in disbelief. "We've come all this way. Frank said we would meet the most important…"

As Weeli spoke, I heard Kareen's voice though his lips did not move.

*You have. Know we are here.*

═╪⁝ ⁝╪═

With that, Kareen was gone.

"Are you fucking kidding me?" Weeli said in disbelief.

Kareen was not kidding. Weeli was furious.

"We came all the way out here. Probably the only civilized people to ever encounter these people and that's it? What the fuck?"

"Half empty or half full, Weeli?" I asked him, hoping to inspire a positive response. In hindsight, I can see the naivety in my aspirations, but hindsight wasn't there to help me at the time.

"Are you shitting me?" Weeli shouted. "Cup-half-full bullshit? We're in the middle of the fucking desert with a once-in-a-lifetime chance to know something about these people, about the nature of everything, and you're giving me cup-half-full bullshit?"

"Maybe we just need to be patient," I suggested. "On the bright side, just like you said, we have experienced a once-in-a-lifetime and never-in-most-lifetimes experience. We found the Shiners. They are real. Who knows what else is real."

"So what?" Weeli screamed. He seemed to be screaming at the canyon walls more than at me. Maybe at Kareen. Maybe at the Shiners. Likely he was screaming at the entire cosmos. "So fucking what? Are we just supposed to go back home? Pick up our lollipop projects and carry on? Fuck that. We are finding them."

"What? You heard him. We aren't finding them if they don't want us to. And we just found them and here we are.

What, are we going to force them to take us in? Tell us all they know? Give us their magic scepter? What?"

"Maybe. You can do whatever you want, but I ain't leaving. I don't care if I have to camp out here and walk this forsaken desert for years, I'm going to find these fuckers. We've come too far."

"I can't do anything I'd like," I pointed out, "we have one car."

"You're an imbecile," he said, shaking his head at me. "After all this, you're worried about a ride home? Take the fucking car if you want. You know I can make a call and have a fucking limousine pick me up if I want. But really, you're just going to go? You're willing to accept that that was it? That's what we came out here for?"

"I'm not saying I'm thrilled, but if they wanted us to stay, if they wanted to show us more or tell us more, they would have. What are you proposing?"

"I don't know," he paused. "Yes, I do know. I'm proposing we go back to town, get more supplies, and plan on hanging out in these canyons 'till we find something."

"Okay," I conceded. Weeli was angry. He was on the verge of crazy and I understood why. I didn't think his plan was a great one, and it could risk any possible connection we might have with the Shiners in the future. Hell, it might even risk our lives, but for the moment that was okay. What I heard were these words: 'back to town.' For me, that meant a chance for Weeli to calm down, for us to have a few drinks, and reflect on the situation.

"Okay," Weeli said.

We started what would be a four-hour hike back through and up the canyon to the South Rim of Bryce. Weeli told me I would need to put in for a leave of absence at work. We both knew he didn't need the job, so he said he would just call Garbway and let him know he might not be back. He explained that he would pay my rent back home and anything else that was needed for as long as it took us to find the Shiners. I had resigned myself to 'yes' him through all of it, at least until we were back at camp and had time to gather our wits. I figured Weeli would be more rational after a few drinks. I was partly right. By the time we made it to the car, Weeli started talking sensibly.

"First stop," he said, "Ruby's. It's time for a drink." I was finishing my third High West Utah Whiskey when Weeli returned from making his round of phone calls. "I bought you a month, and the crazy bastard's going to pay you for it, so pay your own rent. He really loves me. I talked to Laura, too, and I guess I have to be back in a few weeks because the city is dedicating a memorial site to my mother and she doesn't want to handle it alone. So, we have three weeks, Herb. Drink up."

We did drink up. So much so that our return to the canyon was delayed a day while Weeli recovered from his hangover. He spent that time between the pool and the jacuzzi at Ruby's Inn. I spent the time buying supplies, which this time included whiskey and weed.

Our first week back in the canyon was truly an expedition. We were constantly on the move, looking for signs of life, for tracks, for hidden passages to some secret village, but to no avail. By the end of the first week, we were on the move less, and sooner to hit the whiskey and watch the sun go down or the storm roll in and pass. By the third week, it was as if we'd almost forgotten why we stayed. Our time was mostly spent sharing stories of our childhoods and our thoughts about the great mysteries of the cosmos. By the time we made our way back to Salt Lake City International, there was no more anger in Weeli's voice. This was not wasted time and he knew it.

An undeniable gravity pulled on me as I stared out the window and sucked in my fleeting glimpse of the Rockies, Big Sky Country, the Great American West. I'd come to love the thin air, dry and crisp with heat and cold. I'd come to long for the scent of the post-rain desert. I'd come to love so much about the West in such a short period of time. I felt as though I was leaving home. That sadness was quickly devoured by my awareness that nothing would ever be the same.

# CHAPTER 19

# VISIONS OF PLAGIARISM

*When the laughter of humanity*
*Echoes in oblivion,*
*Molecules know no need for Love.*

– POOR JOHN, 1983

Meditating atop a hoodoo, somewhere between the southern edge of Bryce and north of Natural Bridge, where Weeli and I were on our second night of our search for the Shiners, I received a vision. I could see my body in front of me, on the very hoodoo upon which I sat. Liquid lines, some linear, some curved, all seeming to intersect infinitely, connected my body, the canyon walls, hoodoos, ground, and sky. Within one of these connections, a small bubble formed and began to ripple through the lines. At each point where the lines intersected, they burst and began dangling, whipping furiously like a powerful fire hose left open at full blast. As the lines intersecting at my body burst, I watched as my body was transformed into a mass of shiny black liquid suspended in air. What had appeared to be a crystal clear liquid when the lines were connected morphed into a toxic, electrically-charged, cloudy-brown substance as it blew out of the countless severed connections. The murky gas flooded the air. The dangling tentacles continued gyrating violently until, one by one and many by many, they gravitated toward other severed ends and became reconnected. Through the gas clouding the air, I could see everything was connected again, but the lines were now a less transparent, pinkish-gray, and the shiny black mass that was my body had been absorbed by the lines. Connected, these lines vibrated, slowly stabilizing again.

"Herb. Herb!"

And just like that, with the sound of Weeli's voice calling through the night sky, it was gone. Frank had things to say about visions and prophecies. He had once told us that the reason end-of-day prophecies are so popular is not that they give hope and meaning to people, but rather that they serve the purposes of the greedy.

"What do you think has propagated these tales since the beginning of recorded time? Why? If you can make the desperate, downtrodden slave society believe that some other force is going to bring a reckoning, that God, the cosmos, Karma, will bring balance and cleansing, then the people don't have to do it. They simply have to hope and wait... and, in the meantime, they just need to survive. The oldest of religions have the Pralaya. They've embedded a cyclical apocalypse at the end of every Maha Yuga, which is brilliant because it always means there's one coming up. The Old Testament, basis of Judaism and Islam, made sure to include The Book of Daniel, complete with 'Arise and devour much flesh.' And of course, The Revelations of John the Divine cover all modern Christians. When Desert Storm came around, the propaganda machine pushed the idea that the Middle East would implode in a nuclear holocaust, causing massive global catastrophe. When the white flags flew and that didn't happen, a new catalyst arose. The great holy war, brought on by the Islamic State, would bring the final reckoning. They always make sure everyone has something to look forward to. The funny thing is, the most damaging propaganda tool of all time has been The Book of Revelations, which is nothing more than plagiarism, but who gives a shit, right?"

Prior to heading west, Frank inspired me to do my homework, to look back at the prophets and seers, to come to my own opinion about what was and wasn't real. In hindsight, I am certain Frank was simply preparing me for the vision I was to have.

I had always imagined most seers, whether consciously or subconsciously, made it all up, but during my research I came to believe there might be a perfectly viable three-dimensional, scientific explanation. For instance, maybe energies of past and future events exist in the vast majority of our known universe, which is made up of something physicists call 'dark matter,' a term that can be roughly translated as, we haven't got a clue what or why it is, but it is. I could believe that Cayce, Nostradamus, Daniel, and others truly believed they received visions, and maybe their brains picked up waves of dark spatter, but I couldn't believe that there was some intentional design communicating prophecies only to certain individuals with a specific intent. However, I didn't have to look far to agree with Frank about John the Divine's great and tragic plagiarism.

John the Divine's Revelation, written several hundred years after The Book of Daniel, and later published in the same novel:

> *...And in the midst of the throne, and round about the throne, were four beasts full of eyes before and behind. And the first beast was like a lion, and the second beast like a calf, and the third beast had a face as a man, and the fourth beast was like a flying eagle. And the four beasts had each of them six wings about him; and they were full of eyes within; and they rest not day and night...and I stood upon the sand of the sea, and saw a beast rise up out of the sea, having seven heads and ten horns and upon his horns ten crowns...and the beast which I saw was like unto a leopard, and his feet were as the feet of a bear, and his mouth as the mouth of a lion...*

– Excerpt from the
Revelation of St. John the Divine,
The Book of Revelations

Nearly a thousand years earlier:

> *And four great beasts came up from the sea, diverse from one another. The first was like a lion and had Eagle's wings: I beheld till the wings thereof were plucked, and it was lifted up from the Earth, and made stand upon the feet as a man, and a man's heart was given to it. And behold*

*another beast, a second like to a bear, and it raised up itself on one side, and it had three ribs in the mouth of it between the teeth of it, and they said thus unto it, "Arise, devour much flesh."*

*After this I beheld, and lo another, like a leopard, which had upon the back of it four wings of a fowl; the beast had also four heads; and dominion was given to it. After this I saw in the night visions and behold a fourth beast, dreadful and terrible, and strong exceedingly; it devoured and it had great iron teeth; it devoured and broke in pieces, and stamped the residue with the feet of it; and it was diverse from all the beasts that were before it; and it had ten horns.*

– Excerpt from The Book of Daniel

"Herb!" Weeli called, instantly pulling me out of Revelations and back into my body. My body felt different, though. Lighter, connected. "Where you at?" The feeling I had was magical, for lack of better explanation. I didn't want to lose that magic and so didn't respond to Weeli right away. But, as always, Weeli was resourceful.

"There you are," he said, making his way up the canyon to my position. "Why didn't you answer me?" I said nothing as he made his way over. I don't know exactly what words I used to try to explain my experience and feelings to Weeli, but I know they didn't serve their purpose.

"Yeah," he said, "it's beautiful here. It probably inspires many visions. So, I was thinking, whatever I do or don't find out here, I'm done with the bullshit work and story hours with Frank. When I get back, I'm going to find The

Hammer and make this thing happen. I need to get his contacts and I need to get things moving."

This brief moment in our lives was most telling of our relationship. He was my closest friend. We were partners on this path to something, to this idea, this Revolution, to discovery, and self-awareness. As inadequate as my words might have been, even a stranger could have seen on my face, heard in my tone, and felt from a thousand miles away, how transformative this experience was for me.

Weeli summed it up with, "it's beautiful here. It probably inspires a lot of visions." He then went right on to what he, Weeli, was going to do. The word 'we' was no longer part of the story.

As he went on about his life, his family, how everything had led him to this moment, I began to understand how empty Weeli was. All of this was a way to fill a void, to be valuable, at least to himself. While I had thought we were partners on a spiritual pursuit, I was naïve. We never spoke of my vision again.

# CHAPTER 20

# THE TIDE ROLLS IN ON THE REVOLUTION

### *The Atlantic*

*Light.*
*Chilling rain falls gently from silver-gray clouds.*
*Passing.*
*A cool blue breeze.*
*Still.*
*I stand a stone as growls of thunder creek apart*
*the heavens.*
*Crackling.*
*The rumbling roar of ocean and sky meet.*
*Rocks.*
*Smash violently against rocks.*
*Sand.*
*Against my lonesome feet.*
*Earth.*
*Tossed around like wind in air.*

*Weeds.*
*Wrap around me, evolved, moved.*
*Awake.*
*The cold Atlantic takes her course.*
*Still.*
*I am moved.*
*Light.*
*Chilling rain falls gently from silver-gray clouds.*

– S.S. Shelly Stone,
*The Atlantic Contributor,* 1999

Terror.
*Hopeless.*
I don't know how it was possible, but Weeli had even less hope than I.

Panic.

I could see it clear as the setting sun in his petrified eyes.

Certain death.

*Hopeless?* It couldn't be hopeless. I tried to imagine what that meant. *Hopeless.*

*Fuck.*

What began as a body-surfing venture turned deadly in a hurry. We didn't see it coming. We were out playing in the waves, like children in a sandbox, oblivious to the scorpions just beneath the sand. We started out chest deep, just like the night before, but after an hour or so the waves out at sea were just too enticing. Soon it was a competition. Who could catch the waves farthest out? We were children. There was no talk of Revolutions, or Entipop, or saving the world. We were just catching waves and daring each other to swim out farther. As Weeli rode one of the crashers on his back, I swam as hard as I could to get past the line of breakers. When Weeli turned, I gave him the finger.

"Where you at, bitch?" We were competitive. I saw Weeli start power-stroking toward me, then a wave got me. When I came up, Weeli had passed me and was taking advantage of the opportunity to laugh at my expense.

"Where you at, biyatch?" he laughed. Then a wave got him. Weeli came up coughing.

"I guess that one got you."

He wasn't laughing. He wore a concerned look. "You all right?" I asked.

"Yeah," he said, "but maybe we're out too far. I didn't touch bottom at all."

Without looking back to shore, I put up my index finger to say, 'hold on a minute.' I propelled myself below the water to see how far bottom was.

*Fuck.*

There was no bottom. Worse, instead of hitting bottom, I felt a pull.

"Yup," I said as I broke the plane of water and gasped for air, "no bottom. And there's a strong undertow."

"Yeah," Weeli said, "let's head back in."

"Yeah. Fuck," I said as I turned to face the shoreline. My rental house had shifted far to the left. Much too far to the left. We had been pulled well out and to the north.

"Fuck," Weeli confirmed. We swam hard for a good two or three minutes, but it was impossible to tell if we were making any progress.

"I don't think we're moving, man," I said to him. And that's when it hit me.

*Riptide...riptide...riptide.*

The word zinged across my synapses over and over again. I paused for a moment, watching Weeli to see if he was making any progress toward shore.

"Herb, can you touch bottom yet?" Weeli shouted to me as he continued, arm over shoulder. I was hesitant at first, then I submerged myself. A wave got me as I emerged, filling my throat with salt water. *Gag. Cough. Spit. Breathe.*

"No," I told Weeli. "No bottom. And the pull's getting stronger."

*Riptide...riptide...riptide.*

*Zing...zing...zing.*

"No?"

"No."

"Fuck."

Weeli went under. Too long. Panic crept in. Weeli emerged farther out. It wasn't often I saw fear in Weeli's eyes, but he looked scared when he rose out of the water, gasping for air.

"I think we're fucked, Weeli. We might be caught in a riptide." He was having none of it.

"Just fucking swim." We both continued to fight reality, to deny the facts of the matter.

The facts:

**Riptide** *(rip-tīd)*
> *noun. A current opposing other currents, often along the shore. Commonly, riptides pull away from shore while the remaining waters, outside of the current of the riptide, continue to push toward shore.*

The statistics (as I observed them with Weeli, stoned on the couch, watching The Learning Channel a few months prior):

1. *Only one in ten swimmers who attempt to survive by fighting the riptide will survive ('fighting' being defined as 'swimming against the current of the riptide, directly toward shore'). In nine out of ten cases, the swimmer does not progress to shore and utilizes all energy before finally drowning.*

2. *Recommended action if caught in a riptide: swim with the tide, generally moving in a direction parallel to the shore. Do not attempt to swim to shore through the riptide. Swim to the side until the current pulls toward shore again. Swim slowly, sparing every iota of energy possible.*

3. *Of swimmers who do not fight the riptide, the statistics are much more favorable. Eight out of ten survive.*

The facts were important to me. Fighting the tide could mean death. Not fighting the tide could mean death. We had reduced life to a game of chicken with the most powerful force on the planet. She had us in her omnipotent grip. The ocean is blissfully unaware of gay rights, the right of the unborn fetus to bear arms, or a human's so-called right to life. She does not discriminate.

Thoughts zipped across my cranium like comets. *You arrogant fuck. Don't feel like The Shit now, do you?*

*Fuck.*

*Riptide…riptide…riptide.*

*Gonna drown in your own front yard?*

*Moron. Moron. Fucking moron.*

"Weeli," I hollered over to him, "we're in a riptide, man. We gotta–"

"What are you talking about, Herb? Just fucking swim." Weeli was adamant, even confident. Maybe he was confident that we'd make it to shore.

"Weeli, listen to me," I said between deep, panicky breaths. "Do you…a…huh–"

*Crash. Gag.* Another wave. I came up. Caught my breath.

"Most people who die, fucking die because they try to fight it…ugh–"

"Jesus, Herb, we're not going to fucking die," he yelled. There was anger in his voice. The anger seemed to be directed at my use of the word 'die,' rather than at the ocean or our current predicament.

Another wave. *Salt. Spit. Gag. Breathe.* When I emerged, Weeli was under.

"Weeli," I urged as he surfaced, "they…uh…most people die because they try to fight the current and waste all of their energy trying to make it to shore. We're going to wear ourselves out." I caught my breath. "I think we need to make a decision here, man."

"Fuck that," Weeli said emphatically. He continued swimming as hard as he could. For a moment, I pretended I could hide from the facts. I made a halfhearted effort to swim with him toward shore.

"We ain't going anywhere, Weeli," I yelled. "I'm not kidding, man, this is how idiots become statistics. We need to start swimming to the right to get out of this fucking thing." I was getting angry. Angry at the ocean. Angry at myself for being so stupid. Angry with Weeli for being so stoned he didn't remember watching that riptide special whose statistics were flashing before me as clear as that wave...

Under again. *Salt. Gag. Breathe.*

Weeli wasn't having any of it.

"Herb, you fucking listen to me," he shouted over the crashing waves. "Keep fucking swimming. We are going to make it to shore. Just...ah–" The water got him. He was under and then emerged. He coughed. Spat. His tone was less confident. "Uh, just uh...keep fucking swimming. Just swim as hard as you can, man. We're getting back to shore."

Fear of death is an interesting experience. You learn some things about yourself. I was afraid of dying, but somehow I was more afraid of dying alone. No matter what happened, I did not want Weeli and me to split up. At the same time, I felt hatred and extreme resentment toward Weeli for being too ignorant to listen to me. My fear of dying alone would be what led to my death as I stuck it out with Weeli, swimming futilely until our energy abandoned us, reducing our bodies to fish food. As I made careful strokes to spare my energy, I could see Weeli was putting everything he had into making it back to shore.

*Statistic…statistic…statistic.*

I pleaded with him. "Weeli, we're not getting anywhere. We're just using all of our energy to–"

Another wave. Weeli was yelling at me as I emerged.

"…Never get there…are you crazy? Look over there," he said, motioning north, to the right, the direction I suggested we swim. His tone was more desperate. His confidence was gone. "For fuck's sake," he cried out over the waves, "we can't swim over there. It'll just wash us right out into open ocean. Look! Goddamn it!" He was as angry with me for not understanding that we had to swim straight to shore as I was with him for ignoring riptide statistics.

I looked over to my right. Weeli wasn't wrong. He had good cause for trepidation. We were on the point of an inlet, where the bay opens up to the great big Atlantic. If we swam too far north, the natural current would pick us up and pull us right out past the islands. But if we made it out of the riptide before getting that far, we could make it to shore. Maybe.

The waves got both of us. I could hear bits and pieces of Weeli's voice in between my own coughing and the waves washing over. I felt my arms taking on a deadweight heaviness.

"Weeli," I called out again. Desperate. "Weeli, look. Look in front of you, man. We aren't any closer to shore. The tide is ripping us out to sea anyway. We're going to wash out if we don't slow down and start swimming out of this thing."

"Just fucking swim, goddamn you!" he screamed. His tone was adding to my fear. His strokes were losing some of their strength. "We can't just swim out of this thing. It's the fucking ocean, man. We gotta make it to shore. I'm not fucking dying."

"Weeli, listen to me, man." I had to slow my swimming to keep my breath and speak. I pleaded with him. "You were there. Sitting on the couch watching those two guys struggle to get out of that riptide, and the only way they survived was by swimming parallel to shore. We're going nowhere, man. We need to slow down and start swimming to the right. I don't–"

The ocean silenced me mid-sentence. Salt water took the place of the oxygen I attempted to suck down between words. I could see Weeli bobbing like a buoy, but for a minute not swimming. Maybe he was pondering the statistics. A wave got him. He was under. When he surfaced, he drifted farther from me. We had to shout to hear each other. I wondered if it was already too late. If we had surpassed the amount of time and energy required to avoid becoming a statistic.

*Was it already too late and we just didn't know it yet?* My fear and loathing occupied every thought. *What kind of a fool am I? How stupid are we? Well, Herb, now you have all the time in the world to think about how ignorant you are...oh no, wait...that's right, you'll be fucking dead.*

*Statistic...statistic...statistic.*

I had to pull my shit together. Had to give myself every possible chance to survive. I decided. I would not ignore statistics. *Swim with the tide, out of the current.* What I wasn't sure about was whether or not I could do it without Weeli. I needed Weeli. I didn't have the courage to decide alone, to die alone, to survive alone.

"Weeli," I gulped for air, trying to relax. He didn't hear. "Weeli!" I shouted again. Then I heard him.

"Yeah," he hollered, "over here."

"We're just going to kill ourselves fighting this thing. We have to use our energy to get out of it. We have to swim with the tide." The sound of a Seven-Forty-Seven heading for a Logan landing muffled my words. Energy expended for nothing. There was no way Weeli could hear me over the waves and the engines. I thought about how many planes would likely pass over our floating bodies. One by one, planes full of potential rescuers, spotters, heroes, would pass over us without even a thought. Will our bodies float? The plane passed.

"Listen to me, man. Stop fucking swimming for a minute, Weeli, listen to me." Weeli didn't stop fucking swimming for a minute. He swam his heart and energy out. Making no progress, he continued struggling just the same. "Listen to me, Weeli. We need to stop fighting this. We need to use our energy to work with the tide to get out of it. This is how stupid people die, man. We are not going to die." He didn't stop fighting the Atlantic, but he used a great deal of energy cursing me out.

"Fuck you, man. Fucking right we're not going to die. We're going to make it to shore. Now fucking swim! Just fucking swim, Herb. We'll make…uh–" A wave. He was under again.

Panic.

Desperate.

He was shouting again when he emerged. "Fucking swim. We'll make it, man." There was no faith in his voice. No conviction. Just desperation.

*Fuck.*

Did I have the courage to go it alone and leave Weeli? Was Weeli right? Was I the moron who was going to die?

*Fuck.*

"Weeli, I'm done with this. Fighting this thing is how stupid people die. Come on, man, we have to swim with it. You were with me, man. You saw the show. The only survivors of these things are those who swim out of it. We can't fucking fight it."

"Fucking swim!" Weeli shouted. Another wave. I was under. The current pulled me farther down. I fought to get back to air.

"Weeli, we're going to die!" I screamed as soon as I emerged.

"You pussy! If I can fight this then so can you. Now fucking c'mon, man. We're gonna make it. You fucking give up, Herb, and I'll kill you myself, you pussy. Don't you dare leave me, man. We're going to make it."

"Weeli, we can't fight it, for fuck's sake." I was nearly crying. My voice cracked. Our desperation collided somewhere between the waves.

"Swim," he shouted at me. "Goddamn you, swim!"

Desperation bordered resignation. The likelihood of death was overpowering my hope for survival. I was not ready to go it alone. If I was going to die, I didn't want to die alone. So I did the only thing I could think of to try to get Weeli to join me and swim with the current. I cried. I cried like a little bitch and attempted to guilt Weeli into coming with me.

"I can't fight this anymore, man." The tears were real. The salt from my body fluids mixed with the ocean water until I could taste desperation. "I can't fight this anymore, man. I've barely got strength to swim. Come on, man, don't leave me alone. Weeli. We have to swim to the right. I can't make it without you. Please help me. Swim with me, Weeli. I don't want to fucking die, man."

"Herb, you—" He was under. Too long. He emerged violently, panicked and coughing uncontrollably. "Her... uh...Herb," he choked as he spoke, arms flailing. "Herb," he called out as if trying to locate me. Then he was under again. He bobbed up again, yelling for me.

A wave got me. Disoriented. I scraped at the water, pulling myself up, anxious to taste air again.

"Herb." I imagined he could hear me gagging. "Herb," he called again, sounding more desperate. I caught my breath.

"Here," I responded, as if answering roll call at Fort Benning.

*Count off.*

*One, two.*

*Count off.*

*Three, four.*

I cried like a baby.

"Weeli, I don't want to go alone, come on, man. Don't leave me."

"Don't you fucking leave me, man," he screamed right back. A large swell came over my right side. I was under again. Instinctively, my arms began to flail, to pull, and push upward like tentacles. I pushed and pulled, kicked frantically until finally, I made it to the surface again.

"Weeli."

Nothing.

"Weeli!"

"We're not going to make..." I heard in the distance. Another wave. Under again. Fighting again. I'd never tasted water so dry.

*Fuck.*

*I don't want to die.*

From all too far in the distance, I could hear Weeli's desperate fight ensuing.

"No...Her...uh–"

*Under.*

*Salt.*

*Water.*

*Air.*

I emerged disoriented. I gasped for the deepest breath of air I could. Instead, I got a mouth full of salty death. I was done for. Beneath the water I gagged, vomiting the ocean back into herself. Struggling for the surface, I prayed the quickest prayer I had ever prayed to a god in whom I did not believe.

I have read that some folks pray for forgiveness, for mercy, for their loved ones and such, when they believe they are going to die. Even if they have no belief in any god. I prayed for only one thing. Me. Survival.

No, 'Our Father,' no 'In the name of Jesus Christ,' no 'Oh Great Vajradhara,' just *Please save me.* Scraping desperately for the surface, I told myself not to breathe. *No matter how hard it is, if you emerge, don't open your goddamn mouth.* If I sucked in another lung full of salt water I might not make it. Planning ahead didn't help in the least. As soon as air was available, I gasped for the largest gulp possible. The sea was kind to me.

Hope.

No sign or sound of Weeli.

Rolling over onto my back, I eased myself northeast. East was away from shore, but it was also away from the large crashing waves, and hopefully out of the riptide. Slowly, I caught my breath.

I made my choice. I would let the tide pull me out. Struggling with the waves would kill me otherwise. I would float and reserve my strength. The air felt great. Being alive felt great. A warm relief heated every inch of my body like an orgasm.

I looked around in every direction. No Weeli. I knew it was possible that he was there somewhere beyond a rolling wave, beneath a crest or far behind me. As a passing wave picked me up, lifting me above the ocean's horizon, I caught a glimpse of what looked like a small buoy perhaps three hundred yards out to sea. *Weeli? Maybe?*

"Weeli," I tried to shout. What came out was a scratchy, barely audible holler. No response. I hoped. Maybe I hoped for Weeli, but mostly I hoped for me. I hoped for my own selfish reasons, my own selfish survival. If he made it to shore or to rescue, there was a better chance of my own survival, my own rescue.

*Survival.*

I pulled slowly, arm over shoulder, doing the backstroke gently, conserving as much energy as I could while still making progress. Slow and easy like a Sunday morning, I pulled arm over shoulder, left then right. I watched another plane glide above me, breaking up the otherwise perfect sunset sky. As my house floated farther away, I watched a flock of seagulls cross over. I wondered if they'd shit on me. I wondered if they'd pick at me when the time came. *Ravens? Crows? Were ravens and crows the same bird? Would seagulls peck at my eyeballs?* Hell, they were pretty vicious breaking apart crab shells and slamming clams against stones, just for a nibble. There was no telling what they'd do with my sorry ass.

*Would I be washed out where the bay opened up to the ocean just north of Hull? Maybe washed up on one of the islands?* Off the shore of Hull there were three easily-visible islands. There were another four small islands known to anyone familiar with the geography of the area or any castaways who happened to be drifting helplessly past. In all, just off the coast of Hull, there were up to nineteen islands depending on the tide, that season's weather, and who was counting. Most of the islands were believed to have been underwater cliffs and shoals, emerging millions of years ago as the glaciers of the Ice Age melted and receded.

John Cabot was the first westerner known to explore the Boston Harbor. Columbus, of course, never made it far enough northeast to reach the mainland of the harbor. It wasn't until the early sixteen hundreds, nearly two hundred years after Cabot, that John Weston would attempt to colonize the area, which would become Hull. The islands were mysterious, with creepy names like Hangman's Island and Grave's Light. Just to the north, just in from the coast of Salem, witches were burned and hanged. Mostly women, mostly mothers. Beautiful, innocent children hanged in the name of God. The souls of many of those witches were said to have claimed the islands as their home.

The harbor was full of mysterious islands: George's, Gallop's, Lovell's, Nix's Mate, Sunken Ledge (Hangman's), Peddock's, Long, Moon, Rainsford, Thompson's, Grave's Light, Minot's Ledge Light, Boston Lightship, and Deer Island. According to folklore, pirates were hanged on

Hangman's Island. A captain cooked and ate his first mate on Nix's Mate. On George's Island, from whence *John Brown's Body* and *The Battle Hymn of the Republic* came, arose a Union officer executed by his brother, a Confederate prisoner. Castle Island held Fort Independence and buried soldiers. On Little Brewster, the Southern Boston Lighthouse. On Long Island Light, the Long Island Lighthouse. On Peddock's Island, Fort Andrews. On Rainsford Island, the ruins of a pauper colony. Of all of these islands though, the island closest to me, Little Brewster, was foremost in my thoughts. I dreamed, hoped, prayed to be washed ashore.

Hull, surrounded by ocean on three sides, stuck her neck out into the Atlantic in a northwesterly direction with her head hooking west toward the mainland. Hull's portside beaches did not face straight out to open ocean. Thus, it was difficult to gauge the true direction of the tide against the mainland. If not the mainland, if I were pulled too far north and east, the islands were my last hope.

Floating.

Following Little Brewster was Great Brewster Island, Middle Brewster Island, and Outer Brewster Island. If I passed Little Brewster Island, my next best chance might be Great Brewster. Great Brewster was considered the luckiest of all the harbor islands. In recorded history only one ship had ever wrecked on Great Brewster. Everyone survived that shipwreck. Every other island had seen its share of less fortunate seafarers.

Floating.

If I swam northward far enough, while naturally being pulled out to the east, I might make the island. Middle Brewster would be the worst. The terrain on the island was thorny and harsh, the shore rocky and rough. There was almost no inviting beachfront. If I missed those islands, then I had a slight chance of getting washed up onto Outer Brewster Island.

Floating.

My sister's face came to mind. Jenna's dark hair and big, bright, childish smile were as vivid as the plane overhead. I could hear her happy-go-lucky laugh. Thoughts of my siblings ran through my mind. When I struggled desperately, only my survival, only staying alive was on my mind.

Floating.

I cried.

*The Letter...The Letter! Why had I never written a letter?* I'd told myself a zillion times that I would write The Letter. The Death Letter. The note to everyone I knew and loved explaining that life had been fabulous to me in spite of and despite anything I've ever said or done to show otherwise. The letter that would set their hearts and minds at ease. The letter I wished my mother had left us. *My father had God, but what did she have?*

Floating.

Regrets. Out of nowhere, just like the riptide had done, regrets crept in on me. I had always told myself that I had no regrets, that I didn't live life in a way to give cause for regrets. There they were. Just like that, as life was no longer a certainty, as there was no more purpose in lying to myself, they just popped right up. *If I lived*, I promised myself, *there would be no more.*

Floating.

*Hope. Planes. Seagulls.*

Floating.

Sunset. The beautiful sunset. A purplish haze descended on the city, twilight beaming from the steel and glass skyscrapers. Flickering like glitter across the crests, the waning light danced along the waters. Occasionally, I swung my arms as if swimming. Occasionally, I even kicked. If I were to die, the sunset over the ocean, over Boston, was not the worst farewell.

Floating.

Purple faded into a nighttime-gray, blanketing the city. *Did Weeli have a letter? Does everyone?* I wondered. *Was he okay to die? Who the fuck is okay to die? Do I think I'm okay to die?* I thought of the Buddhist death story. There was a great Tibetan monk who spent his entire life studying the death meditation to prepare, to graciously embrace the moment when it arrived. As he lay dying, during his last breaths, his students begged him, "Master, what do you know? What have you learned? Tell us."

"I don't want to die," he replied. "I really don't want to die."

Of course Weeli was not okay with dying. *Was he alive? Were his desperate pleas to me his last spoken words? Would he be rescued and send a rescue team for me? Did Weeli have a letter? That fucking* Letter. *Why didn't I write my simple little…such a simple little…*

"*Dear Family,*" *it would say.* At least I thought it would say as I drifted out on open ocean. I even thought of how the 'F' in Family would be capitalized. *"Dear Family…listen. Sure, it sucks to be dead. I'm not going to lie to you. I fucking loved living. But I had an incredible time. Everyone dies. Not everyone lives well. Thank you. All of you. Love each other as much as you can. Be good to each other. Be good to yourselves. I love you. I hope you die as happy as I have."*

Then I started rewriting the letter. *Wait a minute, what about that time my sister stole my Bible so she didn't get in trouble for not having hers? Do I include that? She has to know I forgave her. What about all the shit I did for them? Will they forget?* I was losing my mind.

I cried at the thought of never seeing my family again. I cried thinking about them finding out I was dead. In that moment it occurred to me that I hadn't once thought of those whom I had lost, those who passed before me. I thought only of the living. Things I believed were of the utmost importance to me when I was not fearing for my life, in that moment of desperation, meant nothing. I hadn't once thought of Sophia, or the Shiners or The Revolution.

Floating.

Selfish thoughts passed. *Maybe they will all appreciate what they have now. What a great brother, friend, uncle he was. How much I sacrificed for them. Maybe they'll...*

Floating.

I wondered what things other than the letter I had left undone.

Floating.

I wondered what the light in the distance was.

Floating.

*Light.*

*A fucking light.*

I stopped wondering about everything except the light. Survival is a powerful thing. All of my cells, senses, and synapses focused on one thing. The light. It had to be a ship.

*A ship?*

The shock woke my body and mind. Singular purpose. Me. *Survival. Get to the light. Don't panic. Control.*

The light. *How far? Nautical miles. Nautical what?*

*Stay calm.*

*Should I swim toward the light? Is it too far? Should I wait? If it's not a ship, then what? Can't waste energy. Think carefully. Be smart.*

"Hello!" I screamed as loud as I could with all the energy I could muster. So much for control. Like the dream where you scream and nothing comes out, the ocean seemed to suck my scream into herself like a vacuum and with it the energy I expended.

"Help!" I tried again. More vacuum. More energy lost. It sounded so hollow, so empty in the vastness of the Atlantic. Not enough energy. A wave got me.

*Fuck.*

White water crashed over me. Panic again. I talked myself down.

*You're okay. Just pull your legs up. Rest your head back against the water. That's all there is to it. Oh, fuck...okay. Extend your arms out to your sides. You will float. You had a plan. Stick to the fucking plan. Just lay your head back like before. Nice and...fuck. No. Nice and easy. There you...*

"Herb."

*Fuck.*

"Herb."

*Weeli? Am I hallucinating? Stick to your plan. You will be fine. You will float. Oh, fuck...okay.*

Floating.

"Herb."

*Fuck. Don't lose your mind. I can't lose my mind.* Still, I was hearing…

"Weeli," I whispered.

*Herb, don't worry about me. I'm fine. The Revolution, Herb. You are The Revolution.*

"Weeli…"

*The light.*

Across my eyes, the light.

"Weeli?"

"Hey, man, Herb!" someone shouted. The light crossed my eyes again.

"Are you alive down there? Say something if you're…"

The light beamed steadily into my eyeballs. The voice was not Weeli's.

"I'm alive." *I'm alive!* There was no describing that feeling at that moment. "I'm alive!"

"Boys, he's alive," the voice called. "We're coming to get you, Son."

In that instant, I forgot about Weeli, I forgot about my family, I forgot about everything except…*I'm alive.*

"Lower that thing down. Boy, say something," the man shouted.

"Right here," I hollered. I rolled over onto my stomach and began to swim toward the boat. With the living beings, the ship and the light right in front of me, I had no flashbacks of drowning. Instead, I had a great sense of energy, of vitality. I swam like I had rested all afternoon.

"Son?"

"Right here."

"You okay, Son?"

"Yeah," I mumbled. I could barely speak. Exhausted and exhilarated to be alive. I was overwhelmed. "Yeah, I'm...I'm great. Thank you, thank you, thank you." I may have repeated a few more 'thank you's.'

There were roars of applause. Even celebration. The men on that ship seemed nearly as happy as I was that I was alive. *What a wonderful world.*

# CHAPTER 21

# FINDING WEELI'S SMILE

*The body is but a fetus in the cocoon of form*
*Squirming, stretching, wrenching life in a cosmic shell*
*Death – the butterfly.*

— ANONYMOUS

The void of the vacant city streets enveloped me. I found myself driving around for hours until the night air was like a vacuum. I sat alone at a red light. The light changed from red to green and back again. Protruding through the thoughts of Weeli consuming me was Frank's voice.

*When you're ready.*

Shortly after Weeli's death, Frank invited me to stay with him, to live his lifestyle for a while, to learn from him.

*When you're ready.*

The light changed back to red.

My brain signaled a nerve, which yanked a muscle, which pushed my right foot down. The light was still red. The cop sat motionless at the other side of the intersection, no more concerned than I was. Maybe he was enveloped in that vacuum, too.

=+ +=

Coping with death is inextricably linked with murder and resurrection, killings and rebirths. As I did after the deaths of my parents, I spent much time going through stages outlined long ago by sociologists, psychologists, and pathological liars before I could arrive at a healthy state of consciousness regarding Weeli's death. Mostly I missed his cocky smirk, his daring grin, his smile. It was gone. Sometimes I think it was just that smile that kept me searching, seeking out truth, hunting down The Revolution. Even a bad idea, if accompanied by a wide-eyed grin that screamed, 'we can own the world!' is inviting. He was dead. The smile was gone. I had to find it within myself. Frank said it would always be with me, that I couldn't kill it if I tried, but if that were true it was well hidden or I was blind as a bat. Dealing with death can make a man 'but a walking shadow.' My shadow of a life was going through those step-by-step stages of births and killings.

First…the births.

The first of new births was the born-again Weeli, a mythological hero. The Weeli that never existed, but was born in my head upon his passing. Weeli, who in death, like so many before him, took on a greatness which he could never have achieved in life.

250

When my mother first passed I did the same. Memories of her stepping out on the porch to watch me take my first bike ride without training wheels kept going through my head. Her proud smile, her waving hand. I can still see it now. I remembered her making me promise to graduate college, to do good things with my life as if I was the chosen one, the promised child, the prince. It took me some time, some predefined stages of mourning, before I realized that her death was probably best for her and all of us given her condition. I remembered the constant pain she was in. I remembered dropping the plastic bin full of her blood-infested urine and feces all over myself as I carried it from her bed up the stairs to the bathroom. I remembered her cursing and coughing from that bed where she spent most of my life. I remembered that she chose to smoke cigarettes by the hundreds, drink vodka like it was water in a desert, drop pills until there were no pills to drop. As I had with her, so with Weeli, I gave birth to a myth.

The deaths...killings.

Murdering the myth was next. After a long period of unknown time, I killed off the legend of Weeli for something more real, memories of Weeli the human being. That, too, came in stages. I had to identify the myths, sort them from the truths, come to grips with them, affect and face their slaughter. Then the rebirth.

I obsessed over the real memories. I gave new life to everything that meant anything to Weeli or reminded me of him. I took on words, styles, actions, which were more his than mine. I found myself using sayings that annoyed me when he used them. I performed the painful exercise of reading the nonsensical psychobabble epic, *Infinite Jest,* just because he did. And so, as with all births, the deaths would follow.

Maybe what helped me through the stages of dealing with death was the timing of it all. I could not kill The Revolution, despite my best efforts. Weeli was certain he would lead The Revolution, but he was dead. There were things I could accept not knowing, but I was most certain that a dead man could not lead. Like many dead before him, his legacy would be to inspire The Revolution.

⋙⋘

Weeli's words stayed with me.

*'The Revolution, Herb. I was just a stepping stone. You are The Revolution.'*

I walked for what felt like days until I arrived at the cemetery on Mystery Hill. Mystery Hill stood at Fort Revere, tall and proud at the end of Hull's neck toward the head of her peninsula, standing guard between the mainland and the mighty sea. Like the islands, the fort was used to keep watch over Boston Harbor during the Revolutionary and Civil Wars. In daylight, Fort Revere had many faces. From the south, at the foot of the hill, the fort was entirely hidden beneath a green front and a variety of headstones, some small and stout, some tall and spire-like. Kind to the dead, Fort Revere provided an eternal view of the seemingly infinite Atlantic Ocean. At the top of the hill stood a stone wall forming a horseshoe-shaped barrier. Beyond the barrier was a tower, the only visible hint that a fort lay beyond the cemetery.

Many days I spent sitting on that wall thinking about Weeli, staring off into the sunset or sunrise, blue sky meeting blue ocean, or gray clouds dropping gray water onto a gray sea, or seeing nothing but my ponderings dissipate in the salty air. This was a revolutionary fort.

At night, moon-cast shadows shift above the dead. The night is always different.

I sat on the wall, staring off into the shifting horizon. Wrapped like sushi in seaweed, The Revolution possessed me.

The waters like putty remained in my mind. Not the muddy waters of the Colorado running through my veins, aching, stretching their red fingers for any sign of life, but the wide-open waters of the crisp Atlantic stinging my brain like a fresh memory of a bright future. It was time.

# CHAPTER 22

# FRANK'S ROCK

*It will be said on that day, 'Lo, this is our savior;*
*we have waited for him, that he might save us.*
*This is the leader; we have waited for him; let us*
*be glad and rejoice.'*

— [ISAIAH 25:9]

Spring.
That feeling of anticipation came over me every year as if I were six years old again, as if my truest desires, likes, dislikes, passions, and feelings about all of life had developed early on and stuck with me for as long as the blood flowed through my polluted flesh. For a period of time, the time it takes thought to appear, mix with the cosmos then vanish, I wondered if The Revolution was just the desire to return to that passion that existed in those early and innocent days.

The spring air, snow melting, mud on the soles of my shoes. I could taste recess, smell summer vacation in the air. Neither was approaching. Still, every year I would imagine what it would be like if all the grown-ups remembered the pleasures of recess and chose random times during the day to run outside and play, shout, fight, frolic, wreak havoc. As those around me grew up, we resorted to more civilized forms of recess like cigarette breaks, during which we would bitch repeatedly about the state of affairs of the average orangutan while killing ourselves slowly, but deliberately.

"You're never going to quit!" Cody shouted across the fishbowl. My soon to be former roommate, Cody, was the only one who knew that my Entipop smoke breaks were coming to an end. Cody and I grew closer after Weeli's death. Cody was suffering from misplaced guilt. The way he saw it, had he never proposed we move into that beach house together, Weeli would still be alive. I tried to impose upon him my absolute certainty that everything happened just as it was meant to and couldn't have happened any other way. And there he was with his big, childish grin giving it to me again.

"I knew you'd never quit smoking." He laughed and slapped me on the shoulder. "So, did you do it yet?" The 'it' he was referring to was turning in my resignation.

"No," I said, "I'm just about to tell Garbway, then I'll hand it in."

"So, Ian backed out. I've got an extra ticket to the Sox game tonight." That was Cody's way of asking me if I wanted to go to the game with him. Cody was a decent, sincere human being. He was also one of those cats that was either too shy or too proud to ask for help or company directly. Instead, he would imply. For instance, when he wanted help with renovations on his sister's house, he didn't ask. He mumbled, "I got to tear down three fucking walls this weekend, man. I don't even think her husband's going to be around to help." I was there. Cody was never going to climb the corporate ladder and he knew it. He didn't want to. He was not a pretend jolly working an angle, rather he was actually jolly and wanted to keep it that way.

"Thanks, man," I said, "but I've got some things I need to do."

"I wasn't inviting you, you douchebag," he said with a big, fat grin. "Now go quit, would ya? You'll shock and inspire the zombies around here. Quitting might be the best thing you ever do for this joint."

I did go quit. Garbway was gracious.

"I understand, kid," he told me. "You got a set of cojones on you. Happy to have you back if a time comes when that's in the cards for you. No need for the two weeks' notice, though. This is a good opportunity for me to discharge a little shock and awe. So do me a favor, let the guys know that you and I have come to an agreement, which you aren't allowed to discuss, pack up your stuff, and go. I'll make sure we pay you through the month. Then I'll head in there and shake up that IT department. You just kind of made my day, Herb. Happy to have you back anytime. Good luck."

With that, I packed my few personal belongings, got in my car and headed north. I was ready. It was time to take Frank up on his offer.

Frank was not surprised to see me, as if I arrived exactly when he expected. We rose with the sun each morning to care for the animals. By five thirty I would have the stalls mucked and the horses out in the field. By eight the wolves, chickens, and other birds were fed. By noon we would have collected wood in the Vermont hills, or repaired a fence, or gathered stones and feathers, whatever was called for on that particular day. When the evening chores were done, and after we'd filled our bellies, our nights were spent with music and books and stars. Frank taught me to play the guitar. There were five chords I needed to know, he said, and he was right. With those five chords, I could accompany him for hours while he sang to the cosmos on his sax.

"It is time for you to sleep with the wolves," Frank said at the end of my first week with him.

"Luca Brasi sleeps with the fishes," I told him. "That doesn't sound promising."

"That's funny. Good to see you're keeping your sense of humor, but no, it's not a euphemism. It's time for you to sleep with the wolves," he smiled. "Come on, let's move your stuff into their stall."

Frank was not joking. He meant for me to sleep with the wolves. Here's the thing, though. *They are wolves.* I fed the beasts, bound to their stalls by massive tow chains, twice a day as Frank instructed. I could pet them, even hug them if they were in the right mood. Frank would let them free only after feeding, when they were full in belly, to reduce their desire to hunt. They would disappear into the Vermont countryside and return religiously at the sound of Frank's whistle. But even Frank kept them chained most of the time. And I didn't see him sleeping with them. Plus, they urinated in their stalls.

"There is much to learn from wolves. Their energy is strong with instinct and freedom, but they are ruthlessly social. They feel the connection between form and formless, and when you are among them you will feel it. Your fear will be their fear. Your love will be their love. It is time for you to sleep with the wolves."

I was bitten twice, urinated on once, and growled at a lot, but by the third night I had grown attached to their warmth and accustomed to the odor. When Frank said the time had come that I no longer needed to sleep with the wolves, I did it anyway. Some nights I slept with the wolves, some nights with the horses. Animals are powerful teachers.

Frank gave me books to read. Even the animals got used to me reading them to sleep. Frank rotated religious and spiritual texts with scientific, historical, and political writings. The first was The Bhagavad-Gita, followed by *Behold a Pale Horse,* then *The Cosmic Landscape.* When he handed me The Old Testament, I retracted.

"You must be joking," I said. "I've read it already. No way."

"You read it before," he explained, "as a Christian text, when you were a different child. You've never read the original translation. It is the foundation of Islam, Judaism, Christianity, and many histories. Read it."

"Can't I just read *Sushi, Sex and Cosmology* again?" I quipped. I read The Old Testament again. Then the Koran, followed by *The History of Capitalism,* then The Talmud. I read The Dharma, followed by *The History of the World,* and then *The Gnostic Teachings.* I read them all in between the farm work and music. One morning, Frank found me as I was cleaning the horse stalls.

"Let's take a walk," he said. His tone was different. I followed him up the hill and into the Vermont mountains.

"You're leaving, Herb," he told me. "The time has come for you to go. The Runners you saw, the Shiners, Weeli, it's all connected. There are folks like me with names like Crazy that help us. Some operate under the radar, some on the grid, some off the grid completely. There are other groups, Herb, which steer the course of human events, that determine the outcome of wars, the survival of religions and races, which tamper with all the things normal folks kill and die, live and love for. The ancient Hindus formed the Incendisti Colla. They're still around steering things this way and that. The Elders, think of them as the Cosmic Knights Templar. There are those who keep in solitude, doing their best to maintain the balance of cosmic energy. The Copper Scroll found at Qumran, the petroglyphs in the south of Chile, the tombs in Kenya. The signposts are there, but some are concealed, some have been controlled, manipulated. Everything is in motion. Choices. I'm here in the mountains instead of out in the world spending my family's fortunes. Choices," he explained. I followed him up a path west of the farm. It was a familiar walk. One we'd taken nearly every day for one reason or another.

"You remember the first time you passed this way?" he asked as we approached a granite boulder the size of a small house.

"I do. I told you I was overwhelmed. I told you it reminded me of the feeling I got at Newspaper Rock. And you nodded as if it meant nothing to you and then told me to go find some good maple."

"It was the stone, Herb, just not that one." Frank walked around the boulder and reached down, rolling over a rock the size of a treasure chest. His strength was remarkable. He removed a piece of tree trunk that lay beneath the rock. I began to feel dizzy, disoriented. It felt like electric, magnetic energy was zipping about me. My head buzzed, tears rolled down my face. As he picked the object up I could see it was wrapped in cloth.

"It is no accident that I have come to be the keeper of the stone, Herb. I am her guardian. When I told you and Weeli that aliens had led me to her, I meant it. Not green Martian aliens, but beings, entities that exist between form and the formless, between this world and the source of everything. If you were blessed to get a glimpse of them, you might call them ghosts, but you would see that they aren't of human form. You'll recall Gehinnom from the Jewish texts, the place Christians call purgatory. This idea originates with what we call Henom, a state between form and formless where the metamorphosis occurs, like the caterpillar in the cocoon becomes the butterfly. There is no punishment or merit system. It is simply a state of transition. These beings exist in that state. It may take time to catch a glimpse of them, but you'll see it for yourself one day. I don't know if they intended to lead me or if they were just attracted to whatever energy this is that you can feel now. Maybe the energy of the stone is what allowed me to catch a glimpse of them at all. I don't know." He held the stone out for me to touch, but I hesitated.

"Don't be afraid. This is why you're here. The energy of everything, Herb, is connected. This is just a piece. You are just a piece and yet, we are, this is, all, everything. I know you want all the answers, Herb, and when the time is right they will come to you."

I fell to the ground. When I came to, I was in the stall lying with the wolves. Frank was sitting in the wooden rocker, my belongings packed up on the floor beside him.

"You'll have Weeli's smile with you," Frank reminded me, "wherever you go. That's just how it is. I can't heal your pain. It will heal itself. When the time is right, we will know and I will see you again."

# CHAPTER 23

# THE DREAMCATCHER, BACK WHERE IT ALL BEGAN

### Dreamcatcher

*Feathers o' wings how symbolize,*
*The nature of flight in our thoughts and mind's eye.*
*Mother Spider has woven webbed flower*
*To protect from dark and keep light to devour.*
*Close your eyes pray Spirit o' all,*
*And know the dreamcatcher will work*
*while you sleep.*

– PROUD JIMMY, THE CANCER WOLF

### The Legend of the Dreamcatcher

*The Native Americans of the Great Plains*
*believed that the air is filled with both good and*
*bad dreams. Historically, the dreamcatchers were*

*hung in the teepee or lodge, and also on a baby's
cradleboard. Legend has it that the good dreams
pass through the center hole to the sleeping person.
The bad dreams are trapped in the web where they
perish in the light of dawn.*

— EXCERPT FROM A CARDBOARD ADVERTISEMENT FOR
ST. JOSEPH'S INDIAN SCHOOL

This was the dumbed-down, lint ball, tourist version of a dreamcatcher. Truth is, there were many histories, lures, beliefs, and mysteries that evolved for the benefit of tourists, whites, foreigners, capitalists, and even the natives themselves, sometimes aimed to mislead, other times to appease, but most times just to increase sales. A number of tribes whose traditions didn't include anything like the dreamcatcher, devised fictional tales and sold dreamcatchers and their made-up tales as their own. It was believed that the closest version to the known truth came from the distorted history of the Ojibwe.

Ojibwe legend tells of a spirit leader, descendant of the first chief of the first tribe. The shaman deprived himself of food and water for two full days. He exhausted his physical energy in those two days ascending one of the sacred mountains. He climbed a great climb requiring the strength and stamina of many men while carrying gifts to be offered to the great spirits of Owani-o-way.

Feathers.

Beads.

A willow hoop.

While meditating on the peak of the sacred mountain, Iktomi, the great sharer of wisdom, appeared in the form of a spider. The language the spider spoke was not the language of the first tribe or any tribe since, but the shaman understood. Iktomi took the shaman's willow hoop, beads, feathers, and other offerings and spun a web around everything. As Iktomi spun his web he spoke of the cycle of life.

"We are before we begin as infants, and we are after we depart this form," he said while weaving the web. "As the blossoming cactus stretches her petals to the sun, we can't but reach for the light, eager for life in any form we abide."

Weaving a meticulous web, Iktomi showed the shaman the ways of the form in this world. The life before the birth, the birth, life, the death, the life after the death, and the rebirth. Iktomi's weave was complete. He gave the web to the shaman. "You see," Iktomi said without words, "through this web the light will shine and be magnified and the dark will be gathered and cleansed, and balance will be."

The different tribes have many versions of the origin of the dreamcatcher, and even the Ojibwe would say this tale is not true. Since Americans knew of 'Injuns' and their dreamcatchers, the trinkets have been bought and sold with all variations of tales and meaning. They have been mass-produced with pictures of Elvis or wolves painted on leather, bark, rawhide, paper, tissue, cardboard, screen, plastic, and just about any other material that could be used as a canvas.

The hoops, according to Ojibwe tradition, were made of wood, whittled into a sphere three and a half inches in diameter. The web was woven from nettle stalk fiber. With the red sap of the bloodroot or the bark of the wild plum tree, the nettle stalk fiber was dyed reddish-brown. The sacred Ojibwe stitch was used to weave the web as a spider would. Their dreamcatchers could be found hung above cradles, the beds of children, and in doorways.

—+ +—

I held the feather Frank had given me. My mission was clear. I needed to return to those waters which took Weeli and spared me. I needed to carry on with The Revolution.

I stepped out into the waters. The waves were mild but, like the wind, they were picking up. My steps were slow, slipping in the sand as I approached her, the mighty Atlantic. I was reverent. If she pleased she could swallow me up instantly into her belly and digest me like a grain of sand sucked up by an oyster. *Maybe I'd become a pearl? Maybe I'd come to know the peace or the horror Weeli had come to know?* The soft, white sand sank, scattering at my feet.

Dark purple-green seaweed tangled its slimy arms and balls through my legs and between my toes. It washed up on the shoals. Thoughts of Weeli, of death, of birth, of The Revolution. *Did she spit him out like this seaweed? Did she embrace him warmly and invitingly, carrying him gently into the cocoon for his rebirth? Did she tear him apart and rip out his humanity and dignity, and bring him to tears and wretched fear at the very end?*

Dancing in mid-air, flirting with the waves, a rush of seagulls and northern sandpipers. The birds danced across the tips of the waves, worshiping Ceres. The waters baptized me, extracting the dark. The wind devoured it and made space for the light. A price had been paid. Many pains. I wasn't ready to become a blissful piece of the balance. It wasn't time for my way through the rebirth. I bid a very temporary farewell to the waters that spared me. It was time for the bright light of The Revolution.

⇥ ⇤

First, one must mourn the passing of the dark and the coming of the light in a mortal fashion with too much drinking and unhealthy thinking and then, maybe, lead. I made my way to the Sea Note for that last frivolous night. Maybe I would drink away the sorrow. Maybe I would drink away the need to drink away anything. As it turned out, I wouldn't drink as much as I planned. The drunken, self-inflated, bloated town clerk had other plans.

"Come on, man, what are you fuh...fuh...uhckin' nuts, kid? I dun even know ya. Sa...so I'd hate to call you supid... stupid. I hain't callin' ya shupid." He slurred his words and spit them out. Slower than I'd ever seen a grown man do. Volunteering at the multi-center nursing home in Brockton years before, I'd encountered a similarly slow, drooling, slurry-speaking man, but he was ninety-one and bedridden. This asshole was just drunk.

"Sah...I wuhint call ya stupid, but...but there's no way the fuh..." He mumbled some ridiculous thing about the town magistrate then warned me of the terrorists moving into Hull to hit the famous Boston Gas fuel tank. I didn't say a word and didn't think it could get worse. Then, he grumbled some absurd thing about killing the mayor and moved on to sports. I had learned in South Boston that the only thing worse than talking to a drunk about religion or politics is talking to a drunk about sports.

*Spit.*

*Drool.*

*Glug.*

"No hu...way the fuckin' Sox are gonna come back from a two game defi...they never win a serious...a series." He gulped down his drink like it was the last he'd ever have. "Two game defithit. Ain't climb that hole. Not the fuckin' Red Sox," he continued. "No...no fu...fucking way." I remained speechless. My third drink arrived.

> *They reel so*
> *To and fro*
> *And stagger like*
> *Drunken men*
> *They are senseless*
> *And at wits end.*
>
> – [107th Psalms]

"No fuh-hukin'...way," he slurred on. Down went my beer, quickly, smoothly. The drunken town clerk mumbled, drooled, slurred on. Desperately hoping to avoid an argument about baseball with a sloppy drunk, I stood up wishing him goodnight. *Why did I bother to stop for a last drink?*

═╪ ╪═

Beneath my feet the crisp leaves crackled, crushed with each step as I walked down Hull's summer streets through the early fall air. The air was particularly dry. Surprisingly dry for the seashore town. The orange glow of the harvest moon lingered in the night sky. I was lonely. Autumn inspired a longing for loneliness, for things past, for death. Sometimes the scent of autumn, the crisp, clear, arousing scent brought memories of making love outdoors on the campus grass of Wheaton College. She was a sparkling spirit of a woman, my first love. We parted ways. It was the sense of parting and lost love that the scent of autumn leaves conjured. The harvest moon, burning a bright orange now, seemed alone in the vast skies of the Atlantic fall evening. A deep solitude was my companion as I made my way down Nantasket Avenue.

Like soft, welcoming thunder, the crashing waves rolled down the beach with a steady rhythm. Routine should have taken me straight across to the boardwalk. From there I'd hook a left, follow Nantasket down to Beach Avenue, then along the ocean all the way to my house. Routine should have dictated that I revere the view of the mysterious moon over the water, within the water, her reflection returning to me twice with every step. Routine did not dictate that night. Energies I did not understand at the time were in control.

*Kish, kish, kish.* The sound of crushing leaves approached. Not the leaves beneath my feet, yet I could hear them as clearly as and in perfect rhythm with my own.

Beneath the dim yellow glow of the street lamp ahead of me, she appeared. The yellow, so harsh, so electric, so loud in contrast to the orange glow lighting the night sky. In the shadow of her silhouette, I could see the frame of an old woman wearing a brimmed hat, carrying a walking stick.

*Kish, kish, kish, kish, kish, kish.*

*Why could I hear her steps as clearly as my own?* In rhythm with my own, with the stride of a young man. *Familiar.* I could feel her getting closer, the familiar feeling growing.

*Kish, kish, kish.*

As her long shadow met the ground near my feet, I rolled my eyes upward, following the fabric of her swaying dress. The familiar feeling grew into something more intense as her energy, compassion, and love began to flood my body like radiant heat from Earth's molten core. I was nervous. Doubting. But everything was so familiar. *Why?*

*Kish, kish, kish.*

She emanated a defenseless energy. I felt her greet me, welcome me, but without words. It was déjà vu, the energy I felt emanating from Sarah, the young child in Exeter. As certainly as I felt the ocean breeze brush gently against my cheeks, I felt her welcome me.

*Kish, kish, kish.*

*Come along.*

I heard it, but her face hadn't moved. I felt her inviting me to follow. I hesitated briefly, but doubt gave way to faith.

*Come along.* Again, her smile hadn't budged.

Lady Mary's energy was too great to deny, almost too much for me to handle. Energies I could only describe as love rolled out of her like a ball of flame, flowing straight into me, washing away any hint of lingering doubt. I was consumed by her strength.

*Oh ah nay-o-way…amazing grace.*

Her frame was stout like the ancient Blackfoot, slightly shrunken-in from years of wear, but strong with wisdom. A thin scarf folded in fourths covered just a part of her silver head. The top of her dress was decorated in a Tlingit potlatch.

*Oh ah nay-o-way…amazing grace.*

*Welcome,* I heard as I walked alongside her, turning down Demare Avenue. "You wonder if I said that out loud?" she asked me.

"I'm wondering…everything, really," I answered. My eyes welled up. Overwhelmed. Confused. She smiled. Nodded.

"Wondering," she whispered as she grabbed hold of my hand. My entire body felt warm as she made contact. There was an electric flow of energy, warmth. "It's a wonderful and exciting thing, you know." She strengthened her grip. I could feel her like I'd never felt any woman before. Beneath the thin scarf, the long dress, and the stringy gray hair was an aged body, but the most beautiful thing I'd ever known. Somehow she let me see her, feel her, and be with her in that instant she took my hand in hers.

⇒⁺ ⁺⇐

We were in her small house.

The stain on the brown crown molding that lined the narrow hallway at the entrance was old and fading. Parts of the original wood, worn and weathered, showed through. The hallway led through the chipped doorframe, which stood naked, no door hanging. There were noticeable holes in the wood where the hinges once hung. Through the frame we went, pausing in the first room, Lady Mary's living area.

"Let me make you some tea, my friend." That time I was positive she actually spoke out loud. Abutting the living room were two more door-less, aging doorframes. One led straight into the kitchen, which was brighter in both lighting and color than the rest of the house. The other led into another small room, maybe her bedroom. Lady Mary turned away and slipped her tiny frame through the weathered crown molding into the kitchen.

The living room was lined with an old, orange shag rug. The chic, natty, hip-in-the-seventies kind of rug. She returned with tea. We sat, silent at first. I drank slowly, feeling it warm me. The energy from Lady Mary, from everything, tingled senses I didn't know existed. There, on the wall leading to the kitchen, she hung.

The dreamcatcher.

Tishi Meh Hamu.

A single, long feather just like Frank's, brown and gray with spots of white, hung from the center of the silky wood, carved so smooth it appeared to be ivory. A meticulously-woven, reddish-brown web like that which Iktomi or the spider may have cast, stretched her thin fingers, forming a tight, open circle in the center.

"Ooh," she sighed in a high-pitched, rhetorical tone, breaking the silence. "Getting restless." She was speaking to the earth. "Just a little shake and bake quake," she smiled. I didn't feel anything shake. Lady Mary just went on as if nothing strange even occurred. The next day I would hear of the quake she should not have felt.

"The painting? You wonder where I acquired my bad taste in art?" She paused. "Paleolithic Stone Age, or so-called 'cavemen art,' is the most sincere realism, longing for the greater knowledge. Some of the Magdalenian carvings have the most radiant energy of any seemingly inanimate objects. And Newspaper Rock, where you were brought to tears by the overwhelming energy. They were born during the Middle Stone Age, an age of rapid evolutionary change. That energy cycles and cycles, reaches and stretches." She turned and motioned toward the far wall. "But this." She reached both hands toward the dreamcatcher. "This is why you're here.

"Oh," she said, as if suddenly feeling a wrenching pain in her gut, "I know this makes them in a bad way. So many lies. So much pain." Looking at the dreamcatcher, shaking her head, she smiled gently. "They were one with the connected energies of all things. Energies without boundaries, within us and through us and all things. They aren't the only ones who knew the art of Tishi Meh Hamu." She paused.

"This is not just about dreams, not just about shining the light. Tishi Meh Hamu," she repeated, cupping her hands together and bowing respectfully to the dreamcatcher. "Tishi Meh Hamu, in the sacred tongue." Her eyes were fixed on mine. "To be the web."

# CHAPTER 24

# DÉJÀ VU

*We Are*
*The Primeval is the Crowning*
*The Alpha is Omega*
*The First, The Last*
*We Are.*

— POOR JOHN, 1992

"Can you feel that?" Frank asked, smiling at me, holding Lady Mary's hand in his own. We were seated on a soft bed of wild grass atop Sarah's Peak on Yakka Island as the sun rose over the Atlantic.

"I can," I told him. The warmth of the energy was tangible.

"Close your eyes," Lady Mary instructed, taking her hand from Frank's and placing her fingertips on the top of my forehead. "You've been here before." She spoke softly. "You remember? You have always been here."

I had spent every day with Lady Mary for nearly a month. She shared her wisdom and her energy with me. She told me of the cyclical nature of everything. That humanity has come and gone before and that our collective memory of those cycles is eternally accessible. That the déjà vu I had been experiencing was my human form accessing this information through the web of Iktomi, the connected energy of all things. That there is no beginning and no end and that time is a 'funny bit of fiction,' except to that which is bound by form. That Buddha, Krishna, and Christ were all onto the truth of the matter, that the spirit of God is not only in us, but is part of us and we, a part of it, of everything, and that everything is in a constant state of creation. That the nature of everything has always been in a state of creating and that there has never been a state of nothing, never a starting point. She shared with me a great many things. It was at the end of that first month that I mentioned Crazy Frank.

"He is on his way," she told me.

"You know Frank?" She just smiled. And I just smiled. Of course she knew him. I would come to see that Crazy Frank and Lady Mary had a great love and respect for one another. When he first arrived, watching them giggle like children and tell stories was a great joy. At the same time, there was a lingering energy of purpose.

"This body is dying," Lady Mary said one night.

"I know," Frank replied.

They turned their attention to the lingering purpose. Me.

"Saint Paul said it best," Lady Mary smiled. "'A man hears what he wants to hear and disregards the rest.' What a sexy little man words made out of that Paul. If only words could capture the truth. But words cannot capture that which is not of words." But she and Frank had words, plenty of words, books, photos, and documents.

I spent the next few days absorbing every iota of wisdom I could, as Lady Mary and Frank spewed like radiation from a supernova.

The Revolution according to Lady Mary and Crazy Frank:

*LM:*
*"The nature of all things is not a truth to be understood by means of the form, with facts and intellect, for those things are not the source of what has always been and always will be."*

*CF:*
*"Most people use facts and figures and scientific evidence to manipulate and control, but you must know the facts as they are purported if you are to affect things rightly. It is important to know the facts. Then, it is important to unknow them, as they are not the truth. They are limited pointers in a three-dimensional world, often misunderstood or manipulated in the context of our true nature."*

*LM:*
*"As with instinct, truth is part of us, that part of us that always has been and always will be. In form, we can only know truth through feeling, not thinking."*

*CF:*
*"If it feels good."*

*LM:*
*"We are born of a perpetual state of creation, creating and being created, infinitely."*

*CF:*
*"Cosmologists refer to the random unpredictability of the smallest known particles as bubbles. These bubbles result in pocket universes, what smart people call 'bubble nucleation,' but they miss the point. There is nothing random about any of it. It is the whole purpose. It is the whole. We are and have always been, that which is being."*

*LM:*
*"The source permeates everything, is everything."*

*CF:*
*"When the Buddha said, 'Look within and you will find God,' he was pointing to the source. It is within all of us and we within it. Krishna said, 'That which pervades the entire body is indestructible.' Nothing can destroy the imperishable. Christ said, 'Look under this stone and I am there.' The 'I' is God, the source. Scientists use words like 'ghostly neutrino' and 'dark matter,' but what they think they know is that ninety-nine percent of everything consists of something they know nothing about, except that it must exist. They have no instruments to measure, to feel the source."*

*LM:*
*"To feel the source, you must let go of the self."*

*CF:*
*"Original sin. Consciousness. The Old Testament tells of Adam and Eve, of original sin. The ancient scripts told a similar tale, but the temptation was that of the formless to bring into fruition form, and out of form, consciousness. The blessed curse. The source is experiencing, we are experiencing, a magical blessing for the energy of all things, in this form, with human consciousness. That blessing is also the curse of consciousness. The identity with the self, with human ego, with self-importance, is like the Great Wall of China between form consciousness and spiritual consciousness, awareness of and being one with the source, the spirit of God. Short of cosmic bubble nucleation, it is necessary to step outside of form consciousness, of form identity, to let go of the self and feel the source, the formless, the nature of us. It is only then that we can truly embody the form. In John's words, 'Even the spirit of truth. Whom the world cannot receive, because it seeth not; neither knoweth not; but ye know; for he dwelleth with you and shall be in you and you in he.' But the words of all the sages have been manipulated by those attached only to form identity for Little Mind purposes. We are of the Big Mind, but to know that mind, we must let go of the Little Mind."*

*LM:*
*"It is good that we experience the blessing of form for the whole, but it is not enough."*

*CF:*

*"The source is suffering. We are all suffering. As the nature of the energy of all things is in a constant state of creation, from the formless to form, from form to the formless, humanity, consciousness, is also creating and being created. In this current cycle, humanity is creating a new dark matter within the Henom, that state between form and formless. This threatens to bring about a self-destructive energy within the formless, the source.*

*The Revolution is Now."*

# ACKNOWLEDGEMENTS

Thanks to Paula M. and BonBon/MamaWest for their reviews of the early and very rough drafts of *Weeli's Smile*. Thanks to all the friends and colleagues who have read editions along the way and provided both their encouragement and critiques. A very special thanks to my friend and editor, Michelle Burinskas, for her constant enthusiasm and passion, and her utter refusal to do anything less than make it to the finish line.

For more works by W.g.Cordaro, please visit wgcordaro. com, ormuspublishing.com, or contact Ormus Publishing.

Made in the USA
Middletown, DE
30 August 2017